THE INDIGNITIES OF ISABELLE

'When I'm naughty,' said Caroline, 'I normally just get a smacking across her knee with my hairbrush.'

Her words left me trembling inside. The idea of her being spanked was bad enough, but the casual, cheeky way she said it really got to me. I could just picture her across Jasmine's knee, with her jeans and panties pulled down and her magnificent, fleshy bottom quite bare. I could well imagine her giggles and squeaks as the spanking began, then her squeals and kicks as her buttocks wobbled and reddened during punishment. Then her contrite snivelling when she stood to massage her heavy, smarting bum cheeks, perhaps even with tears welling in her beautiful brown eyes . . .

A NEXUS CLASSIC

THE INDIGNITIES OF ISABELLE

Penny Birch writing as Cruella

Nexus

This book is a work of fiction.
In real life, make sure you practise safe sex.

This Nexus Classic edition 2002
Nexus
Thames Wharf Studios
Rainville Road
London W6 9HA

First published in 1999 by
Headline Book Publishing

www.nexus-books.co.uk

Typeset by TW Typesetting, Plymouth, Devon

Printed and bound by Clays Ltd, St Ives PLC

ISBN 0 352 33696 X

Why not visit Penny's website at
www.pennybirch.com

One

My last ever report from finishing school contained the line '. . . Isabelle is a quiet girl and much given to introspection . . .' If they had only known what I was thinking about, their remarks might have been somewhat different. I suppose they fondly imagined that my daydreams involved a handsome husband, fine possessions and broad acres. In practice my thoughts would most often be centred on how it would feel to take an old-fashioned tawse to the bare bottom of one of my fellow students.

At nineteen fantasies of sex with other women were nothing new to me. Even the idea of wanting to spank them had been building up in my head for quite a while. There is something about a girl's bottom that simply cries out for chastisement; partly the beautiful shape, but mainly, I think, the fact that a woman's bottom exhibits her sexuality in a way that brooks no denial. Sex is sin, as a thousand sermons have attempted to drum into my head, and sin deserves punishment. A woman's bottom is the very essence of sex, and so she should be punished on it.

In real life, far indeed from the preacher's pulpit, such behaviour is likely to cause far more sex than it ever puts a stop to. Nothing in any sermon has ever convinced me that there is anything wrong with taking pleasure in the physical responses of my body. Indeed, the whole idea that sex is somehow bad has only served to make it seem deliciously naughty. Yet in one important, and ironic, way I have been influenced – to my mind sex should start with a smacked bottom.

It should also be a girl's bottom but not mine. However, despite my dark desires and what I can fairly say is a pretty strong personality, it was not until I had left finishing school that I had my first opportunity to turn fantasy into reality. I was due to go up to university in September and had the prospect of a long, peaceful summer in front of me. I would have been happy to just be alone, walking the moors or simply thinking in my room. My parents had other ideas, having decided that I was already too fond of solitude. So they invited my cousin Samantha Adel to stay for the summer.

Sammy and I were about as different as it is possible to be. I have been told I'm pretty, although I would prefer beautiful or even ethereal. At nearly six feet tall with a naturally slender figure, delicate features and long, fine, near-black hair, I like to think that I at least could not possibly be called ugly. For Sammy there was no doubt that the word pretty was appropriate. Blonde curls, big blue eyes and full lips went with a tiny waist and hips and breasts so full as to seem indecent. A bubbly, extrovert personality put the final touch to her, completing a combination of traits very different from my own and apparently irresistible to men.

It wasn't so much that we disliked each other as that we simply had nothing in common and so, while we never quarrelled, neither did we spend much time together. Instead, while I was out enjoying the solitude of the moors she would be down in the

2

village making friends and flirting with the local boys. One of these, Rory McVeigh, was her favourite, and it was he who provided the impetus for my first experience of the type of sex I had always craved.

My parents had gone into Inverness, leaving the house to Sammy and myself. She had immediately disappeared in the direction of the village for an assignation with Rory, while I had walked up onto the moors behind the house. It was a hot day, and humid, while aside from a pair of walkers on the flank of the distant Ben, I was completely alone. As had been happening more and more often since my cousin's arrival, my thoughts turned to her. She attracted me, as she attracted just about everybody, and it had only been through iron self-control that I had prevented myself from making a pass at her. Not only was she physically lovely but there was something cheeky, impudent even, about her personality that seemed to me to simply beg a smacked bottom.

That was what occupied my mind as I wandered aimlessly up a narrow glen. Sam's bottom was magnificent, a firm, chubby globe; exquisitely feminine. She had come into my room that morning in just her panties, carelessly showing off her big, round breasts. The panties had been black and lacy, also tight with generous slices of creamy white flesh spilling out of them. The temptation to touch her had been close to unbearable as she had chatted merrily about her admirers, apparently oblivious to the effect her body was having on me.

I had hoped that the fresh air would clear my head of such disturbing thoughts, but it had no such effect. Instead I found myself enlarging on the fantasy of having sex with her, and as I did so the urge to masturbate became increasingly strong. I also wanted to do it naked, simply for the exquisite freedom of being nude outdoors and the delightful sense of misbehaviour that it always brought.

Giving in to my need, I changed direction for an area of broken rocks that I knew would provide the cover I needed. I had stripped on the moors before, usually to swim, or sunbathe, occasionally to play with myself. Doing it always produced a thrill that combined simple sexual pleasure with the knowledge that I was being very naughty indeed. Having chosen a safe place among the rocks, I put my rucksack down and peeled my blouse off. The thrill of nudity immediately began to build. My bra followed the blouse, ensuring that I had to remove my boots with my breasts bare. Then it was my trousers, slid down and kicked off to leave me standing in nothing but a diminutive pair of white panties.

I stayed like that for a while, enjoying my near nudity while my excitement rose slowly to the point at which I could no longer resist removing my panties to make it complete. Down they came, peeled slowly over the length of my legs until I was bent into a position that I knew left the rear of my vaginal pouch showing from behind. For a moment I stayed in position, imagining that I was showing off for Sammy. It didn't quite accord with my desire for her, though, and as I stood up and kicked my panties off among the rocks my mind turned to the heart of my fantasy.

What I wanted was for her to kneel between my legs and lick me after she had been thoroughly spanked. I sat down on a rock and parted my legs. My vagina was wet, and with the hard granite pressing into my naked buttocks I put my finger to my clitoris and began to masturbate. In my mind Sammy was licking me. She was nude, her lovely bottom red from spanking as she licked the pussy of the woman who had punished her. I would have told her she needed to be punished. She would have gone down across my knee; contrite, perhaps just a little resentful, but obedient. I would have pulled her dress up, the same dress of clinging black velvet that she had worn that morning. She would have stuck her bottom up, humbly offering me her cheeks to smack and asking if I might spare her the indignity of having her lacy black panties taken down. I would have reminded her that a punishment is intended to shame the transgressor more than it is intended to hurt. Then I would have pulled her pants down, exposing her wonderful, plump bottom for spanking. She would have groaned from the mixture of humiliation and pleasure that was building up in her head, then pushed her bottom yet further up, admitting my right to chastise her as I saw fit.

I would have spanked her, making her lovely bottom bounce and wobble under my hand. She would have begun to protest as the smacks warmed her flesh, and to kick and wriggle. Her movements would have stretched her panties taut between her full thighs, exposing her moist, excited pussy and giving me glimpses of the tight pink knot of her bottom-hole. Ignoring her pleas, I would continue to smack her cheeks until her whole bottom was a glowing pink and she was moaning in ecstasy and shame. Only then would I order her to get up, strip nude and get down between my thighs to lick me to ecstasy while she used a finger on her own pussy.

I came, crying out my pleasure to the empty moor as I imagined how Sammy would feel with her bottom hot and throbbing and her face pressed against my pussy. Only when my orgasm had entirely subsided did I remember where I was. Vague feelings of guilt and hopelessness went through my head as I hastily pulled on my clothes. It wasn't that I saw anything wrong with wanting sex with Sammy, or with wanting to spank her. After all, her compliance and enjoyment were central to the fantasy, although I did expect her to feel genuinely sorry for herself while being punished. Rather it was guilt at being so wanton that I was unable to restrain myself from masturbating and hopelessness because I was sure that she was far too interested in her boyfriends to ever want to play with me.

Knowing myself well enough to realise that if I stayed out on the moors I would continue to brood, I returned to the house. Once there I climbed to the attic, which had been my retreat in times of emotional crisis since my earliest childhood. My family has lived in the house since the end of the eighteenth century and from then to now has made a habit of never throwing anything away. The result of this is that our attic is crammed with boxes and trunks, old furniture and curios dating back pretty well forever. It had fascinated me as a child and still fascinated me now, especially the trunks of old clothing.

Most abundant, and best, were the clothes from the late nineteenth century, when we had been prosperous and my great-great-grandmother seemed to have changed her dress every day. The dresses themselves were gorgeous, and the underwear that went beneath them not only beautiful but of extraordinary complexity. Perhaps most appealing were the corsets, yet sadly the fabric and fittings of many of these had perished and they were really too fragile to wear. More satisfying were the drawers, magnificent creations of linen and heavy lace that reached from the waist to well below the knees. Many of these were in good enough condition to wear, and I had spent many a rainy day dressing in Victorian finery and admiring myself in one of the many mirrors stored alongside the clothes.

I hadn't done this since going to finishing school, and the urge to do so was suddenly irresistible. The feeling of doing something slightly naughty returned as I stripped, not just to my panties and bra as I normally did, but stark naked. Once nude I began to choose the clothes I would wear and was soon lost in a daydream of lace and silk, my earlier preoccupation with Sammy quite forgotten.

My first choice was a combination of chemise and drawers that laced up over my breasts and had a buttoned panel at the rear. The panel could be unbuttoned and pulled through at the front to expose the wearer's bottom and pussy. In reality I knew that this design was to allow a lady in a corset and heavy skirts to use the loo. A much more appealing idea was that it allowed quick access to her bottom whenever she needed chastisement. The idea of how a prim, coy Victorian girl would have felt as her skirts were lifted and her drawers opened so that her bottom could be smacked appealed to me immensely. Nowadays, girls wear jeans that show off the full, glorious shape of their bottoms and even bikinis that leave only the very rudest of details to the imagination. Yet for a modern girl to have even the smallest of bikini pants pulled down for a spanking would be an extraordinarily strong mental experience. How much stronger then must it have been for a woman who would blush to show an ankle to have her most intimate secrets put on show. The actual spanking, of course, would feel much the same for either girl, but the sense of indignity would be far stronger for the Victorian, and it was that which really burned in my mind.

The sound of a door closing in the house below brought me sharply back down to earth. A moment later I heard Sammy's voice calling my name. I stayed silent. Not that there was anything wrong with what I was doing, but it was perhaps a little embarrassing, even childish, in comparison with Sammy's more down-to-earth behaviour. Besides, I only had the combinations on and the front was unlaced to leave my breasts showing, while there was every chance that she had brought a boyfriend back with her to take advantage of my parent's absence.

She had, as the sound of a deep, masculine voice quickly proved. I recognised the voice as well, it belonged to Rory McVeigh. Hearing him I felt a pang of jealousy, although I had to admit that choosing him showed good taste on her part. Rory was big, perhaps slightly raw, but undeniably handsome. His height appealed to me as well, being tall myself, while his shock of red-brown hair reminded me of a lion's mane. There was something wild and untamed about his character, but he was also intelligent. As far as my desire for a male partner went, he would have been an ideal choice.

I also had no doubt of their intentions. During her stay she had already indulged herself with three of the local boys, and had described each encounter to me in a lascivious detail that had left me moist between my legs and more than a little unsettled. Rory had been one of them, and it had been after her description of how the two of them had made love among the beer crates in the cellar of his father's inn that I had come closest to making a pass at her. Now they had a whole house to themselves and were sure to make the best of it.

Girlish laughter from below me confirmed my suspicions and I found a lump in my throat as I heard the door of Sammy's room slam and then the creak of her bed and another giggle. It was more than I could resist, far more. Moving carefully across the attic, I found the junction box from which the wires for Sammy's room light depended. The house had already been old when the electrical system had been installed, and I knew from experience that the ornate piece of moulding from which her light hung contained several holes. My heart was fluttering as I moved the layer of lagging that concealed these. Beneath me I could hear the noises of Sammy and Rory starting to make love; wet, kissing sounds and the occasional sigh of pleasure. I felt guilty about watching them; guilty and wicked, deliciously wicked.

They were together on the bed, their limbs tangled around each other. Sammy's breasts were already bare where he had pulled up her bra and dress. They looked huge, round and firm, each crowned with a rose-pink and firmly erect nipple. Her belly was bare too, a soft bulge of flesh that quivered slightly as his fingers worked at the plump swell of her pussy through her panties. He was kissing her neck and her face was a mask of ecstasy, while with one hand she was stroking the large, pale erection that protruded from his fly.

They had lost no time, indeed I imagined that he must have pulled her dress up before she lay down on the bed. It suggested a wonderfully uninhibited attitude to love-making on her part, which was confirmed as she took hold of the hand that was rubbing her panties and slid it down them. He began to knead her vulva more urgently now that she had made it quite clear that she had no intention of withholding herself from him. Her mouth opened and the speed with which she was jerking at his penis increased. They stayed like that, kissing and masturbating each other, while I moved into a more comfortable position.

I badly wanted to play with myself. Not that this was easy, because the only way I could watch and get at my pussy properly was to kneel on two beams with my head down and my bottom stuck well up in the air. It was an extraordinarily undignified position, and much more a pose that I liked to imagine my partners in than one I liked to adopt myself. I had little option though and was fiddling with the buttons that would give me access to the inside of my drawers even as I bent forward to look once more.

As the panel of my drawers fell away to expose my bottom to the cool air of the attic, Rory was hurriedly trying to pull off Sammy's panties. I had hoped that he would turn her over to show me her magnificent bottom fully nude, or maybe even have her kneel to be mounted from the rear like a dog. To hope that he would spank her was too much, but as it was he simply pulled off her panties and settled himself between her thighs as she spread them to accept him. It was frustrating not being able to see more than his back, buttocks and legs, yet from the expression on her face I knew when he had entered her. He hadn't even bothered to take down his trousers, which added a strangely dirty touch to the scene as his bottom began to move in short, rhythmic pushes, each of which I knew would be moving his cock inside her vagina.

I had slid my hand back and pulled the material of my drawers forward to get at my pussy. I was wet and my pleasure quickly began to rise as I started to masturbate. There was a sense of loss that it wasn't me groaning out my passion underneath him, yet watching Sammy fucked was certainly going to be enough to bring myself to orgasm over. My clitoris was firm beneath my finger and so sensitive that each touch brought a twinge of approaching orgasm. I began to dab at it, using little flicking motions with the top joint of my finger to keep myself on the edge. I was praying that they would do something really rude, something to inspire my darker fantasies and preferably something that involved putting Sammy in a rude or submissive posture.

Just when I was about to give up and bring myself to climax anyway, Rory suddenly pulled out and knelt up on the bed. I heard him ask Sammy to turn over and heard her answering giggle. His cock was standing out from his crotch like a flagpole as she turned and humped herself up into a kneeling position not unlike my own. There is something irresistible about a girl kneeling. It is exquisitely dirty and shows everything, her pussy, even her anus. It is also inherently subservient and a good position for a girl to adopt for punishment.

As Sammy lifted her bottom for entry her cheeks opened and for a moment I was rewarded with a perfect view. She was looking back at Rory, her mischievous face framed in blonde curls and set in an expression of delighted expectancy. Her waist appeared narrower than ever and flared to the breadth of her hips and the full, naked spread of her bottom. Between her cheeks her bottom-hole showed, a wrinkled pink star of flesh, on display to Rory without the slightest thought for her modesty. Beneath, pouted out between her plump thighs, her pussy was swollen and wet with her juices. Rory knelt forward, put his cock to the entrance of her vagina and slid it in.

That was simply too much for me. I came, trying desperately not to scream and give myself away as my body tensed and shuddered in orgasm. For a moment I closed my eyes, then opened them again as a second climax tore through me. He was in her, his front

11

pushed up against her big, naked bottom, his cock pushed to the hilt inside her vagina, filling her, stretching her. I nearly slipped off the beams as my third peak rose up inside me and burst like a bubble in my brain.

The loss of concentration ended my orgasm, but I kept my eye locked to the hole, unable to resist watching them. Sammy had begun to moan and gasp as he started to hump her bottom. He was fucking her with little hard pushes that I could just imagine against my own, more slender haunches. I was a little sore and my breathing was coming heavily from the awkward position that I had been forced to hold. Nevertheless, I considered starting to masturbate again as I watched my beautiful, near-naked cousin kneeling for Rory to fuck her from behind. I probably would have done and even come once more, but before I could get my hand back on my pussy he had pulled out sharply. His cock was slippery with her juice and he grabbed it and began to tug it frantically over her bottom. She gave a little gasp, maybe of expectation, maybe of resentment, and a jet of sperm erupted from his cock to splash over her open, raised bottom cheeks. Then he put his still-hard penis between Sammy's lush buttocks and began to rub it slowly up and down as his erection subsided. She was making a little noise as he did it, like purring, then she put her hand back between her legs and began to bring herself off.

I watched her come, my eye glued to the hole. Never, ever had I seen anything so rude. For me, even the thought of adopting a kneeling position to show my bottom off was so rude that it had me wanting to come. To accept rear entry and be fucked with the man watching his penis slide in and out of my vagina was something simply too dirty to contemplate. I knew how the position left my anus showing as well, which made it even less acceptable and more desir-able. But Sammy – Sammy had not only knelt for Rory and obviously thoroughly enjoyed putting it all on show, but he had come over her bottom and rubbed his cock up between her buttocks. Then she had masturbated over what he had done, playing with herself in a way so wanton, so uninhibited that it caused a physical ache within me.

He pulled back before she came and watched her climax. Her bottom was thrust up high and I could see her fingers as she rubbed frantically at herself. Both her pussy and anus were wet with sperm and juice, and her vagina was so open that I could see inside. She cried out as her orgasm hit her, and I saw her anus pulse and her vagina close as if trying to squeeze on to an imaginary cock. As her muscles tensed her bottom lifted higher still and she let out a long, choking sigh of absolute contentment. Then it was over and she was slumping slowly down on the bed and pouting her lips for him to kiss her.

I sat back. My body was trembling violently with reaction. My pussy and knees were sore and my beautiful Victorian drawers were covered in dust and my juice. Not that I regretted what I had done for an instant, or at least not at a rational level. Deeper was the strong feeling that I had been bad, not only playing with myself but being a Peeping Tomasina as well. For a moment I had the uncomfortable but powerfully erotic thought that it was not Sammy, but me, who deserved to have her bottom smacked. Having always felt that it ought to be me who gave out erotic punishment and not took it, I pushed the idea to the back of my mind along with the flush of shame that came from knowing that if anyone ever did beat my bottom as a prelude to sex, then I would thoroughly enjoy it.

Not that I intended to go and confess my sin to Rory and Sammy. Instead I took my drawers off and dressed as quietly as I could. I waited while they washed and tidied themselves up and then climbed down from the attic and left by the back door. A minute later I returned by the front and greeted them cheerfully. Sammy looked flushed and I would have guessed what she had been up to even if I hadn't been watching. Rory was cooler but perhaps a little flustered by the sudden appearance of the daughter of the house so soon after he had had sex with her cousin.

That is one of the disadvantages of coming from a gentry family that hasn't moved in generations. All the locals looked on us as somewhat apart and so it would have been difficult to make friends even had I been good at it. As it was, none of the locals were ever entirely easy in my presence and so I was not surprised when Rory excused himself as soon as was politely possible.

I think I might have resisted Sammy if my parents hadn't rung shortly afterwards to say that they intended to stay the night in Inverness. For all their determination that I should become more gregarious, they disapproved of Sammy and I spending our evenings at the Black Fleece. Sammy, inevitably, saw their absence as the perfect opportunity to spend the evening there, flirting with Rory and any other unattached males. Of course she needed my connivance to be able to do this.

She made my dinner and did the washing up. She complimented me on my figure and she complimented me on my hair. She offered me the free use of her extensive collection of make-up and even asked if I'd like to borrow any of her clothes, despite the fact that nothing could possibly have fitted. It was nice having her fussing round me, but I remained deliberately cool, all the while wondering how she would take to the suggestion that I would be more than happy to overlook any misbehaviour on her part in return for being allowed to spank her – in advance.

Only when we were actually changing to go out to the inn did my resolve snap. She had bathed and came into my room naked except for a towel. In one hand she had a big powder puff, in the other a container of some expensive and delicately scented talc. Quite casually, she asked if I would powder her and then did something that swept my efforts to resist her away like a feather in a gale.

I had always known that she was utterly lacking in modesty, but I could scarcely believe my eyes as she bounced cheerfully onto my bed, knelt down with her knees well apart, pulled up her towel and presented me with the full, naked spread of her bottom.

'Dry me a little, then powder me, please, Isabelle,' she asked, quite oblivious to the effect she was having on me. 'I can never get at all the little crevices.'

'Don't you think it's a bit rude showing yourself to me like that?' I said, but I was already climbing onto the bed behind her.

'Don't be silly, I haven't got anything that you haven't got too,' she answered.

I took the power puff in trembling fingers and rubbed it into the talc. Her bare pussy was just inches from my face, the furry lips pouted invitingly up as she pulled her back in to present me with the best access to her bottom. Her bum-hole was a pink spot between her glorious, spankable cheeks, which trembled slightly as she moved her knees yet further apart. I patted the powder puff onto her bottom, desperately trying to resist touching.

'I've done my bum, do my fanny and bum-hole please,' she said as if it were a completely everyday remark.

It was just too much.

'I . . . I want to spank you, Sammy,' I stammered, curling an arm around her tight waist and placing my hand against the fullness of her bottom.

'I knew you were like that,' she replied. 'Oh, go on then, if you must, just gently.'

For a moment I had thought she was going to reject me. Then she had given me permission, but not in the needful, wanton way she had spoken to Rory. Rather it was as if she was prepared to take it because it was something I so obviously needed badly. It seemed as if she realised that she had turned me on and felt an obligation to satisfy my dirty lusts, rather as I had felt on the rare occasions that I had sucked boyfriends' cocks. Her response made me feel weak, but I tightened my grip on her waist and began to smack her bulging bottom. She gave a little giggle as the first smack fell. Her flesh was soft and wobbled delightfully, like a big pink jelly.

'Maybe a little harder,' she said. 'Do you like to smack other girls' bottoms then?'

Obviously the answer was yes, so I didn't reply but planted a firmer smack on hers. She squeaked and giggled again. Once more I laid a solid smack on her quivering flesh, this time leaving a pale red hand-mark on one freshly powdered cheek.

'What I really want to do is punish you,' I said.

'If you think I deserve it,' she replied, slightly breathlessly.

'Don't you mind?' I asked.

'Not if it's you,' she answered.

It was such a sweet willing response, the girl wishing to give pleasure to her friend even when it's not her particular thing. Sure that she would say if her punishment became too painful, I took her hard around her waist and began to spank her in earnest.

It was wonderful. Her cheeks bounced and quivered under my hand, her flesh quickly reddening and her squeaks and giggles taking on a tone that quickly revealed her indifference to the erotic pleasure of being punished to be false. I could see every detail of her pussy as I spanked her, and before long a tell-tale bead of white fluid had formed at the entrance to her vagina. Her bottom-hole was pulsing slightly as she contracted her bottom cheeks to the rhythm of my smacks, an involuntary and deliciously rude reaction to punishment that I had never imagined.

Judging my moment to when I felt her ready for a yet more intimate contact, I adjusted my position slightly and slid the hand that was under her tummy onto her pussy. She sighed as my fingers touched her clitoris, a sound of both ecstasy and resignation. I began to masturbate her and increased the force of my smacks. She gave a yelp but made no effort to either stop me playing with her or from increasing the severity of her punishment.

Her giggles quickly stopped to be replaced by groans. Her breathing had been becoming gradually heavier, but suddenly it was coming in short, urgent gasps and I knew she was going to climax. I pushed my fingers against the sopping flesh of her open vulva and really began to lay into her bottom. She squealed loudly, a noise of utter bliss and absolute shame at having come under my discipline.

I stopped spanking as soon as the shudders of her orgasm had subsided. Her whole bottom was a glowing red. Instead of moving she stayed in position, the plump cheeks of her bottom wide apart to show her swollen pussy and tight anus. Then she got up, going slowly back on her haunches to look at me with an expression of breathless pleasure and beautiful submission.

'Do you want your turn?' she asked softly.

'Just lick me,' I answered as I stood back.

I sank back into a chair and without a word she came down between my legs. I had changed into a skirt and quickly pulled this up, urgently wanting her tongue. She waited patiently as I adjusted myself and pulled my panties aside to offer her my bare pussy. Then she put her face in it and started to lick.

In my mind her submission was complete. I had spanked her and now she was kneeling nude between my thighs with her tongue on my pussy. My own clothes were disarranged only just enough to allow myself the full pleasure of her tongue, while she was not only stark naked but had a warm, red bottom to remind her that I had had to punish her.

That was the thought that was uppermost in my mind as I came. I had spanked her, punished her, smacked her naked bottom as she knelt for me, nude and obedient. My orgasm hit me and for one instant everything was absolutely perfect. I knew then that whatever else might be, I needed a lover who would accept my discipline.

Two

Sadly, that one, exquisite encounter with Sammy did not lead to more. She had thought of me as lesbian and been keen to try sex with another girl. When I had asked to spank her, she had been willing but had seen it as something rather perverse which she was prepared to do in order to get to lick my pussy, which was what she was really after. Unfortunately she was completely unprepared for her own response to being spanked. Once she had come down from her erotic and submissive high she was intensely embarrassed. This was not because we had had sex, but because of her own reaction to what she had seen as distinctly unacceptable behaviour.

I had tried to reason with her, but basically we were too different to really see eye to eye. Neither understood the other, and while I was unable to comprehend her complete lack of shame at the exposure of her body, nor could she understand my reasoning that pleasure should be linked with punishment. We parted friends, if not close ones, while her relationship with Rory McVeigh had reached the point of becoming serious.

The rest of the summer passed quietly, and while I had no more opportunity to explore my sexuality, I was confident for the future. Having won a place to read History at Oxford I was sure that my future held a wealth of experience in an environment suited to my perhaps slightly unworldly perspective on life.

I was right, or at least right in part. The majority of my fellow students were dull to the point of distraction. Hearty rowing types; pale, timid intellectuals; obsessive politicals; none of them held the slightest interest for me. Others did, and I quickly found myself among a group who shared my fascination with Victorian clothing. Unfortunately what they didn't share was my web of reasoning that linked such clothes with concepts of shame, violated modesty and, above all, punishment. Indeed, some of them seemed to view the subject as an element of a moral outlook that struck me as priggish to say the least, and I found myself having to hide my true feelings.

Even at finishing school I had been aware that in a sense I am much more highly sexed than many. Yet I had, perhaps optimistically, assumed that more intellectual companions would be correspondingly liberated. If anything, the opposite was true. Likewise, the openly gay women at the university seemed so different from me in other ways that we had little common ground. Indeed, their philosophies were rigid to say the least and accepted neither bisexuality nor spanking as reasonable practises.

So I concentrated on my work and contented myself with long sessions of masturbation and accepting two of the apparently endless stream of men keen to get me into bed. These were fairly crude affairs – flat on my back with some muscular brute humping away on top of me and imagining that the mere feel of his penis inside me was enough to make me come. I suppose it may not be the same for all women, but having a man on top of me never provides enough stimulation to my clitoris to make me come and also prevents me from playing with myself during sex. Some men even seem to object to the idea that I might enjoy some stimulation other than that produced by their cock being rammed vigorously in and out of my pussy. Neither of my choices were quite that bad, but neither were they better than ordinary. Also, neither was loving or even cuddly, one leaving me immediately afterwards and the other simply rolling over and falling asleep.

It was towards the end of second week that I discovered something truly fascinating in the form of an antique shop that specialised in clothing. This was not in Oxford at all, but in the nearby village of Whytleigh a few miles to the north. It stood in a short row of crumbling red brick houses that looked out onto the river Cherwell. A stretch of cobbles separated the houses from the river, while a massive willow at the end of the row covered the whole area in dappled shade. All this produced a timeless air that I found soothing and immensely appealing. The proprietor of the shop was a plump, ruddy-faced man in his late middle age called Walter Jessop, and I quickly discovered that his knowledge of the subject was pretty well comprehensive.

I was fascinated and spent some three hours admiring his wares and then his personal collection. Sadly, I was in no position to buy anything but could only browse and discuss the subtleties of our mutual fascination. I could also tell that he found me attractive, and twice he suggested that I should try something on. Despite his complete lack of physical appeal, I found it impossible to feel threatened by him, he was simply too polite and good-natured. So I went behind an antique screen and put on a set of combinations not unlike those I had worn while watching Rory McVeigh and Sammy have sex. The only difference was that instead of the rear opening being a panel, the cloth over my bottom was bunched and a split was concealed among the folds. This meant that they could be pulled apart to expose the girl's bottom. Mr Jessop pointed this out to me when I stepped out from behind the screen, and the lust in his voice was so transparent that I decided to be merciful and pulled them open to reward him with a brief glimpse of my panties.

It was only done for an instant, yet I could see that my piece of innocent flirtation had had a much stronger effect on him than I had anticipated. His face became red and his eyes looked as if they were about to pop out of their sockets. Feeling slightly alarmed by the effect that a teasing glimpse of my body had had, I dressed quickly and left soon after. This was not because I felt shy or threatened, but because I felt it would be unfair of me to do anything that might lead him to believe that a sexual advance might be accepted.

For all that he didn't appeal to me, the incident had a certain taboo quality about it that I found quite enervating. The idea of giving in to an older man is definitely naughty, particularly when it is quite clear that he is simply after a quick thrill. Disobedience and misbehaviour has always seemed exciting to me, and if I wasn't actually going to do it, then there was no harm in thinking about it. As I cycled back towards Oxford I let my mind run on the possibilities of such an encounter, with my pussy warming on the saddle as I went.

I imagined that he would have wanted me to put on a little display, posing in the combinations. He would have suggested the positions, which would gradually have become ruder. After a while he would have had me take my panties and bra off so that the outline of my body showed beneath the light linen. Then he would have persuaded me to unlace the front and let my breasts free. I would have kept the chemise top closed at first, but gradually relaxed, allowing my nipples to show and then all of my breast. Next it would be my bottom, flashed cheekily between the split sides of the drawers. He would suggest sticking it out, and I'd do it, even though I knew it meant showing him the rear view of my pussy and the dark crevice down by my bottom-hole.

By that time he would be too excited to hold himself and would pull his cock out. He would call me a tease and demand that I took him in my hand. I'd do it, going round behind his chair and gently taking his stiff little penis. He would groan as I started to pull at it, then start to talk to me. He would compliment my body, saying the most outrageously intimate things about my breasts, my bottom, even remarking on the shape of my pussy lips as they showed from behind. I would move round to sit on his lap and he would fondle my bottom as I continued to jerk at his cock. The lacing of my chemise would be fully open, exposing my breasts completely. His hand would slide into my drawers through the slit at the back, finding a bare bottom cheek and starting to mould. I would make no objection but squeeze his cock more firmly and start to tug harder. He would be getting bolder and more intimate, trying to push his hand under my bottom to get at my pussy. I would feel a flush of shame as I lifted my bottom. A finger would touch my anus and another would slide into my wet vagina. He would come and his sperm would splash on my hand as he rubbed me between my legs. Then I'd do it in front of him, sitting down on the floor and spreading my combinations to show him my pussy. I would masturbate completely openly, hiding nothing as I came in front of him.

In fact I nearly had come, because while I had been following this deliciously naughty train of thought my pussy had been rubbing against the saddle of the bicycle. Normally riding a bicycle doesn't do all that much for me, and I was a bit surprised by my reaction. But then I didn't normally think dirty thoughts while riding. It is not a good idea to have an orgasm while cycling down a main road, as I wasn't at all sure if I would be able to stay on. So I stopped and tried to think pure and innocent thoughts until my head cleared. This was partially successful, but I knew that as soon as I was back in the privacy of my room in St George's College I would be on my bed with my jeans and knickers around my ankles.

After negotiating the terrifying series of roundabouts that link the ring road to the road to Banbury I headed for the city centre, where my college stood among the tiny lanes of the original university area. I was immensely pleased with myself for getting into St George's, which is among the oldest colleges, small, select and perhaps the one that captures the atmosphere of the university best of all. Moreover, I had managed to secure a room in a tower. This was actually medieval and lacked all but the most basic amenities, but the atmosphere more than made up for any inconvenience.

Passing the modern colleges with their ugly red brick or even concrete and glass construction always made me feel both lucky and rather superior. There are several of these on the roads leading in from the north, and I was looking at them and feeling sorry for the occupants when I noticed a tall figure with a wild shock of red-brown hair. I stopped, sure that I was wrong, but as he turned from the bicycle he had been padlocking to a tree he became unmistakable – it was Rory McVeigh.

I had not had the least idea that he had got into Oxford. After all, although more intelligent than the other locals, he was simply the inn-keeper's son. Despite the fact that we had never been close, seeing him induced a pang of homesickness in me and I made my way over to him in haste.

If I was surprised to see him, then the same was certainly true in reverse. Even though we had lived within a mile of each other all our lives, from the point of view of education we were worlds apart. I had been at public schools since the age of seven, while he had attended the local schools all his life. In any case it was pleasant to see a face from home and he obviously shared my feelings because he greeted me with a friendliness far greater than he would have done back in Scotland.

We fell to talking and swapping stories of home and after a while he invited me to come up to his room for coffee. The room was very different from mine, a grey box inside a larger grey box which provided accommodation for over two hundred students. As my college had less than one hundred students in total and was basically finer in every way, I simply had to show it off and invited him to come into the city with me.

I suppose that it was inevitable from then that we would end up in bed. I was turned on anyway, and he was cheerful and amusing and seemed so strong and in control. In Scotland I had always felt detached from the locals and must have seemed pretty aloof. Now it was different. We were both first-year undergraduates and equals. For him I am sure that there was an element of satisfaction in suddenly finding the daughter of the local landowner at his own level. I had always had a sneaking fancy for him anyway, and so made no resistance when we had returned to my room and he put an arm around my shoulder and kissed me.

Instead I returned his kiss and allowed myself to be guided slowly down onto my bed as his hand came up to stroke the nape of my neck. With Sammy he had been pretty forthright, rough even. Perhaps that was just the way she made him feel, because with me he was both gentle and careful, as if he were handling bone china. I had no objection at all, and allowed him to lead, using his long, muscular fingers to bring me slowly on heat. First it was my neck, his nails running gently over the skin under my hair until my breathing had quickened and I was beginning to ache for more intimate touches. Only then did he begin to undo the buttons of my blouse, popping them open one by one. My feelings of exposure and vulnerability increased slowly as my blouse was opened, a delicious sensation that made me want to melt and let him do exactly as he pleased.

He did, and there was certainly nothing coy or uncertain about him. When he had taken my blouse and bra off and undone my jeans he pulled his own zip down and produced his cock. Clearly he had no doubt at all that I would want him to, as once both penis and balls were free of his fly he took my hand and placed it on them. I took it all into my grasp and began to knead gently as he slid his own hand down the front of my jeans and into my panties. His cock was stiffening in my hand as his fingers found my vulva. Many men go straight for a girl's vagina once their hand is down her panties. Rory was more expert, or possibly considerate, as instead of penetrating me he began to rub gently at my clitoris.

I sighed and let go of his cock in order to get my jeans down and give him better access to my pussy. He gave an amused chuckle at my eagerness, keeping his hand down my panties and moving closer to rub his now erect penis on the flesh of my thigh. It felt hot, solid, firm and I was more than willing to have it inside me.

As with Sammy, he made no effort to undress himself, which some women might have resented but I found strangely erotic. There was something special about being naked while he was dressed, as if the fact that I had been stripped accentuated my desirability. Suddenly I wanted to be completely naked, without so much as a stitch to cover my body while all he had bare was the cock that he needed showing in order to penetrate me.

As I lifted my bottom to tug my panties down, he moved back and began to undo his shirt. I stopped him with a gesture and told him how I wanted to be. He accepted it without comment, waiting while I stripped and then rising to stand by the bed. He loomed over me, caressing his cock and looking down at my naked body. I pulled my legs up and opened my thighs, eager to be entered. He smiled and moved to the end of the bed, then climbed on and knelt between my open thighs with his straining erection rearing from his fly and his balls protruding underneath.

It looked wonderfully rude and it was all for me. I purred and arched my back, offering my pussy to him without reservation. He came forward, lowering himself onto me. The head of his cock nudged my vulva, nudged again and then found my vagina. He came down on top of me, kissing me as my arms went around his back and my thighs parted to take him in. The tip of his penis was in my pussy, then more and suddenly I was full of cock and he had begun to push, slowly and firmly into me.

For a long time I let him ride me. I was content to simply hold him and revel in the feeling of his cock moving inside my vagina. It wasn't going to make me come, but I was in no rush. Having seen him fuck Sammy I was fairly sure that I knew what he was going to do, and was anticipating the moment when he pulled out of me and made me roll over into the rudest position a girl can possibly get into. Normally I won't let men have me like that, because it is just so revealing and so rude to think that they can actually see the junction between their cocks and my pussy. I also know that they can see my bottom-hole and worry that they might be tempted to bugger me. For Rory, though, I didn't mind. In fact I wanted to show it all to him, to allow him to inspect every crevice of my body while he was still fully clothed. Even if he attempted to put his cock up my bottom I knew that I would at least try and accept him.

He pulled slowly back and I knew it was going to happen. I was breathing deeply as he took me by the hips and rolled me over to lie bottom up on the bed. He put his hands under my tummy and lifted me into a kneeling position. As my knees came forward I felt my bottom spread and knew that it was all showing for him, my open, wet pussy, my bottom-hole, every rude, secret detail of my body. I buried my face in the bedclothes and pulled my back in, making the display I was giving him even ruder. He grunted and put his cock to my vagina.

Once more I filled with penis. I could feel the mouth of my vagina stretched around him, and as he began to push his balls started to slap against my pussy. I was in ecstasy, not just from the physical sensation but because of having been made to adopt such a rude position. His front was smacking against my bottom with each push as well, a sensation perhaps not unlike being spanked, and which I couldn't deny enjoying. The thought of being punished across his knee came into my head, adding a touch of erotic humiliation to my already complicated state of mental bliss.

I put my hand back between my thighs and started to masturbate, determined to come while he was still inside me. His balls slapped against my fingers as I started to play with myself. Suddenly I knew how I wanted to come, a thoroughly dirty idea that complemented my revealing position. As he pushed into me I grabbed his balls and began to rub them against myself. He gave a soft cry, perhaps of surprise, perhaps even of pain. He made no effort to stop me though and continued to move his cock inside me in little jerks as I rubbed his balls against my pussy. I could feel every detail; the rough hair, the wrinkled skin, and the two fleshy lumps that bumped and bumped over my clitoris as I rubbed.

As my orgasm approached he put his hands on my bottom and pulled my cheeks wide. I suppose he did it in order to give himself a good view while he concentrated on my orgasm, but it was exactly right for me as well. I knew that my anus would be showing, stretched wide above where the shaft of his penis disappeared into the gaping hole of my vagina. That was the final touch I needed for my orgasm, which exploded in my head as I squeezed his balls hard against myself.

He began to push again even before I had finished coming, knocking the breath out of me. It was hard and I was already dizzy from my orgasm. For a moment I really thought I was going to faint and then he had suddenly pulled out. Only then did I remember how he had come with Sammy. An instant later his sperm splashed across my bottom, then he had laid his cock in-between my bum cheeks and begun to rub it up and down. My feelings were a jumble of pleasure and a strange sort of satisfying disgust. It did feel good, with the shaft of his cock touching the super-sensitive skin around my anus and between my bottom cheeks, all of it slimy and sticky with sperm and my own juice. It was just the thought of having my bare bottom stuck up in the air, covered in male come and with a fat penis resting between my cheeks that gave me a feeling of outraged indignity.

I didn't move, but let Rory finish himself off between my buttocks as all my feelings of guilt and shame at having been so sexually submissive welled up inside me. Not that I showed it, and the first thing Rory did when he had come down from his orgasm was express his delight and surprise that I had behaved so wantonly. What he actually said was that he was surprised to find me so liberated, but it was clear what he meant.

Once I had cleaned up, which wasn't easy with just an ancient china basin in my room, I made coffee and we fell to talking once more. It was nearly midnight when he left, and I had really been expecting him to spend the night. We parted with a long and intimate kiss, yet as his footsteps faded down the stone stairwell outside my room I couldn't suppress the feeling that for all the pleasure we had taken in each other he still felt that there was a gap between us.

Three

By imposing on myself a degree of thrift so severe that even my grandmother would have been impressed, I managed to save enough money to make another visit to Walter Jessop's shop worthwhile. My aim was to buy a corset. I had always liked the idea of sheathing myself in tight satin, with my waist pulled in as far as possible and my hips and chest enhanced, yet the corsets in the attic at home were all far too fragile to wear. Some of those in his shop had been new, perfect reproductions of Victorian originals, and it was one of these that I wanted.

I felt both shy and guilty as I approached his shop, as if my fantasy after my previous visit had in fact been reality. The cheeky flash of my panties had been for real, so my feelings weren't entirely irrational either. The leer with which he greeted me made it transparently obvious that his own thoughts had run on similar lines, and I found myself blushing as I asked to see his collection of corsets.

He was delighted by my request, and was soon rummaging among his stock with a big smile on his ruddy face. I waited, examining this and that to hide the fluttering feeling in my stomach. We were alone, and corsets need trying on, which was going to mean stripping to my bra and panties – in front of him. It was impossible to feel detached about this, because I knew I would enjoy the process, and not only for the pleasure of putting on such a beautiful garment. On one level the idea of enjoying the thought of giving a dirty old man what amounted to a peep show filled me with self-disgust. On another it appealed deeply to my senses of exhibitionism and erotic shame. I was wearing a panty and bra set that was mostly lace and hinted at both my nipples and the cleft of my bottom, a choice that I now realised had either been foolish or deliberate, depending on viewpoint.

By the time he had arranged a dozen corsets around the shop I was actually trembling and my mind was full of the moment I'd have to ask him to step behind the screen and tighten my laces. I'd be in diminutive, lacy black underwear, nothing more, and even if I kept my back to him he would get a prime view of the way my round little bottom stretched out my panties. His eyes would travel down my back, across my bare shoulders to the bra strap, the catch needing only a tweak to come open and free my breasts. He would take hold of the corset laces and start to pull me in, but his eyes would be on my bottom, admiring the way the top of my cleft showed above my waistband, delighting in the way the lace panel hinted at darker, naughtier secrets below. One little tug and they'd be down, that was all it needed. Some of the corsets had full chests, which would mean taking my bra off and rendering myself even more vulnerable to wandering fingers . . .

I have no illusions about the fact that my body excites men, and I wondered if Jessop would be able to resist me. I hoped he could, because I wasn't at all sure that I wouldn't let him if he tried.

The corsets were beautiful, artworks in satin, silk and lace, without a shred of nylon to be seen. It was impossible to know which to choose, but with a strong feeling of self-reproach I selected a magnificent example in ivory satin, both full chested and long enough to half cover my bottom.

'A beautiful choice, my dear,' Walter Jessop said as I picked the corset up, 'but I fear we have a little problem.'

'What's that?' I asked, half hoping and half dreading that it would be something that meant I had to strip.

'You are rather tall, if I may say so,' he continued, immediately giving me a flush of shame for my dirty mind. 'These are all designed for women of average height, more or less, while you, if I may be so bold as to hazard a guess, are only an inch under six foot.'

'Aren't any of them worth a try?' I asked, realising at once that he was right.

'Not really,' he replied. 'Ideally a corset should be tailor-made, and while I realise that I am losing myself a sale, I would be prepared to give you the address of the corsetière who makes these.'

'Thank you, that would be kind,' I answered, running a finger regretfully over the satin of what I had hoped was going to be my first corset.

'A moment,' he said and disappeared into the back of the shop.

I was left standing in the shop with mixed feelings of relief and regret. Now I wasn't going to have to endure the shame of showing him my underwear, but nor would I have the exquisite erotic thrill that I knew would have come from that very shame. Instead I would be returning to college with an address that would probably prove to be in Wales or somewhere equally unreachable. An added flush of shame came from the realisation that his intentions were more innocent than I had thought. He could easily have had me try on several corsets before pronouncing the task impractical, getting a good look at me in bra and panties even if he did miss his sale. Possibly he had not expected me to do the fitting properly, and the idea that he might be rewarded with a little show had never even entered his head.

He returned with a slip of paper, which he passed to me as he remarked that the address was on the Cowley Road. My enthusiasm returned immediately and after a quick telephone conversation between Walter Jessop and the corsetière I set off with an appointment for that afternoon.

Walter Jessop had told me that the corsetière was a woman by the name of Jasmine Devil but had supplied no more information. As I bicycled over Magdalen Bridge and onto the Cowley Road I was imagining a woman of an appearance so severe that she might actually have stepped out of the Victorian era. I was also imagining someone of at least middle age and so was extremely surprised when Jasmine Devil proved to be in her early twenties and possessed of a delicacy of face best described as elfin. The only detail in which my imagination had been accurate was in her severity of appearance, or at least her attempt at severity. She was of average height and lightly built, almost fragile. Pale blonde hair had been pulled back into a coiled plait and her dress was a tight sheaf of heavy black silk. Neither feature managed to more than slightly alleviate her naturally winsome appearance, yet the haughty look in her eye and the formality of her greeting immediately showed the strength of her personality.

I was ushered upstairs to a long attic room that was clearly also her workroom. Every surface was strewn with cloth, finished and partially finished corsets, other bits of clothing and the apparatus of her trade. Two industrial sewing machines stood at the far end, and at one of these was seated a girl who turned and smiled as Jasmine addressed her.

'This is Caroline Greenwood,' I was informed, 'she will be measuring you and doing the work for your order. Caroline, this is Isabelle Colraine, a student who has ordered a corset.'

'Hi,' Caroline greeted me in a friendly, uncomplicated manner very different from her partner's formality.

That Caroline was Jasmine's partner in more than simply the business sense I quickly realised. They did nothing overt, but their body language was clearly that of not only deep intimacy but also of dominance and submission, with Jasmine clearly in charge. This was clear as they discussed my order and I found myself thrilling to the idea and more than a little envious of Jasmine. Caroline was beautiful, soft, womanly, quite full at the chest and hips but tight-waisted. Near-black curls framed a pretty, vivacious face made somehow insolent by full lips, an upturned nose and large, lustrous brown eyes. In height she was smaller than Jasmine, yet must have weighed several pounds more.

In my mind she was everything I would have liked Sammy to be, and I was quickly wondering if Jasmine made a practice of giving her corporal punishment. The answer came surprisingly quickly, because when Caroline moved a roll of peach-coloured silk to let me touch it something was revealed – a thin, crook-handled cane that could have only one purpose, the application of discipline to a soft, female bottom. It took me a moment to close my mouth and pretend nonchalance, but the look I received from Jasmine made it very clear that she had seen. My face flushed with embarrassment and the picture of how Caroline would look with her bottom bare and decorated with an array of scarlet cane stripes.

At the moment she was wearing jeans, but these were tight and showed off her well-fleshed bottom to advantage as she bent to replace the roll. Beneath the denim, the outline of her panties showed, quite large and demure, like school knickers. I turned away as a shiver went the full length of my spine. Jasmine gave a quiet sound, a suppressed chuckle of amusement at my obvious discomfort.

'Which would you like?' Caroline asked casually, apparently indifferent to the effect her body and the glimpse of the cane were having on me.

'The ivory silk, I think,' I answered.

'Not the peach or one of the pinks?' Jasmine suggested. 'Ivory is perhaps a touch plain for such a pretty girl. It will give a strict look that I feel is unsuitable for you. Something softer would be more appropriate.'

'I . . .' I began, and broke off fully aware that her tone and words implied a desire to see me as sexually subservient to her, in theory if not in actual practice. She had taken me aback though, and no suitable answer came quickly to mind.

'I can see that pink would suit you,' I eventually managed and was rewarded with the sight of a brief trace of ire in her eyes. 'For my own personality I feel that ivory is more appropriate, or possibly even black.'

'Black would be gorgeous,' Caroline put in, only to be quelled by an absolutely furious look from Jasmine.

'You are right, black it is,' I responded before Jasmine could say anything more.

She was going to press the point but at that moment the telephone rang. As Caroline was well in among the rolls and bales of cloth Jasmine was obliged to answer it. Caroline giggled and gave me a cheeky smile as soon as Jasmine had left the room, then pulled a roll of heavyweight black silk out from among the rolls.

'This is the heaviest weight and finest finish we have,' she said, holding it out to me. 'It's expensive, of course, but it is lovely, feel.'

I did, and was immediately captivated. The silk was a pure, lustrous black, smooth and heavy, a texture that went straight to the heart of my love of exotic clothing. I had to have it, even if it meant subsisting on beans on toast for the rest of term.

'It's beautiful,' I told Caroline. 'I'll have it.'

She responded with her mischievous smile and began to step out from among the rolls. Her manner was so open, so relaxed, that it was more than I could resist not to ask the question that had been burning in my mind since the accidental exposure of the cane. Well not a question really, as such an implement could have only one use – discipline. Nor had its exposure necessarily been accidental, I realised.

'Do you and Jasmine ... I mean,' I started clumsily, pointing to where the roll of silk concealed the cane.

'Not often,' she replied gaily, 'normally when I'm naughty I just get a smacking across her knee, with my hairbrush. Now, where's the tape measure.'

Her words left me trembling inside. The idea of her being spanked was bad enough, but the casual, cheeky way she had said it really got to me. As she searched for the tape measure I was picturing her across Jasmine's knee, undoubtedly with her jeans and panties pulled well down and her magnificent, fleshy bottom quite bare. I could well imagine her giggles and squeaks as she was put over, exposed and the spanking began, then her squeals and kicks as her bottom wobbled, bounced and reddened during punishment, then her contrite snivelling when she was finally released and allowed to massage her heavy, smarting bum cheeks, perhaps even with tears welling in her beautiful brown eyes . . .

'You'd better strip off so we can get the measurements right,' she said quite casually as she extracted the tape measure from beneath a half-finished corset of deep green satin. 'Do you know what design you'd like?'

'Full length but leaving the breasts bare would be ideal,' Jasmine spoke from the door. 'Your breasts are really too small to need support, and to leave them bare would enhance your femininity.'

'The majority of Victorian designs covered the lower half of the breasts,' I objected, turning to find Jasmine walking towards us.

'I am aware of that,' she answered. 'In your case though . . .'

'I really want to be as authentic as possible,' I cut in, 'with a straight front that lifts my breasts and pushes them together, not individual cups.'

'I do know how to make a Victorian corset, Isabelle,' she retorted. 'I just feel that with your figure you might feel most at home with your breasts left bare. You'll need to wear a chemise under the corset after all, and that will cover your modesty.'

There was more than a hint of mocking in her voice, derision even, as if the idea of me being shy about having my breasts bare was somehow ridiculous. From my own fantasies I knew full well what she was implying – being bare is appropriate for a girl with submissive sexual tendencies, and to be shy about it is quite wrong. Her attitude was beginning to make me resentful, although I had to admit that the idea of being punished by her in the way she gave

Caroline discipline was uncomfortably appealing. Yet as I was trying to find some suitable answer she turned and addressed Caroline.

'That was Emma, darling,' she said. 'She says her bodice needs adjusting so I'm going over. I won't be too long. Can you deal with Isabelle?'

'Of course,' Caroline replied. 'I'll see you later. Come on Isabelle, take your clothes off.'

I began to undress, with feelings very different from those that Walter Jessop had given me. Caroline was a girl, but it was not her sex so much as her personality that made the idea of undressing in front of her more than just acceptable. She was clearly the submissive partner in her relationship with Jasmine, and although it was me who would be bare it was impossible not to feel excited by the prospect. Jasmine gave me an unreadable smile as she left and presently I heard the front door close below me.

My blouse was already off, drawing a compliment from Caroline on my black lace bra.

'Do you need it off?' I asked, hoping that the answer would be yes.

'I think we'd better,' she answered. 'They're not that small, you know, they just look small because you're so tall.'

'Thank you,' I said as I unsnipped the catch of my bra and my breasts fell free of the cups.

'They look jolly firm too,' she continued quite casually as she admired my now-naked breasts.

'Thank you,' I repeated as I started on the button of my jeans.

'You can keep your panties on,' she continued, 'if you want to . . .'

It was an obvious invitation. There was no need whatever to take off my panties, so it could only be that she wanted me nude. I responded by tugging them down along with my jeans, drawing a little purring sound from her as the furry triangle between my thighs came on show. As I kicked my jeans and trainers off I really thought she was going to grab me as soon as I straightened up, but she simply stood back, running her eyes over my body with unashamed admiration.

'You're beautiful, Isabelle,' she breathed, then suddenly became businesslike. 'Put your arms up and I'll start measuring you.'

I complied, putting my hands on my head to allow her to put the tape measure around my chest. My whole body was trembling and I knew she could feel it. When she touched the tape measure to my breasts my nipples stiffened, and stayed hard, jutting out in blatant betrayal of my excitement as she quite casually noted down my 36B chest in her notebook. She then began to take serial measurements of my body, noting down the circumference at every second inch. Deft touches of her fingers on my back and belly sent new thrills through me and I could feel the moist warmth growing between my legs. She had gone down onto her knees to take the lower measurements and I was sure she would be able to smell the scent of my excitement.

'I think we'll design it to come down just to the top of your bottom,' she said calmly, once more encircling me with the measure.

Her fingers touched right at the top of my bottom cleft, which is an especially sensitive place for me. I like to think it's pretty too, with the roundness of my bottom finishing in a little 'V' shape of soft flesh at the base of my spine. I shivered at her touch, making my bottom quiver and drawing a giggle from her.

'Do you get spanked at all?' she asked, and began to trace a slow line down the cleft of my bottom with a fingernail.

'No, I prefer to give it,' I responded, barely able to control the trembling of my lower lip.

'You know Jasmine would like to punish you, don't you?' she continued.

'I guessed that,' I replied.

'She's good at it,' she went on. 'First she'd dress you up really prettily. Then she'd pull you across her knee, bare your sweet little bum and give you a really good smacking. Or maybe she'd tie your hands behind your back and make you bend over for the cane . . .'

'I'd rather do it to her, or you,' I broke in, no longer able to restrain my desire for her.

She just giggled and went back to measuring me. I forced myself to remain calm while she finished the measurements, aware that she was teasing and determined that I was going to punish her for her impertinence with a well-deserved spanking. Finally she was done and as she closed the notebook with a snap I was already reaching out for her. She giggled and pulled away, but only to scamper towards a threadbare sofa stacked with patterns and pieces of cut cloth.

'I'm going to spank you, you little tease,' I told her. 'Now are you going to take your jeans and pants down or do I have to do it for you?'

'You'll have to do it, if you can,' she giggled and backed against the sofa.

I had been anticipating a giggling surrender to my authority and obedience on Caroline's part. She obviously had other ideas, but she was small and looked soft so I was fully confident of not having the tables turned on me and ending up over her knee with my bare bum red and smarting. I feinted to one side and then made a grab for her as she tried to dash past me. I caught a wrist and pulled her off balance so that she sprawled on the floor. She was trying to fight back as I straddled her, but she was also laughing so hard that she was quite incapable of any real resistance.

I pulled her arms into the small of her back and sat across them, pinning her face down on the floor. Her bottom was right in front of me, a plump ball of blue denim just begging to be smacked. As I bent forward and started to delve under her tummy for the button of her jeans she stopped laughing but continued to thrash. She tried to wriggle away, but it was half-hearted and her breath was coming in sharp little pants, unmistakably passionate. I found the button and her resistance lessened as I popped it open. She knew what I was going to do. I was going to pull her jeans down, then her panties and spank her on the bare bottom. She sighed as I drew her zip down beneath her and stopped wriggling completely, allowing me easy access to her.

I took hold of the waistband of her jeans and began to ease them down, slowly to let her appreciate the full shame of having her bottom stripped for spanking. Underneath the jeans her panties were big, white and rather tight, so that her full cheeks bulged out around the sides of the material in the most delightful way. A small tattoo marked one cheek, a tiny yellow flower outlined in black. I settled her jeans around her thighs, leaving me unrestricted access to her fleshy young bottom.

'You do have a plump bottom, Caroline, don't you?' I taunted, planting a firm smack on a section of full cheek that was spilling out from one side of her over-tight panties.

'Yes,' she whimpered.

'A fat bottom in fact,' I continued, intent on utterly humiliating her before her spanking started, 'it's overflowing your panties.'

'Jasmine likes me to wear them tight,' she responded softly. 'She says if I can always feel them it keeps me on heat and reminds me how easily they can be pulled down.'

'You're a slut, Caroline,' I told her and started to pull her pants down.

She moaned as I pulled the waistband open, lifting her bottom to make the task easier for me. Slowly I eased them down, inch by inch over her lush globe, baring more and more of the chubby bottom cheeks until it was all on show, right down to where the fleshy tucks that met her bottom cleft and the parting between her legs. A tuft of dark hair showed between her thighs, hinting at her pussy.

I inverted her knickers over her jeans, leaving her whole glorious bottom naked and ready for spanking. My own pussy was soaking and badly in need of being touched. I moved forward, pressing myself against her pinned hand. She began to fumble at my vulva, rubbing with her fingers as I planted the first smack hard across the fullest part of her substantial bottom. She gave a little squeak as her flesh shook, and just for a moment her cheeks opened, giving me a tantalising glimpse of dark hair around her anus. I caught her scent too, hot and rich, the smell of excited girl.

Another firm smack followed and then her buttocks were bouncing properly as I set to my task. She quickly began to squeal and kick, but could do nothing to unseat me. As her bottom warmed she also lost all regard for her modesty, bucking her burning rear up and down to give me a fine view of abundant hair, tight brown bottom-hole and pouted sex lips. From the strength of the scent of her sex I knew how turned on she was, but from the way she squealed and thrashed you would have thought the punishment was real discipline and not play. Her struggles were turning me on too, and the more she squirmed and squealed the harder I spanked her.

Finally I stopped. Her whole bottom was red, a fat ball of glowing girl-flesh, hot, smarting and a sight straight from my favourite fantasies. She was breathing hard, sobbing quietly and giving the occasional low moan. She had stopped trying to play with my pussy when the pain of her beating became too great, but now she began again, urgently trying to rub her imprisoned hands against me.

I rose onto my knees and indicated with a gentle pressure that she should roll over. She obeyed, making no dispute of my authority now that I had punished her. As she rolled her pussy came into view, a thickly grown triangle of black curls covering swollen lips. She opened her thighs as I moved my bottom back towards her face, stretching her jeans and panties taut between them. I obliged by pulling them down to her ankles and she sighed as her legs parted fully to expose the moist pink centre of her sex and the reddened tuck of her fleshy bottom. My own thighs were straddled across the soft fullness of her breasts, my naked bottom inches from her face. A gentle kiss just inches from my anus indicated her willingness and I slid myself further back, smothering her mouth in my pussy. An exquisite thrill went through me as her tongue found my clitoris and then she was lapping, sending me dizzy with pleasure.

Shelving my dominance over her, I buried my face between her thighs and returned the favour, tasting the rich, musky flavour of her pussy as I began to lick with the same fervour as she was tonguing me. I had made Sammy kneel to lick me, and she'd been nude while I was dressed, while with Caroline it was me who was naked. Before I was through I was determined to make Caroline adopt an equally humble and yielding position, but not until I'd come, the need was just too urgent.

It didn't take long, with her tongue working on my clitoris with an expertise evidently born of long practice I was soon clamping my thighs around her head in the approach to orgasm. Nor was she far behind. She had started to move her hips rhythmically against my face, a squirming motion that showed off the puckered, brown dimple of her anus each time she did it. I slid my hands under her bottom and took hold of it, moulding her well-spanked cheeks and pulling them open to stretch her anus wide. She immediately responded, her own hands going to my bottom and a fingernail beginning to tease me between my cheeks.

I started to come as she began to tickle my bottom-hole. I felt my pussy start to contract, then the teasing finger was seeking entry to my bottom as another found my vagina. I screamed out my ecstasy into her pussy, coming in her face as her finger probed my vagina. Then my anus popped open and her finger was in my bottom, my ring tightening on the intruding digit as my climax tore through me. For an instant my whole being was centred on my sex, my burning clitoris and my gaping vagina. My penetrated anus too, which sent such a strong and exquisitely dirty thrill through me that I screamed again.

As wave after wave of my orgasm swept through me, I once more buried my face in her pussy, determined to give her the same pleasure. She came in moments, keeping her fingers inside me and emitting a long, ecstatic groan as her chubby thighs clamped hard around my head. I felt the muscles of her buttocks contract in my hand and squeezed them as she came, calling out my name as her climax reached its peak.

As her shudders subsided I stopped licking and turned to take her in my arms. She cuddled up to me, warm and yielding as she burrowed her face into my chest. For a long time we held each other, her arms clamped tight around me as I stroked her curls and held her to my breasts.

Eventually we pulled apart. Caroline, who had seemed full of ebullience and energy from the first, was now cheerful to the point of being manic. The first thing she did on standing up was to go to a mirror and inspect her bottom, admiring her reddened cheeks with immense satisfaction. She then shuffled over to me holding her jeans and panties at knee level and gave me another hug and a kiss, thanking me for punishing her so effectively and placing my hand once more on her bottom. It was still hot from the beating and her skin felt soft and rough with goose pimples. For a long moment we kissed and I explored her bottom, stroking the warm skin in little soothing motions. For the first time I experienced the pleasure of comforting a well-spanked girl, a feeling at once deliciously dominant and also tender.

Again we hugged for a long time before pulling apart. She suggested a shower, taking only a quick glance at her watch. Both of us were sweaty and damp with our own and each other's juices, so I accepted. The implication of her checking the time was not lost on me. Evidently, she didn't want Jasmine to catch us together. The thought inspired a mixture of emotions in me – jealousy, that Jasmine and not I was Caroline's regular partner, a naughty delight in having had such fine sex with Caroline while Jasmine was elsewhere, guilt for just the same reason and apprehension for the possible consequences of my actions.

She stripped with the same indifference to the display of her body that I had noted in Sammy. I like full-bodied girls, and in many ways Sammy and Caroline were similar. Caroline was slightly less full-figured and a little taller, but with the same combination of plump bottom and heavy breasts that I found so appealing. Caroline's waist was also remarkably trim, but presumably trained to corsets where Sammy's was entirely natural. While Caroline was more mature and self-confident, there were also similarities in their personalities and as I watched Caroline strip naked I wondered how it would feel to have both of them naked at my feet, grovelling to me with their fat bottoms red from recently delivered beatings.

I followed Caroline downstairs to the shower, where we played a little more, soaping each other while we discussed our mutual love of old-fashioned clothing. Just as I was fascinated my her big breasts and full, fleshy bottom, so was she with my breasts, which she described as apple-like, and my legs and bottom, which she described as coltish and trim respectively. I couldn't help but giggle when she got down into a squat and asked me to stick my bottom out. As I complied she took hold of my cheeks and pulled them open.

Thinking that she was simply intent on a close inspection of my pussy, I couldn't resist a startled gasp when she buried her face between my bottom cheeks and kissed my anus. As she rose she explained that it was a gesture of thanks for taking control of her and a ritual admission of my dominance. I couldn't help but agree. Just to touch another person's anus has always struck me as an act both

47

intimate, dirty and deeply submissive, but to kiss a partner's bottom-hole was stronger by far, an act of utter submission.

I wanted to continue and was wondering how Caroline would look in combinations and a corset, with the split pulled apart to show her bottom off. She was nervous though and evidently concerned for the return of Jasmine.

'Would she really mind?' I asked as we dressed together in their bedroom.

'Yes and no,' Caroline answered. 'She's ... well, you'll see.'

'How do you mean?' I queried, only to be interrupted by the sound of the door below being opened.

We scampered upstairs in fits of giggles and by the time Jasmine caught up we looked innocent, or at least passably so. If Jasmine suspected anything she made no comment, but I saw her sniff the air and give Caroline a sharp glance.

They took a few more design details for my corset and I paid a deposit, then left, feeling thoroughly satisfied but more than keen to further my exploration.

Four

Caroline's sheer eagerness and lack of inhibition had made having sex with her easier and more guilt free than any of my previous experiences. She was also adept in a way that made my encounter with Sammy seem clumsy, inept almost. It had just been so natural, and I had to admit I was entranced, even a little in love.

The problem was Jasmine. Her efforts to dominate me had been irritating but also compelling. So while I couldn't really say I liked her, I couldn't deny her appeal sexually, nor a sneaking desire to let her have her way. I tried to play this down at first, but it wouldn't go away and so I made a deliberate decision to masturbate over the idea and so try and lay the ghost.

I waited until late at night, then drew my curtains and turned the light off, intent on allowing my imagination full scope. My fingers were trembling as I undressed and let my thoughts wander to find the most satisfying fantasy. Despite my delight in both the idea and practise of spanking other girls, I found the idea of receiving the same treatment myself deeply undignified. I always loved to think how ashamed a girl must feel with her panties pulled down to expose her bottom for punishment, and the idea of being in the same position myself was close to unbearable. It's one thing for some giggly little trollop like Caroline or Sammy to lie across someone's lap and be spanked with her bum bare, but this was me, the graceful, poised Isabelle Colraine, whose whole being demanded that she accept submission from others, not give it.

That wasn't going to stop me doing it, and as I stepped out of my panties to stand naked in the warm air of my room I already knew that although my orgasm might be hard to achieve, it would be superb. I also knew I would feel guilty and ashamed afterwards, but I didn't care any more.

The only light came from the glowing element of my bar heater, which cast a rich orange glow. In the mirror my skin looked red, my hair black and my nipples a deep crimson, like a demoness or succuba from some medieval illustration of the temptations of the flesh. I began to stroke my breasts, watching the nipples harden and protrude, then turning my attention to my stomach, touching my tummy button, stroking my pubic hair but denying myself deeper, more intimate caresses.

Caroline had said that Jasmine would either have put me over her knee or dressed me up and made me bend over for the cane. It was hard to know which position was more humiliating. On the one hand to be thrown naked over a woman's lap and spanked like a little brat seemed gloriously undignified. I would be nude, with my breasts naked and dangling from my chest. When I started to kick and struggle under the pain of my punishment my thighs would part, exposing my pussy and anus to the woman who was slapping my poor, hot bottom. Then again, the sheer depth of shame from being ordered to bend over and obeying would be wonderfully intense. I could imagine just how I'd feel as my skirts were lifted and my fancy drawers pulled open, baring my bottom in a froth of lace and silk. Then I'd be caned on my bare bottom, maybe even made to cry, and left with six or a dozen red lines across the white skin of my nates to remind me of my place and that I had accepted punishment.

I turned, sticking my bottom out for the mirror and imagining the red lines across my buttocks. I had seen their cane and could imagine how much it would hurt and how my poor bottom would throb afterwards. The bruising would last for days, a constant reminder that I had been whacked. I let my hand slip between my legs, finding my pussy moist and ready. Parting my legs I improved my view of my own rear.

Still looking back over my shoulder I began to masturbate, watching the tips of my fingers work among my bush of pubic hair. The centre of my pussy showed deep red in the orange fire light, my anus a dark spot in the shadows between my cheeks. Being slim, I look really rude from the back. Everything shows, while a fatter girl in the same position would at least be spared making quite such a blatant display of her anal charms. It was just how I'd look if I was to be caned, dark brown anus showing, pussy so prominent that my sex lips might even be at risk of feeling the bite of the cane. The only difference would be that instead of being nude I'd have raised skirts and petticoats and split drawers to enhance the fact that my poor bottom was naked.

Once she had me in position, she would beat me, applying the cane skilfully and without mercy, ignoring my pathetic squealing, even ignoring my tears when they started after three or four strokes. Caroline would watch, giggling over my degradation, with one hand down the front of her panties so that she could play with herself while I was punished.

After twelve strokes I would be blubbering openly. My bottom would be on fire and I'd be wriggling my toes and stamping my feet in my pain. My pussy would be wet though, so wet that the juice would be running down my thighs, plain evidence that being beaten had excited me. Then I'd go down on my knees, bow my head to Jasmine, stick my naked, burning bottom out and beg to be allowed to show my thanks by subjecting myself to the exquisite gesture of submission Caroline had given me, the kissing of her anus.

I came, calling out Jasmine's name as my muscles spasmed. My knees came together and I saw my bum cheeks clench in helpless ecstasy, a wonderfully rude sight that helped lift me to a second peak. I was rubbing hard at my clitoris, although it felt unbearably sensitive. Once more I climaxed, then I was falling forward onto the bed, still playing with myself as a great rush of shame for what I had come over swept through me.

At the moment of orgasm I had been imagining myself putting my lips to Jasmine's anus, an act so shameful, so submissive that I found myself sobbing as I sank down, exhausted by my climax.

Masturbating over the thoughts of submission to Jasmine did lay the ghost of my desire for punishment, or at least partially. Instead of a desperate need for it I felt ashamed of myself and aware that I had given in to the deepest, dirtiest corner of my sexuality. On the other hand I knew that as long as I could come over the fantasy I would be able to resist turning it into reality, and so when the time came for my first corset fitting I felt confident of being able to resist Jasmine's attempts to dominate me.

I was, however, concerned about what I had done with Caroline. I had no idea how their relationship worked, and for all I knew Caroline might deliberately be in the habit of indulging in sexual indiscretions just for the pleasure of admitting to them and being punished. The idea appealed to me in any case. As the other guilty party I would be in a very weak position indeed if Jasmine demanded the right to punish me for it. True, I could always just refuse, but such an action would probably spoil my chances of any further pleasures with Caroline. No, if Caroline had told Jasmine and Jasmine demanded my submission as an apology, then I would have to let my panties down or face the end of what was rapidly becoming the most special and exciting part of my life.

As it was, she gave no hint that anything was amiss, greeting me with an easy cheerfulness very different from her initial attitude. I decided that she had accepted that, like her, I preferred to dominate, and had relaxed. Once more I had to strip to my panties for my fitting and being naked in their presence was starting to get to me. The tuile they had made up for my corset was plain calico and lacked erotic appeal, but I was still wearing nothing but a diminutive pair of flowery pink knickers and couldn't help the response of my body. It was only as Caroline was making subtle adjustment to the lower hem of the tuile that Jasmine dropped the bombshell.

'You don't mind that we're videoing this do you?' she asked quite casually.

'Videoing it?' I responded in surprise.

'We usually do,' she continued, pointing to a corner of the attic. 'It makes the making up easier when we haven't got you to model.'

'Oh,' I answered, glancing to where she had pointed.

High among the shadows of the gable end of the room I could see the camera. It was a small device, like a security camera, mounted on a bracket and all but invisible in the dark corner. The implication was at once obvious to me. She was letting me know that everything I had done with Caroline was on tape. Obviously Caroline knew as well and I suddenly realised why she had made a special effort to get me near the couch for our sex – the position we had been in put us directly in front of the lens.

I was immediately furious and gathering my breath to tell both of them exactly what I thought. Then I stopped. For one thing I wasn't certain that the camera had been running on the occasion of my previous visit. If it hadn't, then my accusation would rebound on me with a vengeance. Not only that, but if they had taped me and Caroline then I was in difficulty. Although our sex had been entirely consensual, it wouldn't take a genius to edit the tape to make it seem as if I had forced Caroline down on the floor and spanked her against her will. After all, I'd had her pinned, she had pretended to object when I had pulled down her trousers and panties and she had made a real fuss over her spanking. What Dr Appledore, my tutor, would say if presented with a video that apparently showed me dishing out a bare bottom spanking to a struggling girl I didn't like to think. Rustication was the least I could expect, possibly I would even be sent down. Deciding to play things carefully, I swallowed my anger and put my hands on my head to allow Caroline to pin a tuck under my arm.

What I needed to do, of course, was get the tape back – urgently. If they had done it, then it would be on the main camera tape, while they might or might not have made a copy. I had no way of knowing and although I could not be sure of her good faith, I decided to try and appeal to Caroline as an ally. She returned my pleading look with a wink and the careful application of her finger to her lips. A moment later, when Jasmine was momentarily distracted, she used her finger to trace a pattern on the skin between my breasts and then glanced meaningfully at the camera. It was a W and a J, which could mean only one thing.

Why Walter Jessop had the tape I didn't know. At a guess Caroline had given it to him because she didn't want Jasmine to see it. That raised the question of why she would let me know where it was if she wanted it as a memento, but such minor issues were not my current problem. I had to go to Jessop and get the wretched thing back.

As I cycled north along the Banbury road I reviewed my options. Basically there seemed to be three choices. Firstly, I could find some way to be alone and search the shop and house. This not only had the disadvantage of being illegal and difficult to manage but if the rest of his house was even half as cluttered as his shop, trying to find a video tape, let alone the right video tape, would be like looking for a needle in a haystack.

Secondly, I could take the high moral ground and demand the tape. Whether I would succeed or not was debatable. He obviously fancied me and seemed a gentle sort, yet all he had to do was refuse or simply deny having the tape. It also seemed reasonable to assume that he had watched it, which meant that he had not only seen me naked but in the throes of orgasm under Caroline's tongue. It's hard to be aloof and haughty with a man who has seen you come, and it meant that any prissiness on my part would simply look ridiculous.

The thought of him seeing me nude made me blush with shame and brought my mind to the third possibility – bribery. I had no money to buy the tape with, but I did have something he could hardly fail to want. The thought of offering him sex in return for the tape doubled my sense of shame. It also sent the same naughty thrill through me that I had got when I showed him my panties. Modern girls don't flirt with dirty old men, it just isn't done, but I had, and if he'd seen Caroline and I together then he knew I was no prude.

As I passed the ring road I realised that if I really wanted the tape then the third choice was probably my only option. The realisation gave me a sharp pang of humiliation. Of course I could just ask for it back first, but if he refused I'd have to make an offer. The question was, how little I could get away with and how far I was prepared to go. I could bear the idea of stripping for him and even of posing while he tossed off over me. If he really pushed I'd even be prepared to take him in my hand, just as I had fantasised. I certainly wasn't going to let him fuck me, the thought was just too much. I might just let him put his cock in my mouth though. I hadn't sucked many men's cocks, because it always seems such a submissive act, and I'd never let anyone come in my mouth. The thought of allowing Walter Jessop to put his penis in my mouth was dirty, really dirty, but just on the boundary where the thrill of erotic humiliation made the thought bearable. That would be my limit then, to suck his cock and let him come in my hand. If he wanted more then I'd just have to take my chances with the video.

The prospect of perhaps going so far as to suck Walter Jessop's cock was enough to make my hands shake as I fastened my bicycle to the old-fashioned streetlight opposite his shop. I had decided more or less what I was going to say, and was determined not to back down easily, but it still took a strong effort of will to push the door open and step inside.

The first thing I saw was his head and shoulders protruding above an antique lectern. At the sight of me, his round, ruddy face broke into a broad grin. I tried to read shiftiness or lechery into his expression but failed, finding only unconcealed pleasure and no more than a trace of a leer.

'Ah, Isabelle,' he greeted me. 'I understand that you have ordered a corset from the good Jasmine Devil. So what can I do for you today? Some accessories perhaps?'

'Er . . . yes,' I replied, rather thrown off track. I had expected him to betray at least some awareness of why I was visiting, but of course it was possible that he had no idea Caroline had revealed the whereabouts of the tape.

'You're in luck,' he continued. 'I was at an auction the other day and picked up the most magnificent set of combinations. Only theatrical wear, I'm afraid, not originals. A moderately faithful copy though, made at some time in the fifties at a guess. Pure linen and heavily trimmed with cotton lace, indeed perhaps too heavily for authenticity. Would you like to see them?'

'Yes,' I answered, swept away by his enthusiasm and complete lack of artifice. If he had watched me spank Caroline and come to orgasm with her on the tape then he was being remarkably cool about it.

He stepped down from the lectern and disappeared into the back of the shop, whistling merrily to himself. I stayed where I was, trying to order my thoughts. It is one thing to decide to confront someone on a matter as delicate as that which I wished to broach with him, quite another to actually do it. The thought of describing the contents of the video to him brought the blood to my cheeks, and I wasn't at all sure that I'd actually be able to get the words out to make my indecent proposition. Even with Caroline and Sammy I had felt a little reticent at putting my feelings into words. With Walter Jessop it was a very different matter indeed.

I was still trying to decide on my best approach when he came back, holding the most splendid set of combinations I had seen. Long, and made of light linen, they managed to seem dainty despite being heavily flounced and pleated, not to mention trimmed and embroidered. By comparison, the garments in the attic at home were positively austere.

'It might, in fact, fit you quite well,' he said with obvious relish. 'Would you care to try it on?'

'Yes, but I couldn't possibly afford it!' I remonstrated, torn between desire for the beautiful object and my less than healthy bank balance.

'Nonsense, nonsense,' he answered cheerfully. 'I'm sure we could come to some arrangement. Try it on anyway, without obligation. I freely confess to enjoying the prospect of seeing you wearing it.'

'All right,' I agreed, unable to resist and postponing the real reason for my visit until later.

I took the garment and stepped behind the screen while he began once more to examine the lectern. For some reason – perhaps an unconscious defensiveness combined with the knowledge that I might end up undressing – I had chosen to wear loose canvas trousers and a baggy top but had put on some of my prettiest underwear beneath. This was a silk cami-knicker set which had a looseness around the chest and bottom that I felt gave me a charming, yielding look. I peeled off my trousers and top, then hesitated, wondering whether to go bare under the combinations. Considering that there was a still a possibility of me ending up having to strip, the answer had to be yes. I was trembling hard as I peeled nude behind the screen and threw the camiknicker set across the top of it to make it clear to him that I was naked. If he wanted to make an advance, now was the time and I waited, trembling hard, expecting his ruddy features to appear around the screen at any moment. I felt naughty and as ready as I ever would be.

Nothing happened, and after a while he began to whistle once more. Evidently he had no intention of making such a bold approach, and I reached for the combinations with both relief and regret.

They were really a predecessor to my camiknickers, being the same basic design but with far more modesty, covering me fully from my chest to below my knees. The only major differences were the extra cloth and the split at the rear, designed, of course, to allow a girl in full skirts to pee in comfort, but also convenient should she need to be punished on her bare skin. I stepped into them and pulled them up, then adjusted the laces at the front so that my breasts were not in danger of falling out, even if a good deal of them was showing. The fit was good, if not perfect. The girl for whom they had originally been made must have stood more or less my height but been fuller at the chest and hip. The result was a comfortable bagginess.

'Are you ready, my dear?' Walter Jessop's voice sounded from beyond the screen.

In answer I stepped out and gave him a twirl to which he responded with a smile even broader and more delighted than before.

'You look wonderful!' he declared. 'Your taste is so rare among modern women, you know. You are a gem, Isabelle, a true gem.'

'Thank you,' I responded.

There was a pause, me standing there in just the combinations, Walter Jessop admiring me with an expert eye. Quite suddenly I decided to take the plunge while he was so transparently pleased with me.

'Mr Jessop,' I said carefully. 'I believe you have a certain item in your possession which I would very much like to have in mine.'

'Ah ha,' he answered, his tone a clear admission that my request was not a surprise.

'Unfortunately I am really not able to pay,' I continued, 'but I would be grateful if you would be kind enough not to insist.'

It was carefully worded, with just a faint implication that my gratitude might be tangible. Nor had I actually mentioned the video, the details of which I was hoping to avoid having to discuss. He paused, looking at me reflectively and evidently weighing my words in his mind. Finally he spoke.

'Free, *gratis* as it were, might, I feel, be stretching generosity too far,' he said slowly. 'Yet I have no wish to appear miserly, nor inflexible. Perhaps you have a suggestion for mutually satisfying terms?'

So he was prepared to part with it, but not for nothing. What he was not prepared to do was make me a clear proposition, thus allowing himself to save face should I prove unwilling. His use of the word 'satisfying' was surely a hint though, a hint that I would be able to meet his needs – physically.

'I think we could,' I replied.

Now was the time to act and thus keep control. It was also easier to act than speak. I stepped up onto the lectern, reached out and gently squeezed the front of his trousers, all the while looking straight into his eyes. His genitals felt large, a soft handful within his trousers. For an instant he looked surprised, then his face softened to an expression of eager disbelief.

'Yes please,' he croaked.

Keeping my eyes on his face, I groped for the fastening to his trousers, which proved to be buttons. The front of the lectern hid what I was doing from the door, and I popped a button open, my fingers clumsy and fumbling. He stayed silent as I opened his fly, button by button, until all five were undone and I could slide my hand inside. Once more I squeezed his crotch, this time just through his pants as I tried to pluck up the courage to make the final exposure. Swallowing, I pulled down the front of his underpants, and then it was all in my hand, bare. His cock was small, and still limp, but his balls were huge and they squirmed in their sack as I pulled his genitals free of his trousers.

'Oh God,' he moaned as I cupped his balls in my hand and began to stroke the upper surface of his penis.

Looking down, I found my hand full of his cock and balls, an obscene sight, but one of which I could not deny the erotic impact. It just seemed so naughty to be playing with a dirty old man's genitals, so smutty, so improper, and just the sort of act my parents and various ministers had sought to make me regard as unthinkable. Only then did I realise that I wasn't just going to do it, I was going to enjoy it – whether I liked it or not.

'The door, Isabelle,' he managed.

I gave him a smile and skipped quickly to the door, slipping the bolts into place and pulling down the blind to leave the shop in a dim green light that enhanced my feelings of naughtiness. Turning back to Walter, I found him stepping from the lectern, his genitals still bulging rudely from his fly.

He went into the back room and I followed. It was much like the shop, cluttered with the junk of ages but with a small area cleared for making coffee and a large comfortable armchair positioned to allow him to see into the shop. It was this into which he sank, spreading his legs and favouring me with an inviting smile. His cock was resting on the sack of his balls, still limp but ready for my attentions.

'This may take a while, my dear,' he informed me, 'and perhaps you could call me Mr Jessop, or even "sir", while you do it.'

'Yes, sir,' I replied meekly, his remark immediately triggering a fantasy of my own.

I was wearing only the combinations and my surroundings were both old-fashioned and cluttered, very Victorian. He was also old-fashioned, and could have walked down a street in Victorian times without raising more than the occasional eyebrow. If he could be Mr Jessop, then I could be a shop girl, forced to strip to my underwear and masturbate my employer in order to keep my job. He was perfect for the fantasy, his face red with excitement and his stomach bulging his waistcoat out above the obscene things I was going to have to touch.

He patted the arm of the chair and I went to sit down. His hand cupped my bottom as I reached out, once more faced with the prospect of touching his cock. I did it, curling my finger and thumb around the shaft and starting to tug at it. His other hand came up, pulling at the laces that held my bodice fast. I made no objection, concentrating on my fantasy of being molested. As a shop girl I wouldn't have dared object to his fondling of my bottom, nor to the exposure of my breasts.

My bodice fell open and he pulled the sides apart to expose my breasts. The nipples were already stiff, and as he took one gently between his fingers I couldn't resist a moan. I began to tug at his cock more firmly, feeling it swell in my fingers as he groped at my bottom and breasts. He was right, it was taking a long time. Most of the men I'd been with had erections before I'd got their cocks out of their pants, or even before they had got into mine. Walter's prick was swelling, but slowly, and I began to wonder if he would need it sucked.

I was willing, but I wanted him to order me to take his cock in my mouth, or better still, take me by the hair and force me to do it. He seemed to be enjoying feeling me up though and I realised that he was still unsure how far I would go.

'Must I really kiss it this time Mr Jessop?' I asked pleadingly.

'You must, girl,' he answered firmly, 'and I think now is the time.'

'No, sir, please,' I begged. 'Not that.'

He gave a little chuckle. I'd asked for it, and he knew I wanted it but he also knew I wanted to resist. His hand came up from my bottom, not to take me by the hair but to lock on the nape of my neck. Despite my willingness it felt very real as he pushed me gently but firmly down towards his lap. It was actually quite hard for me, and I felt real shame as my face was pushed close enough to detect the masculine scent of his cock. I'm really not sure if I could have done it without the pressure from his hand, but as it was he simply pushed my face against himself. I was still holding his cock, and with a deep feeling of dirtiness I opened my mouth and let him push my head onto it. It tasted salty and male, an obscene meaty thing that squirmed in my mouth.

I began to suck, his cock swelling more rapidly now that it was in my mouth. It was turning me on properly now, both the sheer dirtiness of what I was doing and my fantasy. I began to move my lips rhythmically on the neck of his cock and encircled the base of his shaft with my fingers, masturbating him into my mouth as a previous boyfriend had taught me. He groaned, keeping his hand on my neck, allowing no escape, while the other stroked my hair in an effort to soothe me despite what he was making me do.

My bottom was stuck out, taut against the seat of my combinations. I knew he could see, because his eyes were locked not on the junction of his penis and my mouth but on the swell of my buttocks. In my fantasy he would have beaten me first, only able to overcome his reserve after becoming unbearably excited by the sight of my naked bottom and the thrill of whipping me. He would have made me bend over the lectern, on tiptoe with my bottom stuck out. He would have opened my drawers, ignoring my sobs and pleas to be allowed to retain at least the modesty of my combinations. My bum would have been exposed, with the rear of my pussy and my anus showing in an involuntary but utterly lewd display. Then he would have caned me – no, he would have used a dog whip on my bottom, a punishment more humiliating still. Then when I sucked him my bum would have been left bare, my exposure and the red marks of punishment adding to his thrill and my shame.

I put my free hand back, intent on my fantasy and his pleasure as I reached behind myself and pulled the split of the combinations open to bare my bum. I did both sides, leaving my naked bottom thrust out and parted so that anyone behind me would have been able to see both my pussy and anus. He gave a sigh of appreciation at the sight. He was hard in my mouth now, his little stubby cock fully erect for my lips to slide up and down. I put my hand between my thighs, delving among the linen folds for my pussy. I was wet and as I found my clitoris and began to dab I knew that my orgasm was not far away.

My fantasy took a new turn as my orgasm started to well up inside me. I was still the shop girl, stripped to her underwear, beaten and forced to suck her obese, sweating employer's penis. Only now his wife had come in and was faced with the sight of the pretty young shop girl with her husband's cock in her mouth. She would be able to see everything, the pink centre of my vagina, swollen with involuntary excitement, the wrinkled dark spot of my anus, the fluff of dark hair that did nothing to hide my secret places. Instantly she would explode with rage, not with her husband though, with me, who she saw as a wanton little slut, always tempting with her young body and pretty face. Before either of us could react, she would snatch up the dog whip and lay it hard across my naked bottom. At that instant he would come in my mouth, too far gone to stop himself.

I started to come, sucking frantically on Mr Jessop's cock as I imagined the utter shame of having my mouth filled with sperm as a whip was applied to my fully exposed bottom. My climax rose as my mind fixed on how the woman would exclaim with disgust at the sight of my excited pussy. Then it burst in my head as I sank my mouth deep on Mr Jessop's cock, taking it all the way in. I could feel the muscles around my vagina and anus in spasm and my last thought as the peak hit me was of the woman's deeper disgust at the sight of my tight brown bottom-hole winking at her in response to the pain of her whip.

He groaned and his grip tightened, making me realise that he was about to come. An instant earlier and I would have let him do it in my mouth, but now I pulled back. His cock popped from my mouth, jerked and a jet of white sperm erupted from the tip. With his hand gripping my neck I had been unable to pull back far enough and it splashed in my face. I exclaimed in disgust as the sticky fluid spattered on my nose and cheeks, pulling back further only to catch his second spurt across my naked breasts. He grunted, grabbing his cock and pulling at it to force out yet more sperm, again catching me across my breasts.

He let go of my neck and I rocked back on my heels, feeling deeply ashamed of myself and thoroughly soiled. There was come on my nose, across my cheeks and on my chin, also on my neck and breasts. I looked down to find a dribble of it hanging from one still-erect nipple, a sight that made me wince in disgust.

'Sorry, my dear, do have a handkerchief,' he said, his voice still coming in pants from the effort of his orgasm.

I accepted the handkerchief and began to dab at myself, saying nothing. I'd done it, and I had to admit I'd enjoyed it, even to the extent that if he had come first I knew I'd have enjoyed having it in my face and probably rubbed the filthy stuff into my nipples while I finished myself off. The thought added to my humiliation and I covered my bottom as soon as my face and chest were clean.

The tape was mine though, by agreement, which – I reminded myself in an attempt to lessen my sense of shame – was why I'd done what I had. Well, partly, I had to face the fact that I'd sucked his cock willingly enough and there had been nothing in our agreement that said I had to masturbate.

'Thank you, my dear,' he said at length after taking the handkerchief and cleaning the last of his come from the tip of his cock. 'It is yours and, should I live to be a hundred, I shall never forget the beautiful experience you have given me.'

'Don't mention it,' I said. 'May I have it then?'

'Eh?' he responded.

'The tape,' I replied. 'Could you get the tape?'

'Tape?' he queried.

'The tape, Caroline and Jasmine's tape,' I insisted, wondering if he was playing games with me.

'What tape is this?' he asked. 'I understood that our arrangement was for you to allow me the pleasure of your body in return for the combinations.'

I didn't reply. His expression and the tone of his voice were so open, so genuinely puzzled that I had no doubt whatever that he was telling the truth. Caroline had lied to me, and I had just sucked a dirty old man off for nothing.

Five

Well, not nothing, because I had the beautiful frilly combinations. Yet I was still furious and felt that I had prostituted myself. The difference was subtle, yet in my mind sucking cock in order to get the tape back would have been a far more acceptable act than doing it for a material reward. True, I hadn't known, but it was what he had thought and so it meant that he basically regarded me as a tart, willing to give sexual favours in return for goods. I was mortified, and my head was a whorl of conflicting emotions, shame, anger and self-disgust predominating. Underneath it all though I knew that I had enjoyed the experience and it was more than I could resist not to masturbate over what I'd done and in particular how it had felt to have his come splashed in my face and over my breasts. At first I couldn't face the thought of visiting Jasmine and Caroline, but finally I had to. Besides, I had paid a deposit on my corset.

For a week I buried myself in my work and the other aspects of my social life that were developing at college. Finally I could put it off no longer, and set off in the direction of the Cowley Road with a determination to get the tape from Jasmine by sheer force of willpower.

She just laughed at me and asked if I'd enjoyed sucking Walter Jessop's cock. I stopped, my fury

changing on the instant to chagrin and embarrassment. I had imagined that what we had done would
stay a secret, but obviously not, he had told Jasmine
and Caroline!

'He taped it,' she continued, 'all of it. He's got a
camera in the back room, just like our one.'

'What!' I demanded, horror-struck by the depths of
their treachery and depravity.

'And there's no good acting prissy either,' she
continued lightly. 'I saw what you did while you were
sucking him. Face it, Isabelle, you're a slut and a
whore.'

I nearly flew at her, but fought the urge down. It
would do no good, and with possession of the two
tapes she had a lot of power over me.

'Now, now,' she chided, sensing my anger. 'Don't
throw a tantrum or I might have to spank you. I tell
you what, I'll play you for the tapes. How about
that?'

'How do you mean?' I demanded, stung by her
suggestion that I might need a spanking but realising
that the remark had been made specifically to goad
me.

'The tapes against your submission,' she continued.
'You do know that I'd like you at my feet, don't you?
I've wanted your little panties off from the moment I
saw you.'

'Maybe,' I answered, blushing but trying to think
logically, 'but how will I know if you've given me all
the copies?'

'You'll just have to trust us,' she responded, 'but
don't get too worried, they're just for our entertainment, we wouldn't do anything nasty.'

She already had, in my view, but then I had had
sex with her girlfriend, so perhaps it wasn't entirely
unfair. In any case, I seemed to have little choice.

'Very well,' I answered, 'what's the game?'

I was expecting some sort of sport, at which I was confident of winning. I was taller than her and obviously fitter, because for all her slim curves and elegant look, underneath she was a wispy little blonde with nothing like my muscle. Then her face set into a wicked smile and I realised that I was being naïve.

'It's simple,' she said, 'and fair. There's a club in Cowley that has strippers on Saturdays, the Red Ox. I know the manager and he'll let us do it if I ask him. The girls get paid by the punters, so whoever makes the most wins, simple.'

'What, strip in front of a load of drunken yobs!' I exclaimed. 'I couldn't! Anyway, I'm a student, I can't do that sort of thing!'

'One thing I promise you,' she laughed, 'is that there won't be anybody from the university there. They look on students as a bunch of stuck-up rich kids and they're not exactly made welcome.'

'Oh, great!' I responded. 'So what are they going to think of me stripping?'

'They'll love it,' she said. 'In fact it'll give you an advantage if you admit you're a student. Don't you realise how much townies would like the idea of seeing some hoity-toity university girl strip?'

She was right. Coming from a genteel and moderately wealthy family I was well aware of how resentful the working classes could be, simply of my birth and what they saw as a haughty, aloof attitude. Undoubtedly the customers at the Red Ox would enjoy seeing a university girl do a striptease. I was dressed the part too, with a college T-shirt, baggy jeans and even my college scarf as the day was distinctly chilly. If Dr Appledore ever found out I would be in deep trouble, but then there was no reason that he should. On the other hand, the

71

thought of peeling nude in front of a gang of working-class males filled me with alarm – but also excitement.

'Come on,' Jasmine urged, sensing my hesitation. 'You must admit it's fair and think how much you want those tapes back.'

She was taunting me, but it was the arrival of Caroline that made me decide to do it. She was delighted by the idea and offered to take round a pint pot to collect the money. I argued for a little more and insisted on defining my submission as an hour of my time subject to her orders and excluding anything dangerous. I couldn't back down in front of Caroline though, not even if it meant once more prostituting myself.

By the time I had showered, dried and put my clothes back on Jasmine had made all the necessary arrangements. We had tossed a coin and she had won, deciding to go second. I could see her logic, assuming that once I had done the ground work and turned the audience on they would be more willing to part with their cash. I wasn't sure she was right though and felt that if I teased and pretended to be coy I could extract enough from them to make them unwilling to give more for the sake of seeing her. I was confident in my looks too, if not so much my ability to dance.

I was on at a quarter to five, and my nervousness grew as we drove up to Cowley in Jasmine's car. The pub was exactly as I had imagined it, a noisy, common place full of beer-swilling townies. There was a stage at one end, garishly lit with coloured spotlights and covered with a threadbare carpet of dull red and gold. This was obviously where the girls stripped – where I was going to strip.

The manager, Mike, was also more or less what I had imagined, a slick-haired wide-boy with a dirty grin and a familiar manner towards us. Knowing Jasmine as a lesbian and fairly refined, I was surprised that she knew him at all, yet it was really Caroline who he seemed to know best and I surmised that she might have worked there at some point, either as a barmaid or stripping.

When my time came I was so nervous that I was unable to stop my fingers shaking. Three glasses of indifferent Cognac – generously provided on the house – had done little to calm me. The music had also been a problem, as I had no time to work out a specific routine. Instead, I had simply asked for something long and slow, reasoning that the more time my striptease took the more money I was likely to get. I was relying on my looks and my ability to tease rather than artistry. After all, as I find other women's bodies attractive I understood how I ought to show off, but then so did Jasmine.

As I stood waiting among the barrels and crates of beer in the tiny back room I could hear Mike announcing me.

'And now,' he shouted, as the jukebox ground to a halt and the buzz of conversation faded, 'we have something special, a college girl!'

There was a chorus of whistles, catcalls and crude remarks and I found myself swallowing on a suddenly dry throat.

'Yes, a college girl,' he continued, 'a pretty little thing from the university is going to strip for you. She says she needs the money, but we know why she's really doing it, don't we? Oh yes, she's doing it because she wants to show off her posh little tush in front of some real men, isn't she?'

There was a chorus of agreement and more whistles and then he introduced me, not as Isabelle, but as Lady Samantha, which I suppose he imagined as an upper-class name. The music started – some lachry-mose love song from the seventies – and I stepped out onto the stage.

I can see how girls who strip professionally manage to be so detached about it. It's not like the audience are real people at all, but simply automata, each identical and driven simply by crude, male lust. After a moment of stark terror I got into the swing of my impromptu display and concentrated on what I was doing and not my audience. My aim was to tease, to hint at the exposure of my body so that more and more coins would go into Caroline's beer glass in the hope of making me reveal more. Mike had made it very clear that I had to go nude, but the crowd didn't know that.

My top went first, peeled off quite quickly to give them something to gape at while I danced and feigned reluctance to undo my trousers. When I finally had the button undone I turned my back and peeled them down, making sure they got a good view of the rather innocent-looking pink panties I had chosen that morning. I gave the audience a shy look as I kicked off my shoes, socks and trousers. I started to dance in my bra and knickers, using my college scarf to tease but deliberately not making any motions to suggest that I was going to go any further. As I had anticipated the calls quickly started for me to strip completely, the cruder among them calling out taunts such as 'Come on love, show us your cunt' and 'I bet she's a virgin'. As I had also anticipated, others made a big show of putting more money in the pot, one offering five pounds for me to take my bra off, another ten if I would throw him my panties.

I teased for as long as I felt I could and then gave them a shy smile and reached back for my bra catch. A fresh chorus of delighted yells sounded as the cups slipped away from my breasts and then I was topless, dancing in just my panties in front of a good fifty men. Once more I played the same game, hinting at the removal of my panties and then hurriedly pulling them back up after revealing no more than a hint of my pubic hair or the top of my bottom cleft. Only when the one who wanted my panties increased his offer to twenty pounds did I decide to give them what they wanted.

I turned my back and looked coyly over my shoulder, trying to imply that the reason I was facing to the front was because I was shy about showing my pussy. Then I dipped my back in, stuck my bottom out and slowly began to take my panties down. Of course the position gave them an even ruder view than they would have had from the front, because it showed off not just the rear view of my sex but also my anus. They obviously thought I didn't realise how much I was showing, because several of them laughed or made remarks at the expense of my modesty.

Despite my detachment, I found myself blushing as I kicked my panties up in the air and caught them. I turned, identified the man who wanted to buy them and held them out, dangled cheekily from the tip of my finger. He extracted a twenty-pound note from his wallet, held it up very obviously so that everyone could see what he was doing and then put it in Caroline's glass. Several people cheered as I tossed him my discarded panties and only then did I become aware that the song was not the one I had started to strip to. For the next three minutes I danced, stark naked on the squalid stage, exhibiting myself. I made sure they got a good look, posing to show off my pussy and letting them look between my bum cheeks.

One curious thing I noticed was that several men simply had their eyes glued between my legs, apparently indifferent to the display of my legs, belly or even my breasts and bum, just as long as they could see my pussy. These also seemed to be the ones who were giving most of the money, so I finished in a squat, with my thighs open to the audience and every detail of my vulva on show. I even touched myself as the last note faded out, finding myself considerably wetter than I had expected.

Caroline joined me as I gathered up my clothes and scampered backstage – or rather into the storeroom.

'You did well,' she said, 'at least sixty quid, I reckon. Jasmine very seldom gets as much as that.'

'Do you mean she does it regularly?' I demanded in sudden horror.

'Sure, every Saturday,' Caroline replied. 'You don't think the corsetry makes enough to live on, do you? No, normally she and I do it, but she told Mike I was on my period and said she'd got you as a stand-in.'

I was left open-mouthed at the revelation. It never occurred to me that the cool, dominant, lesbian Jasmine might lower herself to regular striptease work, but evidently she did. Then again, it didn't mean I'd lost. Even if she had plenty of regular fans in the crowd I had done well and the bet was by no means over. I gave her a dirty look as she came back into the storeroom, but she just smiled back at me. By the time I was fully dressed it was after five, yet Jasmine was still sipping at her drink, apparently in no hurry.

'Well, aren't you going on?' I finally demanded, frustrated by her casual manner.

'I'm just waiting for the football crowds to fill the place up a bit,' she informed me, dropping the second bombshell.

A peep out of the door showed that she was right. The pub was far more crowded than it had been when we arrived and many of the newcomers were in what I assumed to be the colours of the local association football team. Most of them were plainly drunk as well and they seemed almost indecently cheerful.

'Four nil,' Mike announced as he came into the room. 'The lads are well up for it. Come on, Jas, get out there.'

'Sure,' she answered and downed the remainder of her drink.

'You were good, love,' Mike addressed me as Jasmine stood up. 'Fancy a regular spot?'

'No thank you,' I answered frostily.

'Suit yourself,' he replied and stepped out to announce Jasmine.

I have to admit she was good, at least she certainly turned me on. For a start she was a better dancer than I and she was obviously experienced. She also seemed to know half the men in the crowd and allowed some of them little favours like unsnapping her bra, pulling down her panties and having her breasts rubbed in their faces. I had assumed that it was a basic rule that they could look but not touch. Jasmine had other ideas and several times went down into the crowd, responding to pinches of her bottom and touches of her breasts with knowing smiles and gestures at Caroline's glass.

It was the first time I'd had a proper look at her body as well. Naked, her efforts to play down her fragility went to no avail. Her body was delicate, light boned and slight. Her breasts were no bigger than mine, but seemed bigger against her figure, her bottom also, seemed temptingly fleshy simply because her hips were so slender. Her wispy blonde hair added to her appeal, which was certainly having an effect on me.

Like me, she had started in the clothes she was wearing, a figure-hugging dress of blue velvet.

Underneath she proved to have stockings and suspenders, also flouncy underwear in dove-grey silk. As
she stripped I began to wonder to what extent I had
been set up. Unfortunately for me, there was no
question of not honouring the bet, simply as a matter
of pride. Not that I had lost yet, but when Jasmine
finished with an insolent wiggling of her bottom and
stepped back into the store-room I knew that it was
going to be close.

I insisted on Mike counting the money, not at all
sure that I could trust Caroline. My pot had more large
notes than hers, but she had an awful lot of change. In
the end my tally came to sixty-two pounds and
thirty-seven pence, including several one penny pieces,
the presence of which I found unexpectedly annoying.
I watched Jasmine's count with a lump in my throat,
then a sinking feeling as the total passed mine. In the
end it was seventy-three pounds thirty pence, which
undoubtedly meant that without her sneaky timing to
get the football crowd I would have won. It also meant
that I was honour bound to submit myself to her.

We drove back to Jasmine's in a tense silence. My
heart was fluttering and my brain was full of conflicting emotions. I'd been foolish, very foolish, allowing
myself to be manoeuvred into a position where I was
going to be beaten and humiliated. The feeling of
shame for what I'd already done was bad enough, but
it was intensified both by the knowledge that there
was more to come and because I knew full well that
there were several points at which I could have
backed out. I hadn't though, because deep, deep
down I wanted the experience – a piece of self
knowledge more humiliating still.

There was also a feeling of satisfaction at my own
sense of obligation, both because I was going to

honour the bet and because, at the end of the day, if I'm going to enjoy beating other girls' bottoms, then I really ought to allow mine to receive the same treatment.

The first thing Jasmine did on our return was to go into her bedroom and fetch a large copper alarm clock. I had always assumed that she and Caroline shared a bed, and the mixture of female clothes and double sets of this and that showed that I was right. The idea of sleeping with Caroline, or Jasmine for that matter, sent a shiver right through me. Both of them together would be even better and as I followed them back out into the passage I wondered if that was how things would turn out.

I had expected to be put through my paces either in their bedroom or upstairs, and so was surprised when Jasmine used a key to unlock the room next to their bedroom. One look inside changed that surprise to amazement – and not a little alarm.

The room was a torture chamber – or maybe room of correction would be a better description as there were no racks or thumbscrews, but only a selection of furniture and implements clearly designed to bring a girl to the very peak of erotic anguish. The first thing to catch my eye was an upright chair from the seat of which two dildos protruded vertically, one small, one large. To sit on it would mean accepting the dildos up both pussy and bottom. A second similar chair had a large hole in the seat, while a comfortable one in the corner was presumably where Jasmine sat when taking a break from tormenting Caroline. A square box of highly polished wood stood in one corner, its surface broken only by a small iron grill, hinges and a catch that indicated the position of a hatch. The walls were liberally hung with ropes, chain and a variety of implements designed to be applied to soft, round bottoms. A heavy chain hung from a boss in the ceiling, and a thing like a padded trestle stood to one side, clearly designed for girls to bend over during punishment. So, I realised, might the armchair be, as I myself had frequently fantasised about making a girl kneel in an armchair for the cane.

That was more or less what I had been expecting, perhaps kneeling with my panties down for a dozen or so strokes before being made to grovel to Jasmine and perhaps kiss her anus or lick her to orgasm. The sheer complexity of her chamber put a rather different complexion on things and I found myself swallowing hard as I wondered how it would feel to be strung up by my hands or to have the twin dildos sliding inside me as I sat down on the chair. Then another detail of the room caught my eye. A line of video cassettes was arranged on a high shelf, each carefully labelled with an elaborate code. The last two had no code and I could guess what they were.

Jasmine caught the direction of my glance and smiled, confirming my suspicions. She then turned to one of the racks and selected a small but vicious-looking whip with a double end, like a snake's tongue. She set the clock, activated it and turned to me, her expression set in a haughty, amused smile.

'Strip,' she ordered.

So it was to be done nude, I thought as I peeled my top up with trembling fingers. Caroline had sat down in the armchair and was smirking at me, clearly enjoying my discomfort.

'First,' Jasmine announced in a cold, dominant tone, 'I shall punish you for seducing my girlfriend.'

'But . . .' I began automatically, intent on pointing out that it was as much a question of Caroline seducing me.

80

'And that will mean two extra strokes,' she cut in. 'The first thing you must learn is never, ever to answer me back. Also, you address me as Mistress.'

'Yes, Mistress,' I answered while secretly vowing to exact my revenge on her.

'And you needn't sit there simpering either, Caroline,' she continued. 'I shall beat you together. Now get your clothes off.'

It was wonderful to see the change of expression on Caroline's face. One moment she was smiling, absolutely delighted by the prospect of watching me punished and made to grovel to Jasmine. The next her mouth had dropped open and her eyes gone round. She made no protest though and began to strip with an obedient haste that once more made me jealous of Jasmine.

I already had my top off and the catch of my bra undone, but Caroline was naked before me, exhibiting her pretty curves with her hands on her head and her eyes cast down to the ground. I finished stripping and imitated her, waiting for whatever fate Jasmine had in mind for me. For a moment she contemplated us, admiring our bodies and presumably speculating on how best to get the most out of us.

'Get over the armchair,' she snapped suddenly, 'side by side with your legs across the arms.'

We both hastened to obey, getting into positions the humiliating effect of which I was quick to appreciate. Being over the arm forced me to spread my thighs and cock my bottom up, giving Jasmine a full display of my charms. I felt wide open and vulnerable, while I knew that she would be able to see every detail of my sex, every plump fold of hair-covered pussy mound, every little pink tuck and crevice of flesh in my vulva and the moist hole of my actual vagina, also the puckered brown ring of my anus. My bottom was stuck up and felt huge, very big and very exposed.

Of course, Caroline was in an equally unprotected and blatant pose and I wished I could see her from behind. As it was I had to content myself with a sideways glance, finding her dark curls tumbled around her pretty face and one plump breast dangling to the side of the chair arm. Our legs were already touching, and as our eyes met we shared a look of anticipation and sympathy, then took each other's hands.

It was to be my first ever beating, the moment I surrendered the inviolate state of my bottom skin. A frequent element of my fantasies of dominance had been giving corporal punishment to girls when I myself was pristine, my own bottom untouched, never so much as spanked by hand. Now I was going to surrender that and my feelings of impending defloweration were almost as strong as those I had known on the day I lost my virginity.

I could see Jasmine out of the corner of my eye and as she stepped back and raised the whip I shut my eyes and braced myself. The next instant it landed across my bottom with a sharp smack, sending a stinging pain through me and making me gasp. Jasmine laughed, a brief chuckle of amusement at my response. It had been done, I'd allowed someone to apply a whip to my bottom. I was bent over, naked and receiving a whipping, a sensation the pure emotion of which had the tears starting in my eyes. I choked them back, determined not to cry in front of Caroline or to give Jasmine the satisfaction of it.

Jasmine beat me well, applying the whip again and again until I had lost count of the strokes and was panting and whimpering into the armchair. They had stung badly at first, but my endorphins had quickly begun to flow and when she suddenly stopped I was actually ready for more, my feelings very different from how they had been at the onset of my punishment. Nobody before had had the guts to so much as take me across their knee and spank me, let alone make me pose naked and thrash me. Jasmine had done it and she had produced a delicious feeling of compliance in me, a feeling that I would do as I was told and that the ruder and more subservient it was, the better. I was glad she had done it, and was even wishing I'd let myself cry and blubbered out my pain and emotion to her while she whipped me.

Once more she laughed and then a finger invaded my vagina, sliding in easily and making me moan. On withdrawing it she put it to my lips, letting me taste my own excitement before once more standing back and commencing Caroline's punishment. I turned my head to watch, just as Caroline had watched me. Her eyes were screwed tight shut and her fingers were squeezing mine hard, seeking comfort. Then the whip came down across her bottom and she gasped. The blow sent a wave through her soft flesh and by the third stroke her tits were swinging and her whole body was quivering with reaction. Having just been beaten myself I felt for her, yet watching her punished was intensely exciting. Twenty-four times Jasmine brought the whip down, until Caroline was snivelling wretchedly. She also had her bottom high, clearly game for the anticipated finger inside her.

Jasmine did it, then gave me the finger that had been inside Caroline to kiss as well, letting me taste the musky, girlish flavour of pussy juice. I licked obediently, then looked back as Jasmine stepped away to admire the two freshly whipped girls who were hers to do with as she pleased. I looked into her eyes, unable to stop myself pleading for more. She had beaten me, and it seemed that the very act had established her right to do it and now I truly wanted to be made to kiss her feet, her pussy, maybe even her bottom.

She smiled back and turned away, collecting things from a shelf. First she took a mirror, with which she showed us our bottoms. Our skin was red and flushed, decorated with twin blemishes where the adder tongue had done its work. Looking at my thoroughly whipped buttocks I realised why my bottom smarted so much. I was sweating too, beads of it forming on the flushed skin and a single drip running down between my parted buttocks to pool in the dimple of my anus. My pussy was sodden and all too clearly ready for entry. I wished there was a man to fuck me, preferably some over-muscled brute with a cock like a log. At that instant I would have let anyone have me, even some tramp pulled in off the street. As it was, I needed something inside me, anything.

'Fill me, please, Mistress,' I moaned, unable to keep my need hidden.

Jasmine smiled and turned again to the shelf, picking up a huge dildo which she held up for my inspection. It was cock-shaped, and huge, far bigger than any of the cocks that had been inside me. I groaned and stuck my bottom up, then gave a long, deep moan as she touched the grotesque thing to my vagina and slid it up me. My eyes were shut in ecstasy as my pussy filled, then I felt a light twisting motion and suddenly my whole rear was quivering with vibrations.

Barely in control of what I was doing, I began to buck my bottom up and down, revelling in the buzzing feeling that suffused my vulva, buttocks and thighs. Beside me, Jasmine was giving Caroline the same treatment, sliding an identical dildo deep into her and then switching it on. I reached back to play with myself, only to receive a sharp slap across my thighs for my trouble.

'No, you don't, you little slut,' Jasmine said. 'You come when I say and not until I've come first.'

'Yes, Mistress, sorry, Mistress,' I managed.

It was absolute torment. Jasmine sat back on the chair with the hole and watched us writhe. I could just see her, and watched as she pulled up her dress and eased her panties off beneath it. For a while she sat still, casually playing with herself while Caroline and I writhed and whimpered in our pain and ecstasy. Then she stood up and pulled the dildos from our vaginas with an abrupt, pre-emptory motion.

'On the floor, sluts, on your backs,' she ordered brusquely.

I got down on the floor, as did Caroline. It just seemed natural to lie with my legs up and my thighs apart, leaving my vagina wide and vulnerable. Caroline was in the same position, and our legs were intertwined, her skin hot and wet against mine. Jasmine came to look down at us, her mouth set in a derisive sneer as she looked at the state we were in. She stepped forward, placing a foot either side of my head. I could see up her dress, which she had pulled up to the level of her pussy. It was right over my face, and for a moment I wondered what she intended. Then I found out as she began to squat down, lowering herself slowly towards my face. Her thighs came apart as she went, exposing her bottom-hole. I groaned, knowing that I was about to be made to kiss a woman's anus. I braced myself, expecting her to rub her bottom in my face so that I was forced to lick, but she stopped, reached down and pulled her bottom cheeks apart.

Her anus was only inches from my face, a tightly puckered hole, hairless and without the corona of brown skin that made my own bottom-hole look so exceptionally rude. Instead it was pink and slightly everted, like a woman's lips puckered out for a kiss. That was what I was going to have to do, willing, of my own choice.

'Kiss it, then apologise for playing with Caroline,' Jasmine ordered.

I hesitated, my eyes locked on the bum-hole that was being offered to my mouth. I found my head coming up, my lips moving and then as my mouth touched her anal ring I was doing it, the unspeakably dirty, subservient act I had fantasised over but which I had never actually expected to have to do. I sucked in, making it a proper kiss and tasting the tang of her bottom, then pulled back.

'I'm sorry, Mistress,' I said softly.

My breath was coming deeply and I was in desperate need of an orgasm. I knew what would happen if I touched myself though and lay still. For a moment Jasmine stayed poised over my face, letting what I'd just done sink in. Then she sat down, full in my face, naked bottom spread so that her bottom-hole was pressed onto my mouth.

'Caroline, get your face in my pussy,' I heard Jasmine order. 'Isabelle, lick my arse and don't stop until I tell you to.'

I obeyed, too far gone to care anymore. As I started to lap at Jasmine's bottom I felt Caroline mount me, her weight settling onto my body. Jasmine leant back, presenting herself to Caroline, who began to lick with her chin touching mine.

Jasmine really took her time, revelling in the sensation of our tongues and pausing occasionally to rub herself in my face and apply fresh smacks of the whip to Caroline's upturned bottom. Caroline's breasts were pressed against mine and the fur of her pussy was rubbing against my belly, she was squirming, trying to frig herself on me. After a while I took the sides of her breasts in my hands and when Jasmine made no objection I began to caress them. Caroline pulled up a little, letting her full globes into my hands. Her own were on Jasmine's bottom, pulling it open to stretch her Mistress's anus across my mouth.

'In it,' I heard Jasmine order as I felt the first gentle contractions of her muscles against my face.

Resigning myself to what surely had to be the final degradation I rolled my tongue and poked it out, probing her bum-hole with the tip. It went in quite easily and I shut my eyes, at once in ecstasy and utterly disgusted with myself for what I was doing. Jasmine groaned and began to come, squirming herself against our faces. I kept my tongue well up her bottom-hole, feeling her sphincter tighten on it as she climaxed. I heard her call out and then abruptly she had pulled away and I was left gaping, only for Caroline's mouth to meet mine.

We came together in a kiss, her breasts huge in my hands, her body heavy and wet against mine. Then her fingers were groping for my pussy and she had spread her own across my thigh, rubbing frantically to bring sensation to her clitoris.

'You can do it now,' I heard Jasmine say weakly, although both Caroline and I were far too far gone to wait for her permission.

Caroline's fingers had found my clitoris and were working hard, rubbing with an urgency that I knew would bring me off in seconds. She had slid down me to get her thighs across my leg and now took one of my nipples in her mouth. I started to come as her

87

teeth nipped onto the hard bud, screaming and nearly blacking out with the sheer intensity of my climax. Then I was relaxing, my muscles going loose, leaving Caroline to take her pleasure out on my supine body.

She filled her mouth with the flesh of my breast, sucking hard as she humped my leg. I saw Jasmine lift the whip and flick it down on her girlfriend's bottom, once, twice and then Caroline too was coming, moaning out her ecstasy into my chest as she rubbed herself on me and her Mistress beat her.

We collapsed in a sweaty heap, Jasmine's arms coming around us in a hug that gave no hint of the dominance she had been exerting over us. She kissed my cheek, gently, then rubbed her face into Caroline's hair, a gesture full of love and devotion. For a while the three of us lay together, only to be brought back sharply to our senses by the sudden ringing of the alarm clock. I was amazed, because if anybody had asked me I would have sworn that our play had lasted no more than perhaps twenty minutes.

Six

Over the following days my emotions were in a state of absolute turmoil. The experience with Jasmine and Caroline had been exquisite, absolute bliss, from stripping for the men to being beaten by Jasmine and made to lick her anally. It had also been deeply shameful and in direct contradiction to the way I had always seen my sexuality. There was also the matter of the video tapes, which Jasmine had made no move to return. Finally, there was the matter of my bottom, which smarted for over a week, making it even harder to keep my mind off what had happened to me. Temporary relief could be gained by masturbating over it, generally on my knees so that I could admire my poor whipped posterior in the mirror as I came.

Wonderful though my room in the tower of St George's College was, it had the disadvantage of being less than perfectly private. I could lock the door, but that didn't seem to stop people knocking. Before coming up I had read *Tom Brown at Oxford* and had been looking forward to the idea of 'sporting the oak' which meant shutting the outer door of my rooms in a ritual demand for solitude. Unfortunately things had changed since the early nineteenth century and nobody seemed to take the slightest notice. Besides, what had begun life as a set was now two rooms, and my neighbour was a bubbly black girl called Melonie who seemed to have a never-ending string of visitors. Fortunately I had found somewhere else to be alone. My stair ended at a door that gave access to the tower roof, and while the door was always locked I had managed to ingratiate myself sufficiently with the head porter to be allowed access. I had then had a copy of the key made and so provided myself, rather sneakily, with the perfect place for solitude.

It was there to which I repaired to think over my tangled sex life. The real question seemed to be – what did I really want out of it? Mere sensation? Caroline? To be Jasmine's slave-girl? After a long period of introspection I decided that the answer was actually that I wanted Jasmine, and not as my Mistress but as my plaything. True, I had enjoyed what we had done, and I knew that I would do it again, but I would not be really content until she had her tongue wedged firmly up my bottom. I wanted Caroline too, but if I judged her correctly, she would be happy to go along with whatever might happen.

The other problem was the tapes. At least I now knew where they where, and while being tricked into giving Walter Jessop oral sex still rankled, I was at least better off than I had been before. Yet Jasmine kept her punishment room locked and had even been careful to lock it after we had finished having sex together. I had seen where the key was kept though, in her underwear drawer beside their bed.

As I sat on the leaden floor of the tower and watched clouds drift by the peak of the steeple of St Mary's, I realised that in order to retrieve the tapes I needed help. To get into Jasmine's house she needed to be distracted, and then I needed someone bold enough and trustworthy enough to break in and retrieve the tapes. Of course, whoever did it would have to take other things to put me in the clear with Jasmine and Caroline. It was a lot to ask, and I could think of only one friend who might do it – Rory McVeigh.

I had seen him several times since our brief and passionate encounter at the beginning of term, and we had been cordial although we had not gone to bed together again. I was sure he still saw me as rather aloof. After I had explained my predicament to him he didn't, indeed he was amazed – and also fascinated. I had had to admit to everything in order to convince him to help me, yet as he sat opposite me in his room I wasn't at all sure he actually believed me.

'Let me see your bottom then,' he demanded.

I sighed and stood up, slightly put out that he should demand proof of my story. I was in a long woollen skirt, and he watched with interest as I pulled it up and eased my tights and panties far enough down to display my still-blemished bottom. His eyes widened and he sucked his breath in a bit, then gave a nod of acceptance.

'Convinced?' I asked, still holding my skirt up over my bare behind.

'And you enjoyed that?' he queried.

'Yes,' I admitted.

He sucked his breath in again, evidently impressed although I was sure he considered me a pervert. I was about to let my skirt fall when he stood up. Telling him my story had excited me and I hesitated just too long. I dropped my skirt and made to stand, aware not just that his door was unlocked but that the thin walls of his hall of residence allowed neighbours to hear just about any sound.

'Rory!' I protested weakly as he pushed me gently over.

He took no notice and I was lost. My tights and panties were still down under my skirt and I could feel a hard lump where his cock was pressing between the cheeks of my bottom. Then he was lifting my skirt back up, my bum was bare and the hard ridge of his cock was nestling between my cheeks.

'You do have a pretty bottom, Isabelle,' he said and stood back.

I could hear people in the corridor and was close to panic, but I did need it and the very risk of being caught added to the thrill. Hanging my head and opening my legs I waited for entry as he pulled his cock free of his fly.

When he had first had me he had been slow and considerate, but it was not so this time. He was already hard and simply put his cock to my vagina and mounted me with a grunt. I couldn't restrain myself as he began to fuck me and was soon gasping and moaning without a thought for who might hear. He did it hard and urgently, holding me by the hips and pushing himself into me as if determined to get his balls inside me as well as his cock. It was knocking the breath from me and it was all I could do to grip the bedclothes.

Rear entry has always seemed to me dirty and to make the women unequal. Not only was I now being had from behind by the son of my local publican, but he had been turned on by the sight of my whipped buttocks. As my pleasure rose, I started to wish he'd spanked me first, and maybe asked a few friends in to watch me get it. I'd have been over his lap, long skirt up, tights and panties down, my little round bum naked in front of them. They'd have jeered and laughed as I was spanked, especially the girls. Then the men would have taken turns with me over his bed, mounting me one by one with my red bottom turned up . . .

'No!' I squeaked, my fantasy breaking as I realised that he was about to come in me.

He pulled out and put his cock between my bum cheeks, rubbing it on me while his breath came in short, ecstatic pants. Then he groaned loudly and suddenly the cleft of my bottom was wet with sperm. For a long moment he kept his cock in place, rubbing his mess up and down between the cheeks of my bottom. Then he stood back, sighed and sank down into the chair he had been in before.

'I deserved that,' he said. 'Seeing that I'm going to go and burgle a house for your sake.'

'Fair enough,' I answered, intensely aware of his come smeared between my cheeks and running down to my pussy. 'Now, could you wipe me, please. If I stand up my dress will go in it.'

He laughed and complied, using what I suspect was a discarded pair of pants to wipe my bottom clean. I thanked him, turned, sat down on the bed, spread my thighs wide and, I think rather coolly, brought myself off in front of him.

Rory and I arranged things carefully over the next couple of days. Given the contents of her house I felt that we could be reasonably certain of Jasmine not calling the police, but we took every precaution we could think of in any case. Twice Rory started to get cold feet, and twice I was obliged to kneel on my bed and let him mount me from behind. The third time I realised that he wasn't really worried, but just wanted to fuck me. I let him anyway, this time bent over his washbasin with my panties stuck in my mouth so that I wouldn't squeal too much and give away what we were doing to his neighbours.

I could tell that the idea of dominating me was beginning to appeal to him, and he began to give my bottom occasional light slaps, but I didn't make an issue of it. On the day we had chosen I invited Jasmine and Caroline out punting, thus ensuring that they would be well away from the house and unable to make an unscheduled return.

Generally speaking, punting is a summer sport, and even the commercial people by Magdalen Bridge had put theirs away for the winter. St George's punts were simply kept in a locked shack by the Cherwell, and it was no harder to take a punt out in winter than summer.

From the outset Jasmine behaved as if my previous submission to her meant that I now accepted it as my lot. I didn't, but the last thing I was going to do was anything that might jeopardise my plan.

The day was certainly warm enough and we had the river entirely to ourselves. It was also my first attempt at punting, and it proved considerably harder than it looked with an experienced person on the pole. Soon both Jasmine and Caroline were laughing at my efforts and Caroline was using the small paddle to steer us away from the banks, overhanging trees, bridge pilings and other obstacles. Finally, I managed to embed the bow of the punt under the trunk of a half-fallen willow and Caroline was obliged to put the paddle down and push us off.

Jasmine had been reclining in the central section of the punt, propped up on cushions and looking very ladylike while Caroline and I struggled to make the wretched thing do as it was supposed to. Caroline was now kneeling at the bows, with the well-filled seat of her jeans thrust out to within a foot of Jasmine. I couldn't have resisted it, and nor did Jasmine. Taking up the paddle, she gave Caroline a firm swat full across her plump backside. Caroline squeaked and giggled, almost losing her balance.

I was more careful after that, and slowly became more proficient, using the pole like a giant rudder at the end of each stroke and finally beginning to make some headway. Caroline settled down to watch the river, curled up in the bows with her fingers trailing in the water. Jasmine kept hold of the paddle, not using it but admiring its shape and weight in a way that made my bottom tingle. I had already anticipated the possibility that the outing might involve some naughty behaviour, and was resigned to a smacked bottom at the least. The paddle looked painful though and I was relieved when Jasmine eventually put it down and suggested a drink at the Victoria Arms.

One hour and several glasses of beer later we were back in the punt and distinctly giggly. Caroline had been flirting in the pub, a game that I could see was designed not for the benefit of the men in question, but in order to get Jasmine to punish her. It had worked, and in the end Jasmine had threatened to spank Caroline in front of them, speaking loudly enough to make sure they heard. The effect on Caroline was spectacular, turning her mood from one of mischievous flirtation to outright excitement in moments. Suddenly there was no question but that something was going to happen and by unspoken agreement I turned the punt not back towards Oxford, but north, to where the Cherwell runs between open, lonely fields between the Oxford ring road and Islip.

By the time we reached a suitably deserted spot – a narrow channel overhung with willows and well shielded from sight – Caroline was toying with the button of her jeans and Jasmine once more thoughtfully caressing the paddle.

'Right, you two,' she announced as the punt slid in under the green foliage, 'I'm going to spank you both with this lovely big paddle, Caroline because she's naughty and you, Isabelle, just for the hell of it. Now kneel in the front and pull down your pants, both of you.'

I would have preferred to watch Caroline beaten, but was sufficiently drunk and excited to accept the prospect of having my own bottom smacked without protest. Caroline was giggling uncontrollably as she got into position, kneeling with her knees together and her bottom up. I wanted to see her go bare and waited to assume my own pose while she undid her jeans and pulled the whole lot down together, eager to expose her bum for punishment.

She really did have the most magnificent bottom, broad and full, with her slim waist accentuating the spread of her hips. As she pulled her back in her cheeks spread apart, revealing the rich growth of hair between them, with the brown skin of her anus and the pink of her pussy nestled in among it. I dearly wished that I was the one spanking her, but obeyed Jasmine's order, getting down on my knees beside Caroline and pulling up my skirt to show off the seat of my panties. I paused deliberately, wanting the humiliation of being told to drop my knickers.

'I said, pull down your pants, Isabelle,' Jasmine ordered. 'Now do it.'

I put my hands into the waistband and tugged them down, delighting in the rude feeling of showing off my bum. It was for punishment too, not for rear entry, making my feelings even stronger. I knelt down and dipped my back, posing like Caroline with my pussy and bottom-hole showing.

'Good,' Jasmine said coolly. 'First your spankings, then lunch.'

It seemed a peculiar thing to say, although we had brought sandwiches. Then my puzzlement was knocked sharply out of me as the paddle came down on my bottom. It was a hard smack, and a different feeling from the whip. The whip stung, the paddle gave a duller pain, and left my whole bottom throbbing and warm. I had squealed and sat up, putting my hands back automatically to soothe my smarting cheeks. Jasmine pushed me back into position, not unkindly, and then gave Caroline a smack, producing a similar response.

'This is excellent,' she stated, 'I shall make one myself, especially for your bottoms.'

I heard Caroline give a little sob and then the paddle smacked down on my own posterior once more. It was a very different sensation from my first beating. Being drunk and more accepting of Jasmine's right to punish me, it was less emotionally intense, but more sexy, playful even.

Jasmine was merciful, giving us only a dozen each, but by the time it was over my whole bottom was a throbbing ball of pain and an even deep pink all over. It felt wonderful though and I was longing for the aftermath, which I guessed would involve licking Jasmine and then being allowed to play with Caroline. Instead Jasmine ordered me to sit up straight and pull Caroline's panties back up. I obeyed, settling the big pink knickers over Caroline's bulging bottom and allowing myself a quick squeeze of her heated flesh.

'Time for your lunch,' Jasmine announced and pulled out the back of her girlfriend's panties.

Caroline giggled and I turned to look at Jasmine, wondering what she was doing. She had reached back for the bag which contained our lunch and was busily trying to unwrap a sandwich with one hand while holding Caroline's panties open with the other. I realised her intention and watched with a mixture of delight and disgust as she extracted the sandwich – a particularly glutinous one of egg, tomato and mayonnaise. Holding it between finger and thumb, she dropped it down the back of Caroline's panties and then let the elastic snap shut. Caroline giggled again and then yelped as the paddle was once more brought down hard across her bottom. This time there was no smack of wood on girl flesh, but a squishy sound. The panties left a good deal of Caroline's ample bottom spilling out from around the leg holes, and in places the contents of her panties had spurted out, a gooey mess of yellow and white egg and red tomato.

I grimaced as Jasmine reached forward and slowly peeled her girlfriend's panties back down. Underneath was a revolting mess of squashed sandwich, some of it smeared across her bottom, some in the pouch of her panties, but most of it caught between her bum cheeks and in her pussy hair.

'Eat up, Isabelle, there's a good girl,' Jasmine addressed me as she settled Caroline's panties down so that I could eat out of them conveniently.

I'd have been happy to eat the sandwich and I'd have been happy to lick Caroline's pussy, so I suppose I shouldn't have minded combining the two. It was a real mess though and I knew I'd get it all over my face. If I ate it all up I was going to have to lick her bottom-hole as well, which would make her the second girl I'd given that service to.

'Come on,' Jasmine coaxed, 'eat your nice lunch up or I'll give you another twenty with the paddle and make you go the rest of the day with no panties.'

My bottom was still throbbing, and I was sure that going without my panties would also involve her doing something mean like pulling my skirt up to flash my bare bottom. Reasoning that if I'd licked one bum-hole then I might as well lick another I bent down and delicately nipped a piece of egg from the hot red skin of Caroline's bottom.

'Good girl,' Jasmine said.

I took a piece of bread in my mouth, being careful not to soil my face. Without the slightest warning Jasmine took me by the hair and pushed my face in-between Caroline's buttocks. I gasped, immediately earning myself a mouthful of soggy bread, bits of tomatoes and squashed egg. My head was pressed in-between Caroline's fleshy bottom cheeks, the mess all over my face and my mouth right over her bum-hole.

It was what I had needed to make me do it properly, and as Jasmine began to rub my face into Caroline's bottom I started to eat. After a couple of mouthfuls the last of my resolve snapped and I began to tongue Caroline's anus. Caroline gave a low, ecstatic moan and Jasmine let go of my head, now sure that I was fully willing. I pulled back a little so that it was obvious what I was doing and Jasmine laughed at the sight of me so wantonly cleaning her girlfriend's bottom with my tongue. My sense of erotic humiliation was building rapidly. I'd been spanked and now I was licking Caroline's bottom, once more lost to the pleasures of submissive sex.

Yet I was again vowing revenge as I transferred my attention to Caroline's pussy, sucking a fair mouthful of pulped sandwich out of her vagina and then burying my face in deeper to get at her clitoris. I was also thinking of Rory and wondering how he was getting on.

'Not until it's all clean,' Jasmine ordered and pulled me back by the hair only to immediately stuff my face back into the fullness of Caroline's bottom.

I did it properly, reasoning that it was best to let my own excitement build because I was pretty sure what was going to happen to me when Caroline had come. My panties were still down and my skirt up around my waist, leaving my bottom bare, but I imagined they would be pulled up and filled with what remained of the lunch. Then I would be spanked and Caroline would be made to lick me clean.

It was an exciting prospect, and as I licked the smears of mayonnaise and egg from the crests of Caroline's plump cheeks I wondered if Jasmine would allow me to play with myself. I reached back an experimental hand and found my pussy, starting to stroke the outer lips.

'Slut,' Jasmine said and smacked the paddle down on my bottom. 'No, carry on, if you need to wank because you've got Caroline's taste in your mouth I understand.'

I started to dab at my clit, her words bringing a fresh excitement.

Finally, Caroline's bottom was clean, her full cheeks wet and glistening with my saliva, her fur wet and her anus a clean, slowly pulsing dimple in the middle of it. As I buried my face in her pussy I concentrated on the thought that it was me who had shined her anus up so well – with my tongue. She sighed as I found her clitoris, pushing her bottom back so that my face was smothered in the damp, fleshy folds of her pussy. As I licked I felt Jasmine's hand on my bottom. She squeezed a naked cheek, then smacked my hand away from my pussy.

I put my hands on Caroline's bum and pulled her cheeks fully open as Jasmine pulled up my panties. Her fingers found my waistband, pulling it open. Something solid was put down my panties and the waistband snapped shut. The paddle smacked down on my bottom and something squelched in-between my cheeks, soiling my bottom and pussy. Jasmine began to pulp the mess over my bottom with the paddle as Caroline started to come. I heard her call out and her pussy started to spasm against my face. I kept licking, waiting until she had taken a long, leisurely orgasm before pulling back.

My head was spinning with the need to come myself. My panties were full of mess, my bottom hot from beating and my pussy aching to be touched. Caroline had just come, but I didn't see why I should miss out on my licking. Turning, I presented her with my bottom and sighed as she rubbed her face into the damp, sticky rear of my panties.

Jasmine was looking down at me with an expression of utter delight. I could imagine how she felt. The thought of having two wanton, dirty girls playing together at my feet was exquisite, more exquisite even than being one of the girls. I put my face down against the cushions of the punt as Caroline pulled down my pants.

'Slowly,' Jasmine ordered and I felt a firm, wet tongue start to lick me at the top of my bottom cleft.

I groaned, putting a hand to one breast and starting to feel. It was going to be long and slow, a session of sexual torment that would eventually bring me to a glorious peak. My nipple was hard under my clothes and I burrowed my hand into my blouse to get at it, intent on rubbing it while Caroline dealt with my rear.

'Quick, cover up!' Jasmine suddenly hissed.

It took an instant to register, so far gone had I been in my pleasure. Then I realised that something was wrong and sat up quickly, tugging my skirt down over my bottom without thoughts for the consequences. I turned to see what the matter was. Caroline was struggling her panties and jeans up, looking nervously at the thick stand of willow and hawthorn that hid the bank. I caught a movement and for an instant glimpsed the outline of a man carrying a fishing rod.

He moved away, perhaps as embarrassed as us at the encounter. For a moment I felt deeply chagrined, aware of how rude we must have looked and deeply disconcerted by the thought of having been seen. Then Caroline giggled and pointed out that I now had mayonnaise and tomato juice soaking into the back of my skirt. I couldn't help but see the funny side of it, but the man's appearance had broken the moment and there was no suggestion that we return to playing.

I had thought our site secure, but as I poled the punt out from under the willows I realised that there was a clear path running along the bank behind the screen of hawthorns. Given the number of times I had stripped off to swim or even play with myself on the moors near my home, I should have known to check the area properly before doing anything naughty. No great harm seemed to have been done though and we were more amused by the incident than anything as we started back towards Oxford.

Seven

My intention was to visit Rory as soon as I was free.
Unfortunately this wasn't practical. Firstly I badly
needed to change my skirt and panties, which were
still damp and uncomfortable even after I had done
my best to clean up. I walked back to St George's
with Caroline's jumper strategically placed to cover
the wet patch, intending to change and then go
straight to Rory's college.

On arriving at my room, I was surprised to find a
note from Dr Appledore demanding that I see him in
his rooms as soon as I returned. Not only was it
unusual for a tutor to wish to see a student on a
Sunday, but he had signed the note Dr Appledore
while we had been on comfortable first-name terms
for some weeks. I was feeling distinctly apprehensive
as I washed and changed, wondering if one of my
pieces of misbehaviour was about to come home to
roost. There were all sorts of possibilities, ranging
from somebody having sent him a copy of one of the
video tapes, to Rory having been arrested and
admitting to my involvement.

Telling myself that it was pointless to speculate, I
set off for his rooms. I was feeling thoroughly
nervous and had wavered in my choice of dress,
eventually choosing a neat grey two-piece that I knew

made me look sensible and mature. St George's is small, and Dr Appledore's rooms were only at the far side of the quad, so dawdle as I might I soon found myself outside his door on the first floor.

I knocked timidly and responded to his answering call with my hand shaking. He was a big, heavy-set man with a full beard, normally jovial but always rather daunting and undeniably authoritative. Now he looked stern and forbidding, like some Victorian hell-fire preacher about to tell a congregation that they were damned beyond doubt. The whole atmosphere of the room added to my concern, the subtle smell of old books and older stone, the furnishings, little of which post-dated the reign of King Edward VII, the feel of timelessness and scholarship that I had always enjoyed but which now seemed sinister.

As I closed the door behind me I became aware of somebody else standing to the side. Looking round I saw my scout, Stan Tierney, the man who was responsible for cleaning the rooms on my stair. His presence immediately reduced my fears. It implied that the reason I was being summoned was because he had reported to Dr Appledore that I was in the habit of letting men sleep over. This was not technically against the rules, but Dr Appledore was of the old school and I found it easy to believe that he disapproved of such things. Nor was I surprised that Tierney had reported me. He was a coarse, vulgar man with a shabby appearance and a bad habit of making remarks that bordered on the suggestive. I had never liked him and I knew from the male students with whom he got on better that he considered me disdainful and arrogant.

I folded my hands in my lap and waited for Dr Appledore to speak, all the while arranging my defence of my conduct in my mind. Humble apology seemed the best tactic, although my spirit revolted at the idea, preferring an attitude of righteous indignation.

'Ah, Colraine,' he began with far more formality than was usual, 'I fear I have something serious to say to you.'

I looked up, trying to seem contrite instead of defiant, but aware that I was not really succeeding.

'Tierney,' he continued, after a pause in which he seemed to be choosing his words, 'gives me to understand that you have been . . . um . . . ah . . . shall we say . . .'

He couldn't get it out, his shyness having overcome his normally faultless phraseology. I waited, starting to feel sorry for him because he evidently did not relish the task of confronting me with my misdeeds, nor of disciplining me.

'Indulging in inappropriate bodily pleasures,' he continued, his words coming in a sudden rush. 'Bodily pleasures pertinent to some of the looser elements of Aeolic poetry . . .'

'Sorry?' I queried, noting that his face had gone the most furious red.

'I . . . look, Isabelle, this really isn't easy for me,' he stammered as I realised that what he was saying was that Tierney had accused me of lesbianism.

I rallied, determined to defend my right to have sex with another woman and then realised that there were only two ways that Stan Tierney could possibly know I had done anything of the sort. Either he had seen the tape of Caroline and I or it had been him who saw us in the punt. It was my turn to blush as I thought of the intimate knowledge that this implied. No wonder Dr Appledore was having difficulty expressing himself. Still, I had little choice but to defend myself. Remembering how keen Dr Appledore was on the right of the individual to determine their own moral philosophy, I gave my response.

'A Sapphic pleasure as it were,' he continued. 'Oh the devil with it, you know what I mean, sex with another woman.'

'I have done nothing illegal,' I replied, 'nor, I earnestly believe, immoral.'

'Yes, my dear,' Dr Appledore replied in a tired voice. 'But in a college punt? With two girls from the town? With an egg sandwich?'

'Egg and tomato,' I answered, prompted by some mischievous urge before common sense could stop me.

'This is not a matter for levity, Isabelle,' he snapped back, regaining something of his authority.

'No, sir,' I responded, brought sharply back down to earth.

'Nor,' he went on, 'am I particularly concerned with your personal behaviour, although I must confess to being both surprised and shocked. No, what I am concerned with is the good name of the college. I will not go so far as to recommend to the disciplinary committee that you be sent down, but I fear that I have little choice but to advise rustication.'

'I . . .' I began and promptly shut up.

I immediately felt immensely sorry for myself and could feel the tears welling up in my eyes. There was really nothing I could say, yet really I had only been having fun, hurting nobody and doing something that was intensely private and certainly none of Stan Tierney's business. It was really unfair and I desperately wanted to say as much yet knew that such a response would only succeed in making me look like a brat.

'Might we not simply keep it to ourselves, sir?' I suggested instead. 'I promise I will be more discreet in future.'

'Well . . .' Dr Appledore began, only to be interrupted by the scout.

'There was the spanking as well, sir, don't forget the spanking,' Tierney put in maliciously, addressing Dr Appledore in a tone that was at once obsequious and gloating.

'Ah yes,' the tutor sighed, 'Tierney also reports that you allowed yourself to be er . . . spanked, yes, spanked.'

Again he had difficulty getting the indecent word out, but there was a subtle difference in his tone and after he had said it he coloured up and looked quickly away. Tierney was just being nasty, and I had no doubt whatever that he had thoroughly enjoyed watching Jasmine beat Caroline and me. In fact I was somewhat surprised that he hadn't chosen to blackmail me rather than report me. Dr Appledore was different, genuinely sorry for me but intent on what he saw as his duty. It was hard to imagine him getting excited over any pleasure as rudimentary as sex, yet there had been something about the word 'spanked' that had touched a nerve.

I began to wonder if spanking girls was a fantasy of his and with the thought came an outrageous possibility. Maybe, just maybe, he would let me off if I offered to accept physical discipline from him. To me it was infinitely preferable to rustication, painful yet quickly over. Had corporal punishment been even remotely acceptable I would have been over his desk with my panties down like a shot. No, it was too outrageous, he would simply be shocked and have me sent down without further question.

'I would dearly like to overlook this, my dear,' Dr Appledore was saying, 'believe me, yet I fear . . .'

He trailed off, shaking his head sadly. Was it a hint? Was he making me a veiled offer? If so it was couched in language that left him in no danger of accusations of blackmail or coercion if I chose not to accept the offer. Alternatively, his comment might be simply an expression of his regret, nothing more and nothing less. I thought fast, desperately trying to decide on a way of gauging his true feelings without giving myself away. What, I wondered, would a man who liked spanking recognise that a more conventional colleague would not? There was also the problem of Stan Tierney, who was the last man on earth I wanted to make my proposition in front of, never mind watching me take my punishment if it was accepted. At that instant I knew I was really going to do it, it was just a question of how.

'Might we speak alone?' I asked Dr Appledore.

He nodded to Tierney, who returned a respectful bob and walked out, throwing me a dirty leer as he went. An idea came to me as he went, an idea that I at least had to try.

'Dr Appledore,' I said carefully when the door latch had clicked shut behind me, 'do I understand that at present only yourself and Tierney are aware of my indiscretion?'

'That is correct,' he answered.

'Then, sir,' I continued, carefully picking words I hoped would appeal most strongly to the spirit of a spanker yet which held no specific meaning, 'might I respectfully suggest that some more direct form of correction might serve as a better reminder to be less ill-behaved in the future.'

'I am able to impose fines and recommend rustication or expulsion to the disciplinary committee, Isabelle,' he answered. 'That is the extent of my official power.'

The word official was the key. He was playing my game, or at least I hoped he was.

'Perhaps something unofficial,' I suggested, still leaving myself room for a hasty retreat.

'Such as?' he asked, and his eyebrows rose into questioning arches.

He had placed the ball firmly in my court, ending our game of words and demanding a specific statement. His gaze was steady and calm, very different from the lecherous stares of Stan Tierney or the hopeful lust of Walter Jessop. Yet a muscle at the edge of his mouth twitched, just once, momentarily turning the fixed set of his mouth into a lopsided smile. I decided to jump.

'A spanking, sir,' I said as the blood rushed to my face, 'or maybe the cane.'

There was no reply. He continued to look at me, his face unreadable, betraying no emotion whatever. Then he rose to his feet and I stepped back, expecting an explosion of righteous fury.

It never came. Instead he just looked at me, studying my face in minute detail. Finally he spoke.

'Isabelle Colraine,' he said evenly, 'if any other undergraduate had made that proposal to me I would have immediately assumed that an attempt was being made to manoeuvre me into an advantageous position for blackmail. In your case I actually believe the offer to be genuine.'

'It is, sir,' I quavered, still unsure of the nature of his response.

'Then shall we see what is to be done about it?' he replied, his impassive face suddenly breaking into a broad and wicked grin.

'Yes, sir,' I answered.

I was trembling hard, mostly at the prospect of being punished, but also with sheer relief. I was not going to have to endure the disgrace of rustication and the subsequent exposure of my behaviour to my parents, which would have been as inevitable as it was unbearable. Instead I was going to get my bottom smacked, not for the first time, true, but for the first time by a man.

It was worse. After all, I fancied Jasmine as a lover. She was young, beautiful and of course a woman. Being bare in front of her was humiliating for me only because it signified my submission. I could have stripped in front of her for sex or simply in a changing room or shower and never given it a thought. Dr Appledore was very different. I've always felt humiliated by the idea of being bum-up in front of a man, but he was going to beat me. He was also middle-aged and couldn't be described as handsome although he was certainly impressive in a fatherly way. With my sense of erotic humiliation welling up strongly inside me I stepped forward, wondering in what way he intended to punish me and whether he would insist on taking my panties down.

He stepped from behind his desk and walked to the door. I heard the catch click into place, a sound that had a terrible finality about it.

'I think you had better bend over the desk my dear,' he said.

'Yes, sir,' I answered, taking two steps forward and bending at the waist to rest my arms on the polished wood of his desk.

My bottom was up and I was ready, physically if not mentally. I closed my eyes, waiting, shivering. His hands touched me, coming up under my jacket to find the waistband of my skirt. It fastened at the back, and, as he popped the button open and I felt a subtle release of pressure on my tummy, I knew that I was not going to be spared the indignity of exposure.

I stifled a groan as he slipped the skirt down over my hips. It would have been much easier just to lift it if he only wanted to get at my bottom and I began to wonder if he intended to strip me. He stopped pulling with the skirt around my thighs though and refastened the button, effectively trapping my legs and leaving my bottom framed in the grey cloth of my suit. I felt intensely exposed, even with my panties to shield my bottom, and I was glad I'd put on clean ones and chosen sensible white cotton instead of anything fancy.

'I'm sorry, but I really think these had better come down,' he said from behind me and then his fingers were in the waistband of my panties.

This time I could not restrain myself and let out a sob as my bottom was exposed. Then it was bare and my precious panties were being everted around my thighs. I felt the cool air on the rear pouch of my pussy and knew that all my most intimate parts were showing. Leaving my panties, he casually turned up the tails of my jacket and blouse. My exposure was complete.

My breathing had deepened and I was trying to suppress the sexual feelings of having my bum naked. He had stood back and I could sense his eyes feasting on my naked bottom, also on my pussy and anus. I couldn't help but picture the sight – my buttocks round and pushed out, ready for punishment – the fur of my underbelly on show, growing richly on my pussy mound and up between the cheeks of my bottom – my pussy, pouted, swollen and probably wet in the middle – my bum-hole, a wrinkled brown ring, pulsing slightly in my nervousness.

'I see that Tierney was not inaccurate in his statement,' Dr Appledore remarked.

His comment really brought home my sense of exposure and I felt my tears start to well up. It also reminded me that my bottom would still be red from my paddling and even showing traces of my earlier whipping. I swallowed, keeping my eyes shut as I waited for him to start my punishment. He had no implement, so I imagined that it would be done by hand, a punishment less painful than the cane or strap but involving intimate and humiliating contact. There was no sound, but I could feel his eyes burning into my nakedness.

Nothing happened and after a while my curiosity got the better of me and I opened my eyes. I looked back, wondering what was happening and worried that he might lose control and try and fuck me. After all, my pussy must have been a tempting target. He wasn't where I had thought him at all, but investigating a walking-stick stand by the door.

Suddenly the idea of a hand spanking seemed appealing, even if it meant having my bottom fondled. He was extracting a walking stick from the stand, a cane walking stick, true, but very definitely a walking stick and perhaps as thick around as three fingers held together.

'Dr Appledore!' I protested, horrified at what the massive, clumsy thing might do to my poor bottom.

He paid no attention, but tugged at the handle of the stick. To my surprise it came open and he pulled a long length of dull steel from the inside of the cane. As the full length emerged I realised that it was a swordstick, an *épée* in fact, pointed at the tip but blunt at the edges. It was also an ideal implement for enforcing discipline on the bottoms of naughty girls, thin, whippy and undoubtedly agonising.

'Please, Dr Appledore,' I begged, abandoning even the limited dignity of self-restraint. 'Couldn't you just take me across your knee and spank me with your hand or something?'

He turned to me, flexed the swordstick experimentally through the air and tapped it across his palm before speaking.

'Isabelle, my dear,' he began, as he swished the swordstick through the air, 'neither you nor I need be under any illusions as regards the pleasure of what is about to take place. I shall enjoy it, you may be certain, and it is evident to me that you also take pleasure in sensual flagellation. Yet I also wish to punish you and feel that the rather indelicate method of chastisement that you suggest would not only fail to do justice but excite both of us to the point where we might lose our reserve.'

I choked back the angry denial that sprang to my lips. He was right. Once I had been well spanked I would certainly be too aroused to put up more than a token protest should he choose to explore my sex. From there I knew I could easily be persuaded to masturbate him or even to suck his penis. I said nothing, but braced myself as he came to stand behind me and raised the wicked steel cane above my quivering bottom.

'Six of the best, I believe, is traditional,' he said and brought the cane down.

I heard it whistle through the air and the next instant an agonising line of fire sprang up across my bottom. It burned furiously, a searing, hot sensation that seemed to go right through me. I was on my feet immediately, yelping and rubbing at my bottom, squeezing my cheeks and pulling them open in a desperate attempt to lessen the pain without thought for the exhibition I was making of myself.

He waited patiently until I calmed down and I had once more bent submissively across the desk. I was trembling hard and fighting down my sexual response, also crying, with a tear running down my nose from my left eye. He continued to wait and at length I lifted my bottom, acquiescing to the second stroke. Once more he turned up my tails, baring his target.

The first had been laid across the crest of my bottom, striking the plumpest and best padded area. The second came lower, landing on the fleshy tuck of my cheeks where they turn in to meet my thighs. Again it burned crazily and again I yelled out in my pain, but I managed to stay over the desk. This time there was no denying the erotic feeling, and although both my eyes were now wet with tears I couldn't help the warmth of my pussy.

'A little less noise, if you might,' he remarked. 'Neither of us, I am sure, wish the neighbours to be aware of what is happening to you.'

I felt a fresh pang of shame at the thought of anybody else knowing what I was going through and nodded dumbly, determining to keep my squeals to a minimum. My two cane strokes were smarting lines of fire and beginning to throb, increasing my already heightened awareness of my buttocks.

'Sensible girl,' he responded and once more brought the cane down across my bottom.

It landed right across the first one and I squealed again, quite unable to help myself.

'Really Isabelle, you mustn't make such a fuss,' he chided gently.

'It hurts!' I protested.

'Only three more,' he answered cheerfully, 'and then it will all be over. Still, perhaps we had better do something to ensure that you remain quiet. Hmm, a gag of some sort would seem to be called for ... I wonder what might prove efficacious.'

'Use my panties,' I sighed, reasoning that I did need my squeals stifling and that if I had to be gagged then it was better to use something of my own.

'Ah ha, a fine idea!' he responded.

I let him do it, having abandoned any attempt at preserving my modesty. Yet as he reached up under my skirt and pulled my most intimate garment down my legs he still managed to provoke in me a sense of outrage. I was sniffling as I stepped out of them, but opened my mouth when he offered them to me, aware of the possible consequences of not staying shut up.

He pushed the panties into my mouth, wadding the cotton in until my jaws were wide and my cheeks bulging out. They were dry, but tasted of me. Rory had gagged me with my panties to stop me making a noise during sex, and the comparison came home to me as Dr Appledore tucked a fold of cotton into my cheek.

'Three more,' he remarked as he stood back and picked the swordstick up, 'stick it up a little higher please, my dear.'

I obeyed, elevating my bottom as he lifted the cane. Down it came, landing high on my cheeks to make me buck and wriggle, gagging on my panties and trying to kick my thighs about despite the restraint of my skirt.

'Four,' he announced.

Again it came, whipping down across my poor bottom, applied mercilessly hard with the clear intent of punishing me in a way I would not forget in a long time. The pain was less than it had been at first though and I was really having to fight the urge to cock my thighs apart as if offering my vagina for entry. If the pain was less the humiliation was not, and there were tears on my cheeks and a salty taste in my mouth mingling with the musk and perfume of my panties.

'Five,' he remarked.

I braced myself, knowing that with one more stroke it would all be over. An unexpected sense of regret came, as if I was sorry that the beating was about to end. It hurt, of that there was no doubt, but the five strokes had put me in a state of compliant, submissive bliss that my sense of shame and exposure only served to enhance.

'Six,' he said as the final stroke lashed down across my cheeks. The shock went through me and I bucked, then my muscles were relaxing and I was slumping forward.

I was crying freely, lying spread across a desk with my skirt pulled down and my panties stuffed in my mouth. My buttocks were naked and crisscrossed with cane stripes, each burning and throbbing. My pussy was wet and swollen, open to the man who had just beaten me, the first man who had the guts to punish me. As far as I was concerned he could do anything he wanted, make me suck him, mount me, even push his cock up my bottom and sodomise me.

'You may get up now, Isabelle,' he said gently.

I tuned my face to him, my eyes wide, my cheeks streaked with tears, my mouth bulging with white cotton. If he wanted to have me, now was the moment, with my well-thrashed bottom still bare and vulnerable while my head spun with the aftereffect of punishment.

He was stood behind me like a great bear, massive, looming, with a bulge in the front of his trousers betraying his excitement.

'Oh God, I'm going to do it,' he sighed and the next moment he had drawn his fly down and scooped out a thick, half-stiff cock and a pair of sizeable balls.

I relaxed back onto the table and stuck my bottom up, offering myself for entry. He came behind me, tugging my skirt down and freeing my legs. I parted them and something touched the cleft of my bottom, his cock. He began to rub it against the cane marks on my skin, making them tingle. I could feel him tugging at himself as he did it, working it erect for my pussy.

Then it was against my sex lips, rubbing in the wet flesh of my vulva, bumping on my clitoris, touching my vagina, stretching me, penetrating me, sliding up to fill me with solid, swollen penis. He began to hump me, his belly slapping against my bottom, the bottom he had just whipped into submission.

In ecstasy, I lifted my torso and pulled my blouse and bra up, freeing my breasts to swing nude beneath me, the nipples brushing the hard table top. I took them in my hands and began to fondle them, squeezing and stroking as I remembered the way I had been caned.

His pumping was frantic and he was quickly gasping for breath, puffing and blowing with the unaccustomed effort of mounting a young girl from the rear. His weight and the power of his pushes were sending shocks right through me and making me gag on my panties. At that instant he could have come inside me and I simply wouldn't have cared, but his control was greater than mine and at what must have been the last possible moment he pulled out. His hands had been on my bottom, holding my cheeks apart, perhaps to caress my cane marks, perhaps to inspect my anus. As he pulled out he grabbed me by the hair and pulled me round, reaching into my mouth to pull my panties free.

Before I could react he had replaced them with his cock. I gagged as it filled my mouth, pushed to the back of my throat. Then it jerked and suddenly my mouth was full of thick, salty come, an incredible amount of it, filling my cheeks and spurting out from around the base of his penis. I gagged again and then swallowed because it was all I could do, feeling the sticky sperm trickle down my throat as his cock jerked once more to add to the load in my mouth. He still had me by the hair and he finished himself off slowly, pumping his cock in and out until he was completely satisfied. My mouth was full of it and some had already dribbled out to pool on the desk beneath me.

Not only had Dr Appledore beaten me, but he had come in my mouth, taking advantage of my excited and submissive state to achieve another first. Having it done to me was utterly humiliating and exactly the sort of act I felt most appropriate for a girl who had just been caned. Lost to everything but the sensations of my body and mind, I slumped to the floor, spread my thighs and began to masturbate. I had never felt so dirty, and as a trickle of come ran down my chin I reached under my bottom and put a finger to my anus, dabbing at the little tight hole. As I used one hand to alternately enter my vagina and rub at my clitoris I used the other the stimulate my bottom, with the top joint of one finger in my anus while the others stroked the roughened skin where the cane had caught the tender flesh near the crease of my bottom.

He was watching me, and as I started to come I stuck my tongue out, showing him the sperm he had put in my mouth. My back arched and my anus tightened on my finger. I pressed hard on my clitoris, screaming out in my ecstasy, once, twice and then again as my whole being came to centre on the hard bud of flesh beneath my finger.

Then it was over and I was lying back on the floor, soiled, exhausted and deeply ashamed of myself. He was standing over me, for once lost for words, motionless until he suddenly reached out and picked up my discarded panties.

'You might want to clean up a little,' he suggested, handing them to me.

I complied, using the panties to dab off my pussy and wipe my chin and mouth. There was come on my blouse, but too little to look suspicious and a quick check in the mirror in his bedroom showed me to look respectable once more. My panties were sodden and I wrapped them in loo paper before pocketing them, feeling a wry flush of naughtiness at the thought of walking knickerless through college. The touch of humour made me feel a little better and I turned to inspect my bottom, lifting my skirt to reveal six sets of bright red lines decorating my cheeks, each one double like tramlines and flushed deep red in the centre. It looked sore and felt it too, but no one could deny that I had been punished and as I admired the evidence of my chastisement I felt a wonderful sense of catharsis. I'd been beaten for my bad behaviour and now I was pure once more, having expiated my sin.

'Thank you Dr Appledore,' I said as I returned to the main room, still with my skirt up so that he could have a last glimpse of my bottom. 'I actually feel much better for that.'

'Any time my dear, any time,' he assured me with a satisfied smile.

I left, slipping the catch on his door and pushing it open. As I did so I heard a sound from below. Leaning quickly over the balustrade I caught a glimpse of a shabby trouser leg and a brown shoe that had seen better days. Immediately I realised who it was – Stan Tierney. Evidently he had been listening at the door and would have heard, not just my agonised squeals as I was caned but my screams of ecstasy as I came over the experience. Once more the blood rose to my cheeks and as I descended the stair I could feel my furious blushes.

So far it had not been a lucky day for me, having held a great deal of humiliation and punishment for the reward of a helpless orgasm. Of one thing I was sure though, if Rory had managed to get the tapes it would all have been well worth it. My intention was to go straight to his college as soon as I had washed and put on a new pair of panties. As it was I found him outside my room, writing a note on the piece of paper students traditionally attach to their doors.

He had nothing with him, and one look at his face told me that I was due for a disappointment.

'Never again, never,' he said as I hurried up the last few steps. 'You're a liability, Isabelle, you nearly got me arrested.'

For a moment I was furious. After everything I had been through he had failed to do what he was told. Then my anger faded as quickly as it had risen, my mental exhaustion simply too great to accommodate anything more.

'Tell me then,' I sighed as I pushed my key into the lock. 'I'll make us a coffee.'

He accepted my offer, and was presently detailing his adventures of the day. As arranged, he had made his way to the Cowley Road and identified Jasmine's house. To get to the back of Jasmine's house it was necessary to climb the wall of an alley and cross a single, rather wild garden. The back was well shielded from view and it should then have been a simple matter to get inside. By sheer bad luck a constable had appeared at the end of the alley at the exact moment Rory had been pulling himself up onto the wall. A chase had ensued, which had ended with him hiding in a large waste-bin at the rear of a chip shop. He was less than happy about this and laid the blame squarely on me, which I could hardly claim was unfair.

My own tale of woes simply made him laugh, and he frankly admitted that in the circumstances he found it impossible to view me getting the cane as anything other than both appropriate and just. When I had told him everything he made me show him my bottom, which I did with mock reluctance. As I stood there with my dress held up and my bare, whipped cheeks on show to him I felt both an odd pride and a sense of comfort. I also felt both submissive and grateful, despite his failure, and so made no complaint when he reached out and gently took the tuck of one of my cheeks in his hand.

I suppose it was inevitable that from that point we should end up in bed. His experience seemed to have given him new energy, and we made love again and again. At some point during the night he 'punished' me by inserting the handle of my biggest make-up brush into my anus while we made love. Normally such a dirty act would have had me squirming in embarrassment, especially as he had me posing on all fours with the bristles on show in the mirror, protruding from my bottom like some ridiculous tail. As it was, I was simply too far gone to do more than merely enjoy the physical sensation of having my anus penetrated.

Eight

Sexual though it had been, being caned certainly proved an effective punishment for me, serving both the intended functions of punishment – correction for the misdeed and deterrence for the future. My bottom smarted for a week, and although I masturbated over the feel of the resultant bruises again and again, I was a great deal better behaved than I had been. Of course it couldn't last, because I still wanted my corset and there was also the matter of the tapes. My attempt to retrieve them had been a fiasco, and simply added to an already complicated and ignominious position. Now I not only had Jasmine looking on me as her plaything, but also Rory, Dr Appledore and to a certain extent Caroline and Walter Jessop. With the girls, I knew full well that I would end up playing with them again when the time came to collect my finished corset. With Rory, it simply meant abandoning any pretence of reluctance when he wanted to mount me from behind and accepting being gagged with my own panties as part of the ritual. Dr Appledore continued to treat me with professional detachment during tutorials, but made a point of squeezing my bottom when I left. All of this was acceptable to me, and my true worry – being blackmailed by Stan Tierney – came to nothing.

This was just as well, as had he chosen to make life difficult for me I would have been in a serious quandary. He knew both about my naughty behaviour on the punt and about my subsequent caning. True, he was in no position to risk the wrath of Dr Appledore, and perhaps that was why he held back. I was glad in any case, because the idea of being obliged to toss him off or whatever service he might have demanded was both disgusting and appealing. The incident with Walter Jessop had served to fuel my previously mild dirty-old-man fantasies, and my worst concern was not that I might lack the courage to tell Stan Tierney to go to hell, but that he might catch me at the wrong moment and that I might actually do as I was told. The thought of having to take his cock in my hand, let alone my mouth, both repelled and excited me, and it was with considerable relief that the days passed without anything happening.

When a note arrived in my bunker to say that my corset was ready and suggesting bringing my combinations I set off for the Cowley Road with a feeling of resignation. The idea of dressing up and then submitting to Jasmine excited me, that I could no longer deny. On the other hand I still wanted her to submit to me. Unfortunately my previous acceptance of her dominance had made this harder. She now assumed that I would do as I was told, as I quickly discovered on my arrival at her house.

It was just too easy to slip into role, and too pleasurable. When Caroline showed me the corset I was enthralled and couldn't get my clothes off fast enough in my eagerness to try it on. The sight of the fading cane marks on my buttocks amused and delighted both of them. That and the story I was obliged to relate of how I had been punished added to Jasmine's view of me as a natural submissive, something it was becoming increasingly hard to deny.

Dressing up involved wearing just the combinations Walter Jessop had given me, a pair of ribbon-tied black knee stockings Caroline had made as an extra and the corset. It was simply magnificent, a dream of black silk, ribbon and lace, full and heavy, in a style that differed little if at all from that of the one in my attic that had sparked my imagination. Caroline put me in it while Jasmine reclined on the sofa, watching us with a detached amusement. Just being dressed in Victorian clothes was heaven for me, but as Caroline put her knee in my back and started to pull the laces tight I really began to feel the effect.

I was gripping onto the wooden pillar at the centre of the room, with my bottom stuck out and my legs planted apart. Jasmine was eyeing me thoughtfully as I grunted with the effort of having my waist pulled in. The feeling of restraint around my midriff was exquisite, bringing my breasts and hips to a natural prominence of which I was acutely aware. It was as if the sensuality of my body had been enhanced a hundred-fold, and when Caroline tied the laces off and gave my bottom a cheeky squeeze all I could do was moan softly and stick it out further. She giggled but resisted me, instead going for her tape measure. She measured my waist, which came to nineteen inches. This was no record by Victorian standards, but for a girl of my height – and untrained at that – it was impressive. It also felt lovely, as did the position I was in, clutching the pillar with my bottom thrust out.

'Very pretty,' Jasmine remarked, rising to her feet. 'Perhaps we should take you up to the Ox and have you strip. But no, I don't suppose they'd appreciate it.'

'No, they wouldn't,' Caroline put in. 'I think she should be just for us.'

Jasmine had come close. With a gesture at once casual and possessive she ran a fingernail down the nape of my neck, making me sigh and arch my back. Her response was an amused chuckle as she grabbed my bottom in one hand and a breast in the other. She started to knead my flesh, fondling me in a manner that allowed no question that I was hers to touch as she pleased. I let her, enjoying the sensation far too much to want her to stop. As I gave a contented moan her lower hand found the split at the rear of my combinations and slid inside, stroking the bare flesh of my bottom, cupping my cheeks, bouncing one in her hand as if testing the quality and then abruptly pulling back.

'Pleasant, isn't it?' she asked, placing a finger under my chin and tilting my head back.

She had heels on and I was bent forward, meaning that for once her head was above mine. I looked into her eyes. They were the colour of jade, shot with lines of brown, and projecting a cool, haughty dominance. I swallowed, drawn into the beauty of her eyes, yet still, at heart, wanting to see them downcast and meek as she knelt at my feet.

'Let yourself go,' she urged. 'Let your natural need to serve come to the surface. Obey me, serve me, learn to thrill to my word of praise and tremble at my anger, for only then will you be truly fulfilled.'

This was simply too much. A smacked bottom was one thing. My body responded to her skill, and for the pleasure it gave I was willing to play her game. My mind was another matter, and it was that which she evidently wished to possess. Although I had no wish to bring our relationship to an end, I found a hot retort rising to my lips, only to be bitten back as a sudden thought came to mind. She was arrogant, sure of her strength, her ability to dominate by sheer force of personality.

'I think I understand, Jasmine, Mistress,' I answered, keeping my words quiet and slow.

'You're a good little girl at heart,' she replied and tilted my chin up a little further. 'Now tell me what you want to do, how you wish to serve your Mistress.'

'To be, to be at your feet,' I stammered. 'To crawl to you, to beg to you, to be whipped if I'm naughty, to be fed from a dog bowl at your feet, to be tied and used for your amusement, to obey you, to put you first in all things, before myself.'

It was a simple litany composed of some of the things I liked to imagine doing to girls and sprinkled with concepts drawn from various works of sado-masochistic literature. Jasmine's cruel smile told me it was the right thing to say and she was actually purring with pleasure as she stood away from me.

'Tie her hands to the pillar and whip her, Caroline,' Jasmine ordered. 'I shall watch and enjoy her pain.'

'Yes, Mistress,' Caroline answered quickly.

I hung my head and stayed in place with my hands resting on the pillar above the level of my head. It was an exquisite position, intensely sensual and enhanced by my clothing and Jasmine's cruelty. My breathing was becoming deeper, which was no act with the prospect of a whipping from Caroline in view.

Caroline was as enthusiastic as ever, first going down to the playroom and returning with an armload of rope, two wooden poles and a thick leather strap not unlike a tawse. This she held up to my face as she slid her hand into my combinations to stroke my bottom. Then she whispered in my ear, reminding me of how I had spanked her and how she had kissed my anus. She told me that the time had now come for her revenge and pressed the strap to my lips. I kissed it, tasting the leather and something else, perhaps the sweat of girls whose bottoms had previously known its sting.

She made a thorough job of putting me in bondage, strapping my hands to the pillar first and then working on immobilising me completely despite Jasmine having given no such order. The first pole was used to fix my ankles apart. Leather straps at each end attached the rigid pole between my feet, forcing me to stand with my legs well spread so that when my bottom was bared my pussy would be on full show. It was also going to stop me kicking my feet, a restriction that I knew would add to my feeling of frustration during punishment. The second pole went across the small of my back and was tied off on the pillar, making a triangle that forced my back in and made me thrust out my bottom, adding to the indecency of the display I would be giving when my combinations were pulled open. Other ropes added tension to my body, forcing me to keep still and preventing me from doing more than squirm in my bonds during the coming beating.

Instead of simply pulling my combination split open and exposing my bum, she fetched a needle and thread and sewed each side open. The first merely left a slice of one bottom cheek showing, but as the second was drawn away I felt the full intensity of my exposure. The position left me spread wide, pussy stuck out as if anticipating entry, anus stretched, both holes bare and vulnerable should they choose to add to my humiliation by filling them.

Once I was ready, Caroline stood back and Jasmine made a leisurely inspection of my body, walking around me. Coming to my rear, she traced a finger nail down the cleft of my bottom, lingering on my anus to tickle it and make me grunt, then sliding into my vagina. I was wet and her digit went in easily, right inside me until her knuckles brushed my pussy. For an instant she frigged me, wriggling her finger inside me and rubbing her knuckles across my vulva. I moaned and pushed back for more, only for her to laugh and pull away.

Coming back to my front, she put her hand to my mouth and fed me my own juice, making me lick and suck her fingers until they were glistening with my saliva. I closed my eyes and sighed, revelling in the taste as her hands went to the laces that held the top of the combinations closed over my breasts. She tugged the bow and I felt my breasts part a little. With an expert movement, she had pulled my breasts free of my corset. As she pulled the linen flaps apart and bared them to the air they bounced out into her hands, feeling oddly sensitive from their confinement. Now it was all on show, my breasts, my pussy, my bottom, everything secret and rude, flaunted for them, my fancy underwear only serving to enhance my exposure.

Then Jasmine had stepped away and was nodding to Caroline, leaving me bared and ready for punishment. I turned to watch myself beaten, finding Caroline with an ebullient smile on her sweet face. She glanced at me, her eyes glittering with excitement and mischief. Her tongue poked out from between her lips, a gesture of insolence more eloquent than words. I was shaking as she drew the strap back, poising it behind her head with the end held out. It came round, whistling through the air and finding its target on the meat of my naked bottom.

It was a heavy blow, producing a dull, rich pain very different from the bite of the cane or the sting of the whip. I cried out, but it was more a grunt than a scream and carried as much pleasure as it did pain. Jasmine laughed at my response, while Caroline was already drawing her hand back for the second blow. I heard the crack as it landed across my bottom and felt the impact, again making me want to present myself for more as much as pull away. Not that I had any option, my bondage kept me in my rude pose, helpless and available for their amusement and quite unable to either escape or masturbate myself to the orgasm that was rapidly becoming a serious need.

Caroline beat me with a slow and measured pace, aiming her shots to spread the smacks across my bum. When my whole bottom was red and hot and I had started to moan and beg for her touch she transferred her attentions to the backs of my thighs, tucking the rear of my open combinations into themselves so that she could get at the tender flesh where my bottom meets my legs. Suddenly the blows were coming right over my pussy, not hard enough to hurt, but enough for each to make me grunt and buck. It was simply too much. I was desperate to get at myself, to masturbate until I came, rubbing at my clitoris while Caroline beat me and Jasmine watched with her cool, disdainful eyes caressing my wretched, writhing body.

'Make me come, please, Jasmine, please!' I squealed out.

She simply laughed and lay back on the sofa.

'You come when I allow it,' she said, 'and only then. I, as your Mistress, come when I please.'

I watched as she began to tug her dress up. It was black, and made of some shiny material, long and tight at the knee-length hem. She wrenched it up to her waist, exposing stockings, a rather severe suspender belt and black plastic panties. Even as another hard smack landed on my helpless bottom the thought crossed my mind that she must have dressed in such a deliberately erotic way on purpose, as always absolutely confident in getting me where she wanted.

As Caroline landed another heavy smack on my posterior, Jasmine's eyes locked on my body. She slid a hand down the front of her panties and began to play with herself, taking the pleasure that I was denied.

'Me too!' Caroline giggled and I heard a smack as the strap was dropped to the floor.

They abandoned me, which was a worse torment than the beating. I was hung in my bonds, helpless and desperate to come. Yet all I could do was watch Caroline bounce over to Jasmine and bury her face in her Mistress's crotch. Jasmine responded by pulling her panties aside and allowing Caroline access to her pussy.

Caroline's bottom was stuck out towards me, a plump ball in tight blue denim. Having taken their pleasure of me they ignored me, Jasmine shutting her eyes and starting to stroke Caroline's hair as her pleasure rose. Caroline was working on her trousers, popping the button and easing them down over her plump buttocks, taking her big, dark blue panties with them to expose the full glory of her peach to me. She lifted her bottom, spreading the cheeks and taunting me with the show of her furry underbelly and pussy. All I could do was moan as she started to masturbate, making a deliberate display of caressing her pussy and even pulling her bum cheeks open to tease me with a show of her anal charms.

Jasmine came first, Caroline not long after, both girls moaning and sighing in unrestrained ecstasy. Caroline kept her face in her Mistress's pussy long after both of them had come, rubbing herself in a gesture of abased love that added jealousy to my already burning emotions. Finally, they were finished. They stood, kissed and came to stand in front of me, Jasmine cool and poised, Caroline happy as she cuddled onto her Mistress.

'Please?' I begged.

'Patience, little one,' Jasmine answered, 'and it'll be all the better for waiting. Besides, I've come now, and so has Caroline, why should we bother with the house slut?'

'Please, I really need it,' I implored, 'or else leave me here for a while but promise you'll make me come when you return.'

'Hmm, an amusing idea, if hardly original,' Jasmine replied. 'Sometimes if Caroline is really naughty – perhaps for going with a man – I leave her hog-tied in the bath after drinking two or three pints of water. The effect you can guess, especially as she is always fully clothed.'

'No, no,' I said, 'not that, not with my combinations on. It wouldn't be fair.'

She laughed and once more gave me her cruel, amused look, then turned to Caroline.

'Come, Carrie darling,' she said lightly. 'I think we've found little Isabelle's weak spot.'

Caroline giggled and together they left the room, leaving me with a cheerful wave and mocking, blown kisses. A while later I heard the slam of the front door and immediately began to work on my bonds.

It seemed to take forever, but objectively it must have been no more than five minutes. Caroline had made a good job of binding my wrists and also of tying them to the pillar. What she hadn't done was add a loop to stop the ropes moving up and down it. By tugging them down I managed to alter the stresses in the ropes, although it meant maintaining a ridiculous position with my bottom stuck out so far that without the ropes I would have overbalanced.

All I needed was one free hand and the rest would be simple. Working with furious energy, I slowly managed to gain slack, tightening the knot that held my wrists but loosening the coils on the pillar. It hurt, but I was determined and kept it up, ignoring the pain. Finally my hand slid from under the ropes, red, sore but free. The idea of leaving me until I wet myself had amused Jasmine greatly and so it seemed reasonable that it would be some time before they returned. Untying my remaining bonds was easy, Caroline having made no effort to do anything clever, like putting a knot out of my reach.

At last, I was free. A brief rub at my bottom served to soothe the smarting feeling. Barefoot, I ran down the stairs and was soon rummaging among Jasmine's underwear for the playroom key. It was at the back, and concealed in the folds of a lacy body. Moments later I was pushing open the playroom door and then the video tapes were at last in my hands. I was trembling by the time I had got to the living room and was kneeling on the floor eagerly feeding a tape into the machine. I knew what it would show – either Caroline and I indulging our mutual taste for spanking or me sucking Walter Jessop's penis. I was still high from Jasmine and Caroline's treatment of my body and was wondering if I could risk the time to sneak a quick orgasm as the tape began to play.

White noise showed on the screen, then a brief flicker of colour, then more white noise. With my ears straining for their return I worked frantically at the remote control, searching for the compromising views of myself that had exercised my mind so strongly for weeks and resulted in my acceptance of my own submission.

There was nothing. Both tapes were blank, neither containing so much as a bit of old soap opera, never mind the rude and dramatic images I had been expecting. My first thought was that Jasmine had tricked me once more, leading me to think that these were the tapes while the real ones were concealed elsewhere. Then another thought occurred to me and I was running upstairs, leaving the decoy tapes on the living room floor.

In the attic, it was the work of a moment to pull Caroline's sewing machine underneath the camera. Climbing onto it I reached up, examining the device in the dim light of the gable end. It was as I had suspected. The wires leading from it ended at the wall, the lens was a mere plastic bubble, the body contained neither working parts nor controls – it was a fake, a dud, no more capable of recording pictures than a brick.

Nine

On the return of Jasmine and Caroline I was back in bondage, exactly as I had been when they left. After I had been untied and allowed to come in front of them I was told that I was now Jasmine's maid and junior to Caroline. I was burning with anger at the trick that had been played on me, yet so great was my need for the pleasures that came from associating with them that I found myself quite unable to allow my fury to surface. Instead I accepted, simply because not to do so would mean abandoning the only relationship I had ever known which really suited my sexuality. True, it was the reverse side of the coin, but time would tell.

My maid service involved spending the majority of my spare time at Jasmine's and basically doing as I was told, both in the form of eroticised domestic chores and sexual service. Not that it was really that simple, because they had put me on a specific regime, which required that I perform certain tasks and received certain punishments for mistakes. These were posted on the wall and included instructions such as me having to make Jasmine's bed and then take a stroke of the strap for every crease she could find.

When I wasn't with them, I was often with Rory, who was now my regular bed-mate, although we had

made no definite commitment. We often slept together and also made a habit of turning ourselves on
by the device of masturbating together while I related
what Jasmine and Caroline had made me do.

Between them they kept me satisfied if not perfectly
fulfilled, providing two worthwhile facets to my sex
life. I was keen to keep these apart, but fate decreed
otherwise.

The incident started with my Thursday afternoon
tutorial. This was at five o'clock, and as I had spent
most of the previous evening scrubbing Jasmine's
kitchen floor with a parsnip pushed up my vagina I
had given less attention to the essay than I should
have done. On arriving at Dr Appledore's room I
found him looking at it with a mild frown.

'Sit down, Isabelle, my dear,' he greeted me, then
tapped the top sheet of the essay with his forefinger.
'This is fair, but not really to your normal standard
and, frankly, a little short.'

'I'm sorry, I was a little distracted,' I answered,
truthfully enough.

He seemed to accept my answer and we began to
discuss my essay, remaining deeply involved in the
intricacies of the seventeenth-century French court
system until six o'clock.

'Enough, I feel, the hour grows late,' he announced
suddenly and pushed his chair back from the desk.
'Now, my dear, if you would be good enough to come
across my knees, I feel that you would benefit from a
smacked bottom.'

'Duncan!' I protested automatically, completely
taken aback by the suggestion despite my earlier
caning.

He gave me a curious look, both plea and command. I stood up, swallowing, not entirely averse to
the idea of a good over-the-knee spanking, but not

really ready for it. The thing was that Jasmine's taste ran to whips, straps and occasionally the cane but not really hand spanking. I had always favoured two types of punishment, formal beating with a tawse and crude, impromptu spanking with the girl across my knee. With his big, powerful frame and large hands Dr Appledore was just the man to dish out the latter, especially as his age and authority would provide all I needed in the way of mental stimulation while I was punished. So, telling myself not to be prissy and to seize the moment, I got up and walked to the door. He may have thought I was going to walk out of it, but when I clicked the catch into place and turned back his expression was both stern and satisfied.

'Yes, sir, I realise I need to be spanked,' I told him, making it very clear that I was going to play along.

It was as brusque and matter-of-fact as I could have hoped for. As I came close he took me by the wrist and pulled me sharply down over his knee, then twisted my arm into the small of my back to render me helpless. He was humming cheerfully to himself as he pulled my skirt up to expose my panties. I was dressed up because I was going to meet Rory later, not to make a pretty display during punishment from my tutor. Beneath my skirt I had on silk panties, stockings and suspenders, all in pure white. The exposure of all this gave me my now familiar and exquisite twinge of erotic humiliation, but I had little time to dwell on my position and the fact of my fancy underwear being on show.

My panties came down with a swift jerk, exposing a lot more than just intimate clothing. I moaned at the sensation of the silk sliding down off my bum and gave a little whimper as he cocked his leg around my calf and forced my legs apart. I could feel the panties stretched taut between my thighs and knew that the position left my pussy and anus on full show – always an important element of humiliating a girl during punishment.

Once more, he gave me only a brief pause to contemplate the indignity of my position and then landed one heavy, bear-like paw hard across my naked seat. I yelped and bucked, only to catch the next, then another as he began to spank me with a pace and vigour that instantly robbed me of all self-control or dignity. I began to kick, squeal and thrash my legs as slap after slap landed across my bottom. It was smarting, then burning, my meat bouncing with the impacts so that I could feel the waves in the soft flesh of my thighs and midriff. In no time I was blubbering and had begun to beat my free fist against his legs and the floor. All this was futile. He continued to spank me without mercy, applying heavy, authoritative swats to my bottom that were clearly intended to punish as well as titillate.

I could really feel my bottom, which I was sure was swollen and red and somehow blatantly indecent. As my endorphins kicked in, the feeling became increasingly sexual, joining the mental pleasures of humiliation, exposure and the sense of having been naughty and getting what I deserved. My squeals turned to moans and the urge to masturbate had started to build up. Yet he took no notice of my obvious arousal, continuing to spank me and speaking only occasionally to tell me that I was a bad girl.

Finally it stopped, leaving me snivelling over his lap, my hot, red bottom stuck high in the air. How many he had delivered I have no idea, but it had certainly worked. I felt chastened and compliant, deeply sorry for myself yet eager to submit to the penetration of my vagina or whatever else he chose to do to slack the excitement of having beaten me. At some point I had started crying, although I had barely noticed through the pain of my spanking. Now, as I slid to the floor, I turned my tear-streaked face up to him, waiting to be told what to do.

He said nothing, but simply opened his fly and pulled out his cock. I took it in my mouth, circling the base with my fingers. As I began to suck and simultaneously masturbate him into my mouth I was already rummaging among my disarranged clothing for my pussy. My panties were only a little way down, stretched between my thighs just below the tuck of my bottom. The front was still half over my pussy, and as I slid my hand into them I was thinking of how I would look from the rear. My legs were spread and my skirt was up. Every detail of my bottom would be on show – the pink opening of my pussy with my fingers working in the wet pink folds, my anus, a ring of puckered brown flesh around the central hole – my buttocks, round and girlish and above all, freshly spanked. All of it would be framed by my raised skirt and lowered panties, with my stockings, suspenders and demure combination of skirt and blouse adding a final touch to the image of violated modesty.

His cock was hard in my mouth and I was tugging at the base, willing to accept a mouth-load of come because I had been so expertly spanked. Once he'd come in my mouth I wanted my own orgasm, not before. He took a good while, something that I was learning to appreciate as an advantage of older men. This allowed me a long, leisurely suck on his cock while I took turns to dab at my clitoris, finger my vagina, tickle my anus and stroke my smarting bum cheeks.

When he did come it was with a great jerk and a grunt of pleasure. My mouth filled with hot, salty come, which I swallowed. Feeling it in my throat gave me such a strong feeling of wanton, dirty pleasure that I simply had to have my orgasm. Nestling my face into his crotch, I reached back, eased the top joint of my middle finger into my anus and started to dab at my clitoris in what I knew would be the climb to an earth-shattering climax. He began to stroke my hair and I gulped his cock back into my mouth, wanting it there when I came. The first shiver of approaching orgasm went through me and that was the exact moment which the bursar chose to knock on the door.

Half-an-hour later I was cycling north up St Giles in a state of extreme frustration. The bursar had been intent on discussing some complex matter of college politics and I had had to leave with my bottom hot and red under my skirt and my head spinning with the need for my orgasm. My first thought was to go straight to my room and play with myself, but I was supposed to be meeting Rory and decided that he could be made to oblige me with a nice lick of my pussy instead.

He did, making me come as I lay on his bed with my knees up and my panties around my ankles. By the time I came his cock was hard and he mounted me without troubling to ask, taking his pleasure of my pussy and coming all over my belly and suspender belt. After cleaning up we decided to go for a drink and set off across Port Meadow with the Perch in mind.

We became somewhat confused while trying to get to the far side of the river and ended up walking along the tow path by the canal. It was a chill November's evening and distinctly cold, and so we had just decided to chose a more convenient pub when I realised that the three figures coming towards us were familiar – Jasmine, Caroline and Walter Jessop.

From the moment I had completed the introductions I knew that there was going to be mischief. Jasmine asked if Rory was my boyfriend and gave me an arch look when I replied that we had no definite arrangement. They then put us right on our route to the Perch and joined us, having originally been coming back from a friend's houseboat. Once we were settled into the warmth of the pub and had progressed to the third round of drinks, Caroline was flirting openly with Rory and giggling at Jasmine's increasingly suggestive rebukes. They were also teasing me, making references to my love of Victorian clothing and spanking that quickly had me blushing.

After five drinks, a complex set of tensions had developed among us, tensions that were distinctly erotic in nature. Rory stood as the admired younger male, basking in the attentions of three girls and joining Jasmine's efforts to keep me in a submissive, pliant role. I tried hard not to seem resentful, aware that it would only turn Jasmine on, yet could not help responding to their admiration even though it was designed to put me on my knees. Caroline was clearly angling for sex with Rory followed by formal punishment from Jasmine and informal punishment from myself, teasing and flirting to get her way. Jasmine was cooler but clearly keen on Rory, which surprised me as I had thought her sexual liaisons confined to women. Walter Jessop remained in a detached, somehow paternal, certainly voyeuristic role, lapping up the sexual nature of the conversation and sipping at his ginger beer with a pleased smile on his ruddy features.

I was pretty drunk by the time I became aware of my hunger and realised that if I continued to down shots of malt whisky on an empty stomach I was going to end up incapable. At my suggestion of food Walter offered to drive us back to his house and make us dinner. We accepted gladly, especially Rory and I, who had stood our rounds but were both in danger of running out of money.

The drive up to Whytleigh passed in a drunken haze. Walter had bought a round of bottled brown ale, which the rest of us passed round, increasing my feeling of warm naughtiness. Jasmine had arranged things so that I was in the back between her and Caroline, and by the time we got onto the ring road they had my breasts out with my blouse and jacket pulled back my shoulders to trap my arms. Jasmine was feeding me beer while Caroline licked what spilt over off my chin and chest. Rory was watching this from the front, fascinated to see three girls playing together and clearly excited. Walter, fortunately, remained remarkably cool.

By the time we reached Whytleigh, I was in a fine state. Encouraged by my response, they had pulled my skirt up and taken down my panties. These were now round my ankles while Caroline rubbed a beer bottle against my pussy. My breasts were bare and sticky with beer and the girls' saliva, while they had used my bra to tie my hands behind my back. Jasmine was kissing me and tormenting my nipples with her finger nails, and I would soon have come had we not arrived at Walter's.

The other three houses in the row were all shops only and closed, so there was little chance of our being disturbed. Certainly Walter seemed to think so, because he made no protest when they refused to let me make myself decent. Instead I was made to stand in the street with my breasts bare and my skirt tucked up into its own waistband so that my bottom and pussy showed. Only then did Jasmine and Caroline realise that I had been spanked earlier and I was made to stick my bottom out and show off the still flushed cheeks under one of the streetlights.

I was glad to get indoors, but by the time we had gone upstairs to Walter's tiny flat I found myself firmly the centre of attention. More beer was broken out, and when Jasmine ordered me to strip and serve it I made no objection. I'd done it before for her and Caroline, both nude and in my Victorian underwear, but it was different in front of men, and more humiliating. I was too drunk and too excited to care though and was soon crawling on the floor, naked and eager.

Caroline, perhaps jealous of the attention I was getting, opted to join me, and quickly stripped nude to join me on the floor. The sight was making Rory's eyes bulge and I could see the lump in his trousers, not just the swelling of a half-stiff cock, but a solid bar that hinted at a full erection underneath. Caroline had noticed this and turned to Jasmine, kneeling up to beg with her hands, like a puppy dog.

'My slut would like to play with your cock, Rory,' Jasmine said after a good minute of Caroline's frantic panting and whining. 'Would you enjoy that?'

'Yes, thank you,' Rory answered, trying to remain suave and cool but not really succeeding.

'Go on then,' Jasmine conceded, patting Caroline's head, 'do it. You too, Isabelle.'

I was in a thoroughly dirty mood, and keen not just to take Rory's lovely big cock out, but to suck it and let him come in my mouth. Besides, he was my friend and lover, and if anybody was going to play with his erection I wanted it to be me. So even before Caroline had responded I was scampering across on all fours and already had Rory's fly down when she arrived. We pulled his cock out and I took hold of it, placing the end to my mouth as Caroline began to fondle his balls.

That was how we were when Walter emerged from the kitchen, both naked, licking and sucking eagerly at Rory's cock, both not just oblivious to the display we were making of ourselves but actively revelling in it. Walter put the plates down on the table and paused to admire our bare bums, which were thrust out right at him, mine neat but pink from spanking, Caroline's broad and fleshy but pale and un-blemished.

'Come on, you two, dinner time,' Jasmine ordered commandingly. 'Walter, put their bowls on the floor, they can eat like that.

We did, slurping up our dinner with our faces in the plastic bowls Walter had placed on the floor. Walter had made a pasta and flavoured it with pesto sauce, a really messy thing to eat the way we were. The others laughed at us and took plenty of oppor-tunity to fondle our upturned bottoms and dangling breasts. That I should do something so rude and so supposedly degraded I can only put down to the quantity of drink I had consumed and the slow build-up of excitement since Dr Appledore had first suggested that I would benefit from a spanking. Benefit I certainly had, although perhaps not in the way he imagined. The spanking and the subsequent events had enabled me to shed my last vestiges of reserve, to really enjoy the pleasures of submissive sex. Although I still felt a keen humiliation at being made to behave like a puppy, there was nothing in the emotion that made me want to stop. Indeed, when Jasmine unexpectedly took me by the hair and pushed my face into the bowl of pasta and sauce all I could do was reach back and start to play with myself from the sheer delight of being so thoroughly abused.

This earned me a smack on my bottom and an order to be patient. Jasmine then pulled me up by the hair and put a bottle to my lips. It was not beer, but some rich red wine, more of which splashed in my face and over my breasts than went in my mouth. Caroline's tongue touched one of my nipples and I simply lost control completely. Grabbing her, I rolled her over and mounted her, hearing her squeal of delight abruptly silenced as I sat myself down on her face. She began to lick, sharing her attentions across my pussy and bottom with a frantic urgency. I returned the favour, sinking my face between her plump thighs as they came up and apart to offer her pussy to me. I started to lick, concentrating on Caroline's delicious pussy but still aware that our position left my bottom spread wide for the inspection of the audience.

'Little sluts,' Jasmine said from behind me. 'You do know you'll both be whipped for this, don't you?'

Caroline's response was to put her hands on my bottom and start to tickle my anus. Her own bottom-hole was just inches in front of my face, a puckered brown spot in its nest of hair. I popped a finger into it and another into her vagina, wiggling both as I licked at her clitoris. Not surprisingly neither of us took long to come. When we did it was together, with our behaviour more or less a mirror image. Both had our tongues on the other's clitoris, both had two fingers in the other's vagina and both another finger in the other's anus. The only real difference was that while my legs were splayed out on the floor, Caroline's were rolled up in the air.

My orgasm was simply exquisite. Dizzy with drink and the scent of Caroline's pussy, my head was already swimming. As I came the sensation became stronger, building to a blinding crescendo that had every muscle in my body locked in ecstasy and left me weak and panting, only vaguely aware that Caroline had come too.

After that, events became somewhat blurred. I recall climbing off Caroline to find that Jasmine was sitting in-between the two men with a cock in either hand. Rory was erect, Walter still half-limp, yet both men's faces were set in bliss. There was something deliciously rude about the cool, dominant Jasmine playing with two men's cocks, giving them hand service, as it were, while they watched Caroline's and my dirty little floor show. Caroline and I were ordered to suck cock and I am sure I got Rory's yet my next clear memory is of sucking desperately on Walter's in order to get him stiff. Caroline was standing with her magnificent breasts held out into his face, smothering him in flesh to help arouse him. Slowly his cock was filling in my mouth, expanding to the stubby erection of which I knew him to be capable.

I'm not sure who suggested dressing me up, but they put me in a chemise and drawers, only with the back panel undone so that my bum showed. Caroline took over the sucking while Jasmine and Rory spanked me in front of him. I was lying across their locked knees with my arms twisted into the small of my back while a hairbrush was used to bring my cheeks up to full colour. In my drunken, sexy haze it just seemed pleasant, like the little pats a girl might expect on her bottom as a show of affection from a friend. It must have been effective though, because the next thing I knew Caroline was clapping with delight over the sight of Walter's cock, now rock hard and wet with our saliva.

Jasmine, I think, suggested that he should be allowed to fuck one of us, and it was certainly her who made us draw lots for it. I lost, which just made me giggle. By this time we had somehow got into his bedroom and I remember throwing myself back on the bed and spreading my thighs, quite happy to be mounted. Walter came up to kneel between my legs and entered me, holding me by the thighs and pushing himself into me with little, short thrusts. I protested that I was all sloppy and could hardly feel it, to which the little bitch Jasmine responded by suggesting that I be buggered.

Walter dismounted and before I really knew what I was doing I had rolled over and was sticking my bottom up. I was anally virgin, yet all I could do at the obscene thought of his cock being stuck up my bottom was giggle stupidly and wiggle my hips from side to side. Had I balked, I am sure that the others would certainly not have gone along with Jasmine's suggestion. As it was, they thought it was the most wonderful idea.

Someone, I think Caroline, greased my bottom, using what I later discovered to have been lard. The feel of her fingers in my rectum removed any last misgivings I might have had about accepting a cock in the same hole and as she withdrew them all I could do was lift my bum and wait. I remember thinking how my anus must have looked, open and glistening with lubricant, the normally tight brown ring of flesh wide to show off a darker centre, ready for penetration. Somebody called me a slut and smacked my bottom. I felt a hand pull at my drawers and sensed him changed his position. Then his weight was settling onto my buttocks and I could feel his cock between them, short and hard, ready for my anus. He probed at me, grunting as his cock bumped against the crevice of my bottom. The head found my bum-hole, pressing into the greasy ring. He pushed and for an instant it hurt, a dull pain that came with a odd pang of despair that I would no longer be able to take pride in my tight, unviolated rosebud. I know I groaned aloud at the strange popping sensation as my sphincter gave in and the first inch of his penis entered my bottom.

It was in, I was being buggered. I sighed, giving in completely as he began to work his erection deeper up my bottom. It slid in a little more each time he shoved, and each time it made me grunt and pushed the breath from my lungs. Finally, it was right up, stretching my anus and filling my rectum. I had always thought of Walter's cock as small, but it didn't feel like that up my bottom, it felt huge, a great bloated thing that was swelling inside me and knocking the breath from my body.

Once well in, he took my legs and pulled them apart as far as they would go. With one last push he pressed his erection into me, right to the hilt, so that I could feel his huge balls lying against my empty pussy. Then he began to bugger me, slowly, firmly, with an insistent rhythm that quickly had me clutching at the bed and panting out my ecstasy through a mouthful of his coverlet. I was scarcely aware of the others watching, nor really of who was buggering me. All I could think of was the weight on my back and the feel of the cock in my back-passage. It was bliss, to deny it would be foolish, yet it was also dirty, humiliating and quite unspeakably rude.

I wanted to get at my pussy but couldn't because of his weight. Trying to do so I became aware that there was a pillow under my tummy, undoubtedly put there to keep my bum high but I had no idea when or by whom. Bracing my legs I tried to lift and felt him respond to the pressure. My hand slipped down, found the front of my drawers and went in, through the puff of my pubic hair and onto my pussy. Finding my clitoris I relaxed and began to rub, purring to myself as he once more began to ride my bottom.

My desire was to come when he did, to feel the spurt in my rectum as my anus locked on his intruding shaft. His rhythm had quickened and I knew he was getting there. It was hard though, as the sheer power of having him in me was threatening to make me lose control. Also as his pushes became faster and more urgent it became a little painful, making me want to wriggle on his cock instead of concentrate on my orgasm. His balls were slapping on my hand as I frigged though and the hot, stretched feeling of my anus kept what was in it firmly implanted in my mind.

Suddenly I was coming. The muscles of my sex began to clamp. I felt my anal ring squeeze on his cock. I screamed and bit hard on the coverlet, my fingers clutching frantically at it. His cock jerked in my back-passage and I knew he had come up me. That was when my full awareness of his identity returned, unexpectedly and with agonising force. Walter Jessop had just come up my bottom. I'd been spanked, licked out, stripped, spanked again, fucked and finally buggered, buggered by a dirty old man whose erection was still wedged up my bottom. I screamed as I came again. I hit my climax and just stayed there, writhing and thrashing underneath him in total abandonment until it all simply became too much and I passed out on the bed.

They went on after that, because I can vaguely remember being cuddled by Caroline and Jasmine's squeals of ecstasy as she was mounted by Rory. Nothing further happened to me though, or at least I don't think it did, although I doubt I'd have noticed if they'd tied me in the street and invited the villagers to take turns up my bottom.

I awoke with the most appalling hangover. My head was throbbing, I felt sick and my mouth seemed to have the texture of sandpaper. My bottom was sore too, and not just the cheeks. I was in Walter Jessop's bed, with Caroline and Jasmine. Of the men, there was no sign. I was naked too, at some point having been divested of my drawers and chemise.

The girls were fast asleep and I left them, dragging myself painfully to the kitchen. My bottom was so sore that I was limping, and as I poured myself a glass of orange juice I came to understand what people mean when they described something as 'buggered'. What I had done was rude in a way that transcended any previous experience. I had always felt that there was something deeply rude about even touching a man's cock, and a lot of effort had certainly been expended in the cause of making me believe it. All they had done was make me enjoy the feeling of being naughty, yet I would never be the sort of woman who can have sexual contact for the simple physical pleasure. If touching a cock was rude, then sucking one was really dirty, maybe even dirtier than one taken inside my vagina. Yet even allowing a man to come in my mouth and swallowing his sperm was an act of saintly innocence compared with accepting a cock up my bottom.

I'd done it though, and I couldn't deny my pleasure in the experience. Still, in the cold morning light it was hard to be rational, and try as I might I couldn't help but feel a good measure of shame. I'd done it in front of an audience as well, writhing and squirming in ecstasy while they watched – Rory, Caroline and Jasmine.

Jasmine, of course, was the one who had suggested it, that much I was sure of. So, I might have been buggered and maybe I would be again, but I would have my revenge on Jasmine if it was the last thing I did, both for having me sodomised and for all the spankings and humiliations she had given me.

As I reached this conclusion I remembered a detail from after I had passed out. Rory had fucked Jasmine, I was sure of it. Not only had she let him have her, but it had been from the rear, the way he liked to enter girls best. So much to Miss high-and-mighty dominant lesbian Jasmine, I thought, not just accepting a man but from behind in a position that I knew she considered inherently submissive.

Ten

By the Friday evening my feelings were very different. My head had cleared and I was working in my room in college. It was cold outside and already dark, with a fresh wind driving flurries of rain against my window. I have always been sensitive to the weather, and nature in general, and it now gave me a sense of loneliness, even desolation. By contrast the previous day had been so warm, so intimate. Far from regretting what had happened, I was missing it, and quite badly. It had really brought out the submissive in me, and despite a sullen resentment towards Jasmine I was keen for more.

I also felt nervy and a little fragile. Objectively, I knew that this was due to my approaching period, but that didn't prevent it from contributing to my mood. What I wanted to do was seek Rory out and be given a hard spanking followed by a long cuddle, yet I really did have to keep my work up, as Dr Appledore's treatment of my bottom had shown me.

By midnight I had done enough work to satisfy my conscience and my desperation had risen to fever pitch. I needed to do something naughty, also submissive. My mind was running to all sorts of fantasies of humiliation and punishment, mostly impractical ones, but then that is what imagination is for. When

I masturbated in my room I generally made use of my mirror, taking pleasure in the reflection of my own body, which never failed to inspire my sense of rudeness. Now it was simply too cold, despite my fire. Also, while the memory of being buggered the night before was making me keen to once more experience the feeling of having my anus stretched taut around some intruding object, I was still a little sore and not sure whether it was a good idea. Soothing my bottom-hole did seem a good idea though and I decided to go to bed naked with a tube of cold cream by the bed.

Soon I was in a warm dark cocoon of bedding, naked and feeling thoroughly naughty. My mind had begun to run on old-fashioned punishments, as it often did. The difference was that this time I was not the stern, highland schoolma'am using a tawse to impose necessary discipline to the soft, naked bottoms of her sixth-form girls; nor the matron of a nursing home, dragging her squealing charges across her knee for bare bottom spankings in front of their friends and colleagues. Instead I was the victim, a Victorian schoolgirl with her dress lifted and her drawers pulled open while her bottom was thrashed in front of her classmates; also the unfortunate junior nurse, kicking and sobbing across the matron's knee with her uniform off and her big frilly panties down around her thighs while her bottom was turned a blazing shade of red.

My thighs were open. A finger was tracing slow circles over my clit, while others held my sex lips open. My nipples were erect under my other hand, with the softness of my little breast wobbling underneath. Imagining that I was the nurse, and that my punishment was for masturbating, I reached for the tube of cold cream and took it down under the covers. Intent on soothing my bum-hole, I turned over and stuck my bottom up, applying a long worm of cream directly to my anus. It felt wonderful, cold and slimy, immediately easing the soreness that came of permitting a cock to be put inside my rectum.

As I began to rub, I imagined myself being caught like this – bottom up, well-lubricated anus glistening, pinkish brown in the sudden light, finger rubbing in that most secret of places. I purred as I gently popped a finger up my bottom-hole, wriggling it in and letting my thoughts run to men's cocks. My nurse fantasy seemed inappropriate for buggery, unless the matron were to take me with a strap-on. But no, I wanted a live, hot penis and besides, I had been imagining the matron as a cold, self-righteous woman, beating me because I was a dirty, wanton little slut.

One fantasy did suit it though, that of being put in the pillory. I slid a hand under my belly and found my pussy, masturbating eagerly as my finger slid in and out of my bum-hole. The public flogging of women was abolished in the 1790s, yet I could imagine it continuing in remote villages, perhaps in my own highlands or the more rustic counties of England. Certainly I could imagine it happening on the tiny village green at Whytleigh, perhaps as late as the 1860s. I would be the daughter of the local great house, magnificent in flounced crinoline and petti-coats, every square inch of my flesh below the neck hidden from prying eyes. Tired of my haughty airs and aloof disdain, the villagers would catch me one evening. First it would be the duck pond, thrown in and pushed under so that my perfectly coiffured hair was ruined. When I was finally pulled out my beautiful dress would be a bedraggled mess, smeared with mud and hung with weed. There would be no mercy though. They would drag me to the village pillory, clamp me into it despite my furious protests and dire threats. My dress would be cut open at the front, leaving my breasts dangling naked to be pawed by rough-handed yokels. I would howl with rage and shame as my dress was turned up, the pannier inverted to form a huge ring around the bulging fullness of my bottom. My entreaties would be ignored as my petticoats were pulled up, one by one until all I had left to cover my modesty was my long drawers. My shame would become unbearable as these were pulled open and I would burst into tears as my precious bottom came on show. Somebody, a woman, would tell me that the rear of my vulva showed, calling it a cunt and laughing as she gave my buttocks an experimental smack.

Then I would be beaten. Some would use dog whips, others freshly picked willow. Some would use just their hands, and take the opportunity to have a good feel of my squirming buttocks. They would nettle me too, tickling my bottom and thighs until my whole rear was throbbing and burning, doing my pussy last. While they did it, others would pelt me with refuse, smearing old eggs and worse into my face and hair and over my breasts. Finally, I would be left, sobbing brokenly, my buttocks aflame and my face and breasts soiled and filthy. My dress would be ruined, a torn, dirt-smattered rag that the lowest of beggars would have refused.

Then, in the dead of night the men would come, taking turns to make me suck their cocks and then use me from the rear. Soon I would have come in my mouth and up my pussy, on my buttocks and down my drawers. The last would be a swineherd, a massive man with the manners of his pigs and a cock like a cucumber. When I sucked him hard and he had entered me he would express discontent, calmly stating that my cunt was too well battered for his tool. Then he would bugger me, licking my anus and putting a finger in, then forcing his erection up me, stretching me, filling me, making me gasp and squeal until he came deep in my rectum . . .

I came. I had two fingers up my bottom, imagining that it was the giant yokel's cock. I was imagining that my fingers were his too, he having decided to frig me for the thrill of feeling my anus contract around his cock when I came. I almost screamed and had to bite the pillow to stop myself. Three times my orgasm rose and faded, leaving me limp and gasping as my fingers slipped from my gaping bottom-hole.

I awoke to the knowledge that if I didn't do something to assert my dominance soon, I was going to end up as Jasmine's plaything and like it. I was getting more and more submissive, and the memory of the previous night's fantasy and how I had frigged my bottom had me blushing with shame for my abandoned role as the cool, dominant lady. I needed to reassert myself – badly.

There also seemed only one way to go about it – the seduction of Caroline. With her bubbly personality and relaxed attitude to sex, she seemed indifferent to the more subtle interplay of dominance and submission, while I knew from experience that she enjoyed my attentions. The problem was to avoid Jasmine.

The idea gave me a sudden burst of energy. Feeling deliciously mischievous, I made for the bicycle sheds while my plan developed in my head. In the saddle bag was my street-map, a glance at which showed the existence of two Alma Roads. One was in Somers Town, the other near the station. Neither was particularly long, which made them perfect for my purposes.

Cycling out along the Headingly Road, I found a convenient call box and telephoned Jasmine. Putting on my most girly voice, I enquired about corsets and asked if it was possible for her to come out and measure me accurately. She fell for it hook, line and sinker, and when I gave my measurements as roughly 38D 24 38 – similar to Caroline's – she promised to be there as soon as she could. I gave the address as 179 Alma Road, thanked her sweetly and hung up.

Five minutes later, I was standing behind a van as I watched her leave her house and drive away in the direction of Somers Town. Grinning uncontrollably, I approached the house, my only concern being that Caroline might not be in.

She was, and greeted me effusively. Although anything but jealous by nature, I was sure that she was at least a little put out by having her girlfriend going off to measure a girl as beddable as I had made myself out to be. My timely appearance altered all that, putting her on an even footing with Jasmine. From the moment she opened her mouth under mine as we kissed in greeting there was no doubt in my mind that she would be willing to play. As we had their entire collection of sex toys to play with it was more a question of what to do.

Caroline was at her giggliest, and looked good enough to eat in a big jumper and red trousers that were baggy at the legs but clung to her ample bottom. My first thought was simply to spank her and see where things led, but the sheer innocence of her look gave me a better idea. It was also an idea that avoided the possibility of Jasmine coming back early from her wild goose chase and catching us – I was going to take Caroline flashing.

Conscious that public exposure was perhaps more my fantasy than hers, I suggested the idea to her. She responded with her normal giggly enthusiasm, but pointed out that it was perhaps not a very safe thing to do for two women on their own. This had simply not occurred to me, perhaps as a result of my genteel upbringing, yet I had to admit that she was right. My disappointment, however, was short lived, as she then suggested that I might like to give her a public spanking.

At first this struck me as even more dangerous than my suggestion, but as she explained what was evidently a well thought out fantasy I became increasingly keen on the idea. When she had finished, my only reservation was the painful memory of what had happened the last time I had been naughty outdoors. Such was her enthusiasm that I found myself unable to resist, reasoning that we could easily get well clear of the city and that it was hardly likely that we would stumble across Stan Tierney twice.

So we set off, taking a bus south towards Reading and getting off at a point that overlooked the broad spread of the Thames Valley and the Vale of White Horse. The view was impressive, the more so because of the cool, clear air. True, it was a great deal less grand than the bens and moors of my home, but there was an appealing softness to it only partly spoilt by the great cooling towers at Didcot. The downs even gave me a slight pang of homesickness, their high, open slopes evoking images of the space and air that I had always loved. There was also a distinctly autumnal feel to the air, which I found melancholy.

Caroline seemed entirely unaffected by the atmosphere, bouncing merrily off the bus and opening the map to find a suitable site for her punishment. The plan was essentially simple, to find a stretch of river without bridges, go to a place with a suitable audience at the far side, for me to give Caroline a bare bottom spanking that looked like a genuine punishment and to retreat. Obviously the audience had to be carefully chosen, but otherwise the idea seemed faultless and highly stimulating.

A pint of strong, sweet beer and a dram of malt dispelled both my pensive mood and my last misgivings. Checking the map once more, we set off down a footpath that led towards the river. Half-an-hour later we were still walking and had seen nobody. We could have walked naked and nobody would have been any the wiser, we would just have been colder. What I had managed to do was grill Caroline on Jasmine's sexuality. Unfortunately her response wasn't encouraging for me. Jasmine, it seemed, never submitted to other girls. She did submit to men, occasionally, and what she liked was the feeling of not being physically capable of resisting. She therefore only submitted to men she could trust but who wanted to punish her, these being few and far between. Women, she felt, could simply not induce the feeling of helplessness that she craved. When she did go down it tended to be with a bump, but it was a rare event. I also learned that she accepted occasional spankings from Walter Jessop, which surprised me.

What she had never done was kiss anybody's bottom-hole, a gesture of submission to which she attached exceptional importance. She had had hers kissed many times – including by me – but not once had she given the same in return. I had found the act shameful, submissive, dirty and – once her puckered bottom-hole had been presented to my lips – irresistible. Certainly it was an act of deep surrender, yet to me little more so than offering my bottom for spanking.

After a while the Thames appeared to our right, a broad expanse of ruffled water that reflected scattered sunlight and clouds. To our left a beech wood rose up the side of a chalky down, the few remaining leaves stirring in the breeze. It was beautiful and lonely and I was starting to feel tempted to abandon our plan and just have Caroline then and there, down among the leaves beneath the trees.

I dare say there would have been no resistance, but at that moment we found what we wanted. Across the river, and some way to the front, three widely spaced green umbrellas showed the presence of fishermen. I stopped, my heart suddenly in my mouth at the prospect of what we were going to do. All three were male, two who looked as if they might have been retired businessmen, one younger.

'Come on, let's do it!' Caroline urged from beside me.

'All right,' I answered, trying to seem calm but feeling more than a little nervous. 'What do you want me to be, a jealous friend whose boyfriend you've pinched?'

'An angry aunt,' she replied.

'Your aunt!' I responded. 'What do you mean your aunt? Do I look like your aunt? I'm younger than you are Caroline Greenwood!'

She laughed and ran, calling back to taunt me in a voice loud enough for the three fishermen to hear. With her little legs and fleshy figure she had no chance and I had caught her and grabbed her by the arm before she was half way to the point opposite them.

'Right, you little brat, I'm going to teach you a lesson!' I stormed as I tightened my grip and began to drag her towards a fallen beech. 'I'm going to pull down your pants and spank your fat bottom.'

'No, Auntie, we're being watched!' she squealed in outrage, trying ineffectually to pull away from me.

'Don't be prissy!' I snapped back. 'Do you think it matters if they see your bare bottom?'

'Yes it does!' she objected. 'I'm eighteen, auntie! I can't go bare in public!'

'You should have thought of the consequences before you misbehaved,' I answered, seating myself on the tree trunk and pulling her towards me.

'No! Please no!' she squealed as I tugged her down across my knee. 'No, Auntie Isabelle, not a spanking! Please, not in front of other people!'

'Stop whining!' I ordered and put my hand under her belly to find her trouser button.

It felt glorious to have her across my knee, and exquisitely naughty to know that we were being watched. Her bum was towards them, a plump peach straining against tight red cotton but shortly to be bare. They were going to see everything, yet from far enough to make our act more realistic and more of a tease. She put up a good struggle too, kicking and squealing in her efforts to stop me undoing her trousers.

'Not with my trousers down! Please no!' she begged when I finally had the button undone and her zip down.

'You won't appreciate it properly on your trouser seat,' I answered, 'not with the amount of padding you've got.'

'That isn't padding, that's all me!' she squealed and redoubled her efforts to prevent the disgrace of having her trousers pulled down and her panties put on show.

I managed though and was soon tugging them down off her behind. This sent her into a real fit, thrashing her legs and cursing me as her plump globe was slowly exposed with the cheeks stretching out a pair of bright pink panties. I simply twisted her arm more firmly and took the trousers down to her knees, thus quietening the worst of her kicks.

'Now for your panties,' I announced loudly. 'I might have let you keep them up, but as you've made such a scene you'll take it on the bare bottom.'

'No!' she yelled and gave a frantic lurch.

It was all I could do to hang on and as it was I had to haul her back across my knee. Twisting her arm still harder and cocking one leg up to raise her bottom into an even more undignified position, I took hold of the waistband of her panties.

'No,' she repeated, only this time as a forlorn plea to be allowed to retain her last scrap of modesty.

'Sorry, my dear, but they're coming down,' I replied and did it.

In my fantasies there are two ways to pull down a girl's panties in preparation for spanking. The first is brusque, matter-of-fact and quick, as if the exposure of her bottom is inconsequential, her cheeks being bare a mere convenience to improve the salutary effect of her spanking, her pride and modesty nothing. The second is to do it agonisingly slowly, peeling them down over her cheeks because we all know that having her bottom bared really does matter to a girl about to be spanked – it matters a lot.

I chose the second technique, although the first would have perhaps been more in keeping with our little act. It was certainly right for Caroline, because I could feel the tension in her body as her lovely big globes were revealed inch by inch to the fishermen and when I had settled the panties well down around her thighs she gave a sigh of pleasure that I hope they mistook for resignation – if they heard at all.

She was bare over my knee, her lovely rounded white bottom thrust high with a hint of dark hair showing between her cheeks. From their position I knew they would be able to see at least a hint of pussy, although they were too far away for any real detail. Resisting the urge to feel her first, I lifted my hand and brought it down on her bottom with a most satisfactory slapping sound. She squealed and her big cheeks bounced and parted, giving me a rude glimpse of her brownish bottom-hole. It was supposed to look like a punishment, so I delivered the second immediately and then set to work to spank her properly.

Her response was wonderful – kicks, squeals, yelps, pleas, everything a girl ought to do while she's being spanked across the lap of a stern and vengeful aunt. Not that Caroline was faking it, because I certainly wasn't being easy on her. I knew how hard Jasmine spanked her and that it was usually with a strap. Keen not to seem inadequate in comparison, I really let Caroline have it, spanking and spanking until her whole bottom was an even, glowing red and her skin was hot to the touch. By then she was sobbing and panting, clearly excited. My intention was to let her up, give her brief lecture while she stood there with her panties at half-mast and her big red bum on show and then simply walk on, leaving the three fishermen with the memory of an unexpected and deliciously rude pleasure.

From their reaction, anybody would have thought that it was they and not we who had done something improper. All three had watched our little display, but all three were also pretending not to have noticed, as if to have watched openly might have laid them open to a charge of voyeurism. Somewhat stung by their lack of reaction, I ordered Caroline to take off trousers and panties. She obeyed and I could see her body shivering as she peeled off. Bare from the waist down, she made a very cute sight indeed, with her chubby bottom peeping out from under her jumper, the cheeks red and evidently freshly spanked. I made her walk like that, hoping that somebody would pass us and see that she had been punished.

Perhaps fortuitously nobody came and when we reached a thicker section of wood I decided that my sexual need could wait no longer. Pulling her in behind me, I found a suitable place and quickly peeled off my own lower garments. With both of us naked from the waist down I ordered her to lie on her back. Squatting over her face with my top pulled up so that I could play with my breasts, I had her lick me, taking a long, exquisite orgasm in the pale afternoon light of the beech wood. Keen to maintain my dominance I declined to return the favour but had her strip naked and masturbate standing while I added to her punishment with a whippy hazel twig.

Having both come we felt thoroughly satisfied and also pleased with ourselves for the show we had made. It had excited her as much as it had me, and she was exceptionally cuddly on the way back, insisting on holding my hand and frequently stopping to kiss and hug me. My attempt to seduce her had been a complete success, but as our bus neared Oxford I began to worry about Jasmine's reaction.

I was right to do so, because she was less than happy. Having discovered that there was no 179 Alma Road in Oxford, she had returned home with the intention of taking her frustration out on Caroline's bottom. Caroline – with a typically easy-going attitude – had not so much as left a note to say where she had gone, nor who she was with.

Caroline's response was to tell her to stop sulking and give a detailed account of our dirty afternoon in the country. Inevitably Jasmine wanted to punish us and I once more found myself faced with the choice of confronting her or submitting. Reminding myself that I, at the least, had had Caroline's unqualified submission, and that I had, after all, played a pretty mean trick on Jasmine, I consented. My immediate contrition and acceptance of her right to punish me made her so self-satisfied that I simply had to tell the truth.

To Caroline's delight and Jasmine's consternation, I explained how I had invented the imaginary customer and drawn her off on a wild goose chase. By the end she was right on the cusp between play vengefulness and real anger. She turned away, spent a long moment gazing out of the kitchen window and then turned back. It wasn't obvious, but in one corner of her eye I could detect the hint of a tear. I immediately felt a complete bitch, both for having tricked her and for having seduced her girlfriend. True, she had done worse to me, but at that moment it simply didn't matter.

'I was only playing,' I assured her, holding out my arms. 'I'm sorry, I didn't mean to upset you.'

She smiled, stood forward and came into my arms. For one delicious moment she melted and was soft and yielding against my body. Then she had pulled back and the moment was gone, a fleeting impression of what it would have been like to have her surrender to me.

'So then, your punishment,' she said, once more cool and in command, 'although it's hard to know what to do with such a dirty pair of sluts.'

Caroline and I spent the next hour cleaning the bathroom. We were naked and obliged to stay on our knees, while Jasmine stood over us with a long-handled bath-brush which she would apply to our bottoms from time to time. My cheeks were soon red and smarting and I was becoming increasingly turned on, yet Jasmine seemed less than satisfied. Finally she called a halt to the operation and fetched collars from the playroom. These she attached to our necks, then led us upstairs and tethered us both to a post in the attic. She then fetched herself a long drink and sat down to mull over our fate.

Kneeling naked on her attic floor with a warm bottom and a wet pussy, I was game for more or less anything. Caroline was the same, and in fact the worst punishment she could have given us would have been to simply leave us unsatisfied. As it was, I was pretty sure that she would do no such thing and was reflecting on what she might have in store for me. Possibly she would call Walter Jessop and have him sodomise me again, only this time with me fully sober, Caroline too. Alternatively she might take us up to the Red Ox and make us strip in front of the rowdy uncouth men who drank there, keeping our money and maybe even making us offer blow-jobs in the pub toilets afterwards. The idea made me shiver, but I knew that to Caroline it would be of no great consequence. I also suspected that they were in the habit of allowing Walter Jessop at the least an occasional feel, simply from the intimacy they had shown in front of him. Not that I imagined that he regularly buggered Caroline, yet his expertise in getting his cock up my bottom had suggested that I was not the first. Finally, her thoughtful expression turned into a smile and she stood up.

'So,' she announced, 'as you two evidently like each other so much, perhaps you'd like to spend the night together?'

She said it with a great deal of satisfaction, which made it clear to me that the statement was not so innocent as it first appeared. So did Caroline's reaction, which was to give a little whine of apprehension and turn her soulful brown eyes to me in sympathy.

I soon found out Jasmine's intentions. Caroline and I were led downstairs and into the playroom. Here Jasmine unlocked the square box that I had seen before and ushered me inside. I obeyed, although somewhat tentatively as I could already see what was intended. Sure enough, Caroline was chivvied in after me and the hatch locked in place. Inside, we were squashed together, our bodies in an enforced intimacy of contact. All I could see of Caroline was her face and one breast, illuminated by the faint light from the wire grill in the top. Her eyes were wide and her full lower lip shivering, suggesting a reaction stronger than that which I felt appropriate. Then Jasmine turned the light off and closed the door, bidding us a cheerful goodnight as she went.

My assumption was that we would be left about an hour, roughly until Jasmine wanted her dinner served. Caroline and I were squeezed into a close embrace, our thighs locked together so that my pussy was pressed against her leg. Intent on making the most of the experience I cuddled her to me and was rewarded with a warm and trembling kiss. There was something urgent about her response, almost desperate, as if her need for comfort was as great as her need for pleasure. This caused me to feel protective as well as excited, making me want to stroke her head as much as explore her body.

It was a strange experience, and rather an awkward one, yet intensely sensual. In the close confines of the box there was no getting away from the contact between us, nor the scent of aroused female bodies that built quickly as we played. We could neither stretch out nor get into any but a few positions. Yet we could kiss, and did so fervently while we explored each other. Caroline was so different to me, with her full curves, that I found a particular fascination in touching her, a fascination which she returned. Her breasts in particular were wonderful to touch, big, heavy globes of flesh with large, prominent nipples. Even her pussy was different, plumper and softer than my own, with larger labia and an enticing, squashy feel to the flesh.

We masturbated together, bringing each other to orgasm with our fingers. By the end, we were sticky with juice and sweat, locked together with our bodies touching in several places and our tongues in each other's mouths. As my orgasm subsided it occurred to me that if this was a punishment it contained very little of the pain and humiliation which Jasmine normally liked me to accept.

When we had finished, Caroline still wanted to hold me and I was happy to respond. She was shivering, clearly more affected by our confinement than I, and I began to stroke her back as we waited for Jasmine to return.

She didn't, and after a while I was beginning to wonder what was happening. It was dark and quiet, the only sounds were our breathing and occasional movements. I had no idea how long we had been in the box, nor of time in general. Deprived of freedom, light and sound, the only immediate realities were Caroline and the box, also Jasmine, who although not there had total control over our freedom. I began to appreciate the intensity of Caroline's response to the punishment, and that it was, truly, a punishment.

I had been in a sensitive, highly strung mood anyway, but as I squatted curled up in the box, with Caroline pressed close to me, I began to experience increasingly strong emotions, some of them unexpected. The first was an intimacy with Caroline, the only other occupant of my personal universe. There was also a sense of having been naughty, and of having been disciplined, remorse, self-pity, also exposure, because although confined I was completely naked – save for the collar which Jasmine had fixed to my neck. Further beneath the surface were a heightened sensitivity and a faint sense of panic, presumably my body's automatic responses to the situation. Finally, and surprisingly, there was a sense of dependence on Jasmine, a sense that was becoming alarmingly strong as our imprisonment wore on.

We had sex again several times, urgent, uninhibited grapples that did as much to assert our reality as to provide physical gratification. I got to know every inch of Caroline's body, and she mine. Her face, her feet and hands, her breasts and waist, the folds of her pussy and the tight hole between her bottom cheeks, all of it I stroked and caressed, until every last shred of distance between us had been erased. I would have done anything for her, touched her anywhere, given her any service she needed.

Events blurred, cuddles, kisses, sex, long periods of huddling together in the dark without saying a word. For a while I was cross with Jasmine, not so much for locking us up, but because she evidently knew that the experience would inspire dependency in me. Yet the anger passed and the dependency became stronger, threatening to overwhelm me . . .

Eleven

I sat in my room, staring blankly out of the window and feeling the trembling of my fingertips. It had been the early hours of the morning when Jasmine had released us, and we had crawled from the hatch to kiss and lick her feet, disorientated, dizzy, damp and pathetic in our gratitude and need for her. She had ordered us to scrub out the inside of the box, still nude, and then to wash.

In bed she had lain between us, completely in control as we cuddled, shivering onto her chest. I had let her stroke my hair and hug me to her breasts, then eagerly responded to her command to lick her pussy. I had worn my collar all night, marking me as Jasmine's property, yet when I had taken it off in the morning I had felt not release, but loss. Since I left their house I had not stopped trembling and I could not clear my mind of thoughts of them, love for Caroline, dependency on Jasmine. In my room I had masturbated until my pussy was sore, calling out their names each time I came. For over eight hours I had been kept in close proximity to Caroline and no longer having her by me produced a sense of wrenching loneliness. Nor did I have Jasmine to serve and grovel to, to wash and pleasure with my tongue, or simply to gaze at in adoration.

The mood broke with my period, which began that afternoon. By supper time I was pretty well back to my normal self, although acutely aware that Jasmine had come within an ace of making me her plaything. Neither did I have any illusions about her ability to do it. Her knowledge of the intricacies of sexual dominance and submission were far beyond mine, and I had little doubt that her devious mind was not exhausted. I had three options, succumb, walk away or conquer. The first was what she expected of me, and the one to which I was being drawn. The second was the sensible route, but one against which my pride and desire both rebelled. The third was what I wanted, and as I sat in hall, listening to my fellow historians prattle lightly of this and that, I decided to keep trying.

I had seduced Caroline and only succeeded in entangling myself more thoroughly in Jasmine's web. Caroline, for all her girlish innocence and boundless sexual enthusiasm, was far from stupid, and might well have been fully aware of the likely outcome of our behaviour. Neither could I trust Walter Jessop to help, nor even Rory. Both men took a lot of pleasure in my submission and were unlikely to do anything that might spoil it. I wanted Jasmine dominated, and to see it done, yet she was evidently not going to let me do it. Indeed, judging from what I had seen and heard she only ever allowed herself to take sexually subordinate, or even passive, roles with the rare men she chose to gift with her favours. Rory had been one of those, and I knew she was keen on another, more leisurely encounter. Possibly I could wait until Rory had made her too high to resist and then join in as a dominant third party. Jasmine might respond, or they might turn on me and share me as their plaything. If they did I doubted I could resist and it might be the last straw.

The rest of my Sunday was spent pondering the problem, yet I could find no viable solution.

Monday morning was busy, with lectures and a tutorial, then a discussion group after lunch. By the time I returned to college I was feeling confident and also more detached, enabling me to make a more objective assessment of the problem.

It proved fortunate that I was in a strong and self-confident mood, because that afternoon Stan Tierney made his long-awaited move. Had he done it on the previous morning I would probably have ended up on my knees with his cock in my mouth, and felt grateful for it. As it was I coolly pointed out to him that if I chose to complain the loss of his job would be the least of his problems. His response was surly and he was reluctant to give in, arguing that if I was prepared to be beaten by and have sex with Dr Appledore, then giving him what he chose to describe as a 'jerk off' should be acceptable. I simply laughed and told him to get lost, leaving him to ponder on my motives and stew in his frustration.

I sat down to work on my essay, quickly losing myself in the complexities of eighteenth-century French culture. Only when I chanced to use the word 'Mistress' did my thoughts return to Jasmine, and suddenly an idea had come to me, a delightfully wicked idea.

Jasmine had told me, quite blatantly, that she intended at some point to humiliate me by making me watch her and Rory have sex but not letting me join in. That this might even extend to letting him lead I knew from the way she had offered herself on her knees the might Walter had buggered me. Later, Rory had suggested that I might enjoy being buggered by him, but I had declined, alarmed by the size of his cock.

My first move was to visit Rory and ask for his assistance in return for the pleasure of putting his cock up my bottom. He loved the idea, and wanted to do it then and there, but was less keen on the idea of helping. I pointed out that on this occasion he would run no risk of arrest and that he would have to wait until afterwards to take his prize. We finally compromised, with me posing my naked bottom for him to come over and he agreeing to do as he was told. Hoping that the offer of anal sex was enough to make him trustworthy, I set off for Jasmine's.

When I arrived, she was feeding sweets to a naked Caroline from the palm of her hand and insisted that I strip and join the game. I did as I was told, with my sense of submissive pleasure once more rising as I nuzzled the treats from her palm with my lips. I then explained that I had asked Rory to come round on the Thursday evening, and that she might confidently expect to have sex with him while I watched. I added that the idea of having her take the passive role to a man while remaining firmly aloof to me really excited me. She was delighted at what she saw as my deliberate self-effacement and accepted, even going so far as to postpone the dozen strokes of the strap she had intended to give me. Instead I was allowed to watch Caroline receive a beating, which left me more than a little turned on.

The next step had to wait until the morning, and I returned to college with a mischievous smile on my lips and a knot of tension in my stomach.

On Thursday I was finding it hard to concentrate on my lectures. At the tutorial my essay was well received, yet I suggested to Duncan that a spanking would do me good in any case. He agreed cheerfully and put me across his knee, raising my skirt and pulling down my tights and panties for fifty firm swats on my naked bottom. This left me warm-bottomed and feeling dirty, and as my period was now over I joyfully let him have me. I lay on my back in an armchair with my legs rolled up, pulled my blouse open and was mounted while I played with my breasts. He came across my belly and asked if I would like to be licked. I declined, intent on retaining the sexual tension we had built up for later.

Although it was always me who got spanked, I now felt a friendliness and sympathy with Duncan Appledore that was very different from the mixture of love and resentment which Jasmine inspired in me. In Duncan, I had a friend as well as somebody who could provide me with the ecstasy of discipline. Maybe it was because he was older and senior to me in the college hierarchy, or because the idea of punishing men has never appealed to me, but the fact that he was now giving me regular bare bottom spankings in no way reduced my impression of him as equal at heart.

I met Rory in a pub near Jasmine's and we took a couple of drams of malt each, then set off with me explaining to him exactly what he was supposed to do. We arrived at Jasmine's to find her looking enticing to say the least. Instead of her usual rather severe look, she had made up and dressed her hair to give a soft, winsome image. Her dress was a sheath of crimson velvet, short and clinging, which made the most of her breasts and hips while leaving plenty of leg showing. High heels and what I was sure were stockings completed the ensemble, while I was certain that her underwear would prove as feminine as the rest. Rory was pleased in any case and could scarcely keep his eyes off her. Caroline, like me, was dressed in a long skirt and a jumper with tights and sensible shoes, a choice presumably dictated by Jasmine in order to ensure Rory's full attention.

She got it and basked in it, making no secret of her intentions but not hurrying either. Occasionally, she would throw me an arch look, deliberately taunting me with her power over my boyfriend. Never having been more than marginally possessive towards Rory, I felt none of the humiliation which she imagined, yet returned downcast looks to order. Caroline and I had already fallen into our chosen roles for the evening, serving them wine and watching but holding back.

Jasmine and Rory were soon kissing, then tentatively exploring each other. Their urgency increased, Jasmine allowing him to unzip the back of her dress and ease it down over her shoulders. Her bra followed, tugged roughly up to let her breasts fall loose into his hands. Not long after her panties were down, pulled to the level of her knees while his hand worked up her skirt, stroking her pussy in a way that was making her moan and writhe against him.

Only when his cock was out and erect in her hand did he teasingly suggest blindfolding her and tying her, asking it as a particular favour. She complied, laughing and throwing me a satisfied smile as Caroline fixed a length of black silk around her head. Rory took control from there, having Jasmine bend over a chair and slipping his cock into her mouth. Caroline tied Jasmine's hands behind her back and as she began to suck I rose and slipped from the room, replying to Caroline's concerned glance with a quietening gesture.

In the hall I made a quick telephone call and was rewarded within five minutes by a quiet knock on the door. I opened it, finding the man I had been expecting – Stan Tierney.

He looked as disreputable as ever, although he had put on a suit of sorts and combed his scraggy grey hair. I motioned him inside and led him to the living room, putting my finger to my lips as Caroline's mouth opened in astonishment. Rory grinned at me and continued to fuck Jasmine's mouth. He had his hand twisted into her hair and she seemed to be in ecstasy, with her cheeks pulled in as she sucked greedily on his cock as it was fed in and out of her mouth. I gestured to Stan, indicating his fly. He gave me a leer in return, undid his fly and pulled out his cock and balls with an flagrancy that made me wince.

I had told him what would be happening, tempting him with the thought of sex with a beautiful girl even if it was not me. As it happened, he knew Jasmine, or at least of her, having seen her strip at the Red Ox. The prospect of having her suck his cock had been hard for him to resist, yet he had been suspicious, certain that I intended to lead him into some sort of trap. Finally, I had had to take him in my hand to get my way, judging the experience a small price to pay for my revenge on Jasmine. It had been hard, because I really didn't like him, but I had done it. He actually had a fine cock, big and fleshy. Once I had overcome my initial squeamishness at exactly who I was touching I had found it exciting to hold. Shamefully so, as I had pulled him off while he sat beside me on my bed.

Now I looked like having to repeat the performance, as while Rory's cock was rock hard in Jasmine's mouth, Stan's was still limp. With a shrug to Caroline and Rory I took hold of Stan Tierney's cock. It felt thick and meaty and squirmed in my hand as the blood came quickly to it. Making a ring of my fingers, I held it just below the foreskin, as he had shown me the first time. He stiffened quickly and was soon firm in my hand, a big, pink erection thrusting out from his fly.

I found myself grinning maniacally as I gestured to Rory to pull back. He did so, but kept his hand in Jasmine's hair. She stayed gaping, evidently wanting her mouth filled with cock. As Stan stepped forward and slid his erection into her waiting mouth I felt a wave of fierce elation sweep through me.

It was wonderful. Jasmine – haughty, pretty Jasmine, who had beaten me and humiliated me, who had had me buggered by Walter Jessop and who had almost brought me to my knees completely – was sucking eagerly on a dirty old man's cock!

I wanted him to come in her mouth but that was all, just enough for her to really appreciate the dirtiness of her act and to bring out the same submissive feelings in her that she had in me. It was working, as she was getting more and more excited by having her head held while she sucked. I was planning on pulling her blindfold up at the moment he came, yet as he took hold of his cock and started to masturbate himself into her mouth events began to take on a momentum of their own.

Rory was standing to one side, his hand locked in Jasmine's hair and his erection in his hand, straining as if about to burst. He seemed a little uneasy in close proximity to Stan and moved round, towards Jasmine's rear. Her panties were well down and her skirt rucked up, leaving about half of her pert little bottom on show. Rory could have had a good feel without giving the game away, yet instead he let go of Jasmine's hair and moved behind her to pull up her dress and rest his cock between the cheeks of her bottom. I made a desperate gesture to stop him but it was too late.

'One of Isabelle's college friends,' Caroline said as Jasmine flinched.

It worked, Jasmine immediately sticking her bottom up for entry in a gesture as wanton as anything I or Caroline had done. Rory put his cock to her vagina and took hold of her suspender belt, using it to pull himself in by. She increased the urgency with which she was sucking on Stan Tierney's cock as Rory began to fuck her.

'How about you two joining in?' Stan asked, addressing Caroline and I.

I suppose it was the accent – uneducated and local – that alerted Jasmine, because she immediately pulled her head back and shook it to dislodge the blindfold. The manoeuvre didn't really work, but Stan Tierney completed the job for her, completely ignoring what I had told him to do.

'Yeah, get a good look at the cock you're sucking,' he drawled as he pulled the blindfold up over Jasmine's eyes.

She looked up, gave a little gasp and then he had fed his cock back into her open mouth. For a moment she looked furious, a wonderful sight as her mouth was still full of penis. Rory was riding her hard though and the light of anger quickly died in her eyes. Resignedly, submissively, she went back to the dirty, smutty task of bringing Stan Tierney to orgasm in her mouth. I was elated, grinning and laughing as Jasmine accepted her fate. Caroline was in rapture too, giggling and smirking at her Mistress's shameful behaviour.

'Suck it, Jasmine!' she urged. 'Make him do it in your mouth!'

Jasmine moaned around her mouthful of penis and began to suck more eagerly still, drawing a hoarse grunt from Tierney. Suddenly he jerked and white sperm erupted from around her lips, splashing onto his balls and the carpet below. Her eyes were screwed up and her face set in an expression of utter disgust, yet she sucked and swallowed as squirt after squirt erupted into her mouth. Finally he pulled out, wiping his cock on her cheek as she swallowed her last mouthful. His come was smeared on her face and nose, also dribbling down her chin, a sight that simultaneously repelled and delighted me.

'Oh yes,' Caroline breathed, 'that's right, Jasmine, swallow it.

She crawled forward, her mouth meeting her girlfriend's in a deep, sticky kiss to which Jasmine instantly responded.

Rory was still behind Jasmine, taking his time in her pussy with firm, even pushes that kept her nicely high without ever giving her the chance to reach orgasm. With her hands tied there was little she could do, and I was determined to have her begging to be touched before she was allowed to come. Yet I was no longer really in charge of the situation and hesitated, uncertain whether now was the time to exert my own dominance. Caroline, I knew, would cheerfully accept me as the dominant female in the group. Rory would play along yet not really be under my command, while to Stan Tierney the concept would simply be unfamiliar. Jasmine might succumb, or not.

For all my need, I decided against it, determined that when the time came her submission to me would have to be complete and rather more personal. For now the sight of her allowing herself to be thoroughly used by the two men would be sufficient, and indeed it had already done a lot to reduce my awe of her. I could also at least take advantage of her excitement and take my pleasure with her in a way that was neither painful nor humiliating for me.

Stan Tierney had sat down and was stroking his cock while he watched Rory fuck Jasmine. Caroline was kissing Jasmine and fondling her breasts, while her bottom was stuck out more or less in my face. Giving in to my own need, I began to pull Caroline's skirt up, exposing chubby thighs and then the plump, panty-clad ball of her bottom. I slid my hand between her thighs and began to caress her pussy through her panties. She wiggled her bottom, evidently eager for my touch. I grinned up at Rory, whose expression showed that he was not going to take long to come. He smiled back, then reached out and grabbed me by the hair.

I let out a squeak of protest but it was half-hearted. Responding to the pressure I let him pull me close, until my cheek was pressed close to Jasmine's haunch. I still had my hand on Caroline's pussy, which I could feel through her damp panty crotch. I began to rub over her clitoris as Rory pulled his cock from Jasmine's pussy and fed it to me. It was wet with Jasmine's cream, which I could taste along with the more masculine flavour of his cock. I thought he was going to finish off in my mouth, but he pulled back and once more slid it inside Jasmine's pussy. Still holding me by the hair, he repeated the process, again and again feeding me her juices on the rigid shaft of his penis until my mouth was rich with her taste and my face was sticky with her juice.

Caroline was coming under my fingers, and I really wanted to attend to her, but Rory wouldn't let me, instead pulling me closer to himself. I was dragged round until my face was behind Jasmine's bottom, then Rory took the scruff of my neck and pushed my head in-between Jasmine's thighs, our earlier agreement evidently quite forgotten. He made me lick her pussy and anus, then turned my head and apparently quite casually, with a quick flourish of his hand, came full in my face. I shut my eyes just in time to stop his sperm going in them, but it splashed over my face so that I had to keep them shut. I felt his cock bump against my lips and opened my mouth, letting him slide it in and drain himself into my throat. As my mouth filled with the salty taste and slimy texture of male come I was very aware that this was not at all a dominant thing to be doing. True, Jasmine had perhaps been given the worst treatment, yet the men were firmly in charge.

It stayed that way for the rest of the evening. They sat back to watch while Jasmine, Caroline and I played on the floor. Our need was too urgent to bother with stripping, but we had quickly pulled off our pants and opened our tops to allow access to our main erogenous zones. Nor was there any real opportunity for me to assert myself. Even as Rory had been coming in my mouth Caroline had turned her attention to me, lifting my skirt and tearing down my panties in a frenzy to get at me. Being licked from behind in a kneeling position is hardly dignified, and it was made rapidly less so by Jasmine when Rory had untied her. She rolled off the chair, sitting down on the floor with a bump. Her legs were apart, with her skirt up around her waist and her panties at ankle level. Sliding forward on her bottom, she tucked my head into her pussy and trapped me with her panties, leaving me little option but to lick. Caroline's tongue was doing amazing things at my other end and I was in no mood to try and change the situation.

I came quickly, full in Caroline's face, and was immediately mounted by Rory, who had managed to get his cock hard again in an impressively short space of time. Jasmine came when he was inside me and released me so that I could get into an at least marginally more comfortable position in which to accept Rory. He rode me slowly, taking an age to come, by which time I was sore and dizzy with sex. By then, Stan had managed to mount Caroline and was humping away on top of her as she lay rolled up on the floor with her breasts out and her panties dangling from one ankle.

When both men had come a second time the whole thing simply ran out of steam. I was left in a sticky, exhausted heap on the floor, well satisfied sexually but only moderately satisfied with the outcome of my wicked plot. True, Jasmine had been made to submit and been well and truly used. She had enjoyed it as well, and seeing her in such a state of submissive ecstasy had made me feel stronger. Yet it was only half a victory, as she had not submitted to me and in the end I had been just as wanton and uninhibited as her.

I paid for what I had done as well. When we had cleaned up Jasmine ordered me to return the following evening. Once more faced with the quandary of confrontation or obedience, I followed her orders and on the Friday night was put on my new domestic regime. This involved an increased load of domestic chores, done naked as usual and with carrots pushed up both my vagina and anus. Inevitably they found fault and I was put across Caroline's knee and spanked before being fixed to the ceiling chains in the playroom by my hands. Jasmine put me in a pair of rubber pants with a vibrator built into the crotch and proceeded to whip me while I came again and again. It was an extraordinary experience and left me too weak to stand, yet it failed to return me to that state of abject submission she had had me in after the box treatment. Even when she was sat on my face afterwards, with her dress lifted and her panties pulled aside to let me get at her bottom-hole, I found that in my mind I had the image of her blissful face with the mouth stretched wide around Stan Tierney's big, pale cock.

Twelve

I slept at their house on the Friday night and stayed with them the following day. It was the end of eighth week and term was technically over. My time was my own, yet I was in no great hurry to go home. It took no effort at all to persuade Jasmine to let me stay for a week and I even managed to convince her to forego rent in return for my use as a domestic. Despite her eagerness to keep me around she was in a curious mood and twice made remarks about needing to fully reassert her authority. This pleased me, as it showed that my piece of black mischief had worked, yet it also made me nervous because I knew that any such reasserting was likely to be at my expense.

As I cycled into town to sort things out with the college lodge, I pondered the situation. My status was improved, at least in my own eyes, and I felt more confident, certainly confident enough to want to continue to play my part. I still needed Jasmine's long-term surrender though and could see no way of getting it. The problem was that what-ever action I took simply produced a correspondingly forceful reaction. I had seduced Caroline and ended up locked in a box with her. I had tricked Jasmine into sex with a dirty old man and ended up with my face in her pussy, not to mention a future of scrubbing floors in the nude with both my pussy and bottom filled with some suitably phallic vegetable.

No, what I needed was for her to acknowledge my right to punish her just as I acknowledged hers to punish me. Only that would reset the cycle, and that was what I needed to do, although I now realised that I would still want to taste the pleasures of my own submission. The acceptance of that change in myself also made me realise that my ability to accept my darker fantasies was not limited to submission. Coming over the thought of dirty old men doing rude things to me had always made me feel deeply guilty and ashamed of myself. It still did, yet I had now actually done it, not once, but four times, and the reality had been little more disturbing than the fantasy. The thought that I – Isabelle Colraine – should have had the penis of disreputable old goat like Stan Tierney in my hand still made shiver, but it had been a small price indeed to pay for having him come in Jasmine's mouth.

With that happy thought, I arrived at the lodge. As I wheeled my bicycle under the arch, the porter called out to draw my attention. To my surprise, he was indicating the most enormous parcel, which was for me. Both pleased and puzzled, I laid it across the seat of my bicycle and took it with me. The feel of it suggested cloth, while an attached note revealed that it was from Walter Jessop. Evidently it was an article of clothing, and from the weight it seemed likely to be pretty grand.

Fired by a sense of excitement that made me want to skip, I hastened to my room, locking the door behind me and hurriedly opening the parcel. As I had suspected, it was clothing, and exactly the sort of clothing that I was so in love with but could not possibly afford. The first thing I saw was a great expanse of crimson brocade with an elaborate pattern of gold and black. This proved to be the most magnificent Victorian evening gown, evidently new but perfect in every detail. It was simply beautiful yet that was not all. Below it were three petticoats, one in plain cotton, one in flannel and one in taffeta. These surrounded a box which held a pair of neatly made square-heeled ankle boots, again an accurate reproduction of 1890s originals. A cape and bonnet for outdoors completed the outfit.

I was in a state of rapture. With everything laid out on the bed I stripped naked, gave myself a hasty wash at the basin, applied powder and perfume and began to dress. I started with my knee stockings and combinations, as always delighting in the soft feel of the linen and gentle tickling of the frills. My beautiful black silk corset followed, not the easiest garment to put on alone, but I managed with the ingenious assistance of my long-handled hairbrush as a lever. Once I had pulled my waist in to the nineteen inches of which I knew I was capable, I began to pull the petticoats on one by one until I could feel the weight of my clothes and the mirror showed me with my clothes flaring out from the waist with a prominent bulge of cloth over the bottom that in 1896 would have been the dying echo of the fashion for bustles. My boots followed, then the dress itself, which again was cut to my favourite era, the last few years of the old Queen's reign.

After a fair bit of twisting and pinning of my hair I looked perfect, every inch the refined young Victorian lady, dressed for a ball. Looking in the mirror I admired my reflection and could find little fault in what I saw. I was as I wanted to be and, while my bust might perhaps have been a little fuller, there was no doubting the delicacy of my facial features nor the elegance of my gentle curves. Had I been able I would have made a pass at my own reflection, and was already wondering how best to exploit the erotic potential of my new dress.

My first thought was to return to Jasmine and beg to be allowed to dress Caroline as a maid. Once she was suitably attired I would punish her, perhaps with a riding whip, and then make her crawl under my skirts to lick me to heaven. The only drawback, and not really a drawback at all if I was honest with myself, was that Jasmine would undoubtedly want to give me some yet more elaborate and humiliating punishment afterwards.

An alternative was to go to Walter and give him exactly the sort of thank you he would most appreciate. There were all sorts of fantasies we could play out, with me as a distressed gentlewoman or a bored rich girl, perhaps submitting reluctantly to a caning or being made to suck his cock, full of bashful protestations and shocked pleas as I was pushed to my knees and presented with his penis and balls. The thought made me shiver, yet Whytleigh was over half-an-hour's ride away and I wanted my fun immediately.

I was even considering going to Stan Tierney's house. Although he would not have appreciated the effect of my costume, it was easy to imagine him as a Victorian street rough. I could then extend my distressed gentlewoman fantasy, imagining myself forced to accept the unendurable shame of selling my body. I had just decided that I needed to come too badly to do anything elaborate when a knock at my door and the sound of Rory's voice solved my problems. Here was not only the most attractive of the men I knew, but someone to whom I was genuinely obliged and in front of whom I need have no inhibitions.

Nevertheless, I was a little shocked when he came in and promptly put a pot of petroleum jelly down on the table. I had not forgotten our bargain and knew full well what it was intended to lubricate – my bottom-hole. My expression of alarm must have been well in keeping with my dress, as his grin and appreciative gaze made it clear that he liked not only my appearance but also the idea of my being shocked by what he had in store for me. Thinking of how a real Victorian young lady would have reacted to the prospect of being sodomised reinforced my reaction and I put my hand to my open mouth in my best look of mortification.

'Not too keen now it's payback time, eh?' Rory drawled, immediately falling in with my game. 'Well, I did your dirty work so I want my reward, so let's have those fancy skirts up for a view of your pretty arse!'

'Sir! No!' I squealed as he advanced on me after locking the door and checking that it was properly done.

I backed against the bed and sat down heavily. He stood in front of me, splay-legged and grinning. Slowly, with his eyes fixed on mine, he drew down his fly, dug within and pulled out his cock and balls. I gave a gasp of shock and drew further away, pressing my back to the wall.

'No use being mawkish,' he said, 'now you can lift your skirts or we can do this the hard way. What's it to be?'

'You are horrid!' I exclaimed but began to lift my dress, exposing my silk petticoat and ankles.

'My, quite the fine lady, aren't we?' he sneered. 'Come on now, I don't want lace and frills, I want cunt . . . and then it's one for your breech.'

'No, sir, please sir, anything but that, sir!' I stammered.

'Best be obedient, then,' he responded. 'Come on, let's be seeing your purse.'

Trembling, and not entirely by choice, I lifted my petticoats until he was faced with the tucks and fold of the drawers part of my combinations, the sole covering to my modesty. As he took hold of my knees I shut my eyes and turned my face away, concentrating on the feel of having my pussy exposed in such a delightful way. He pushed my thighs apart, roughly, then delved for the split of my drawers. I felt them part and a waft of cold air crossed my pussy. I was bare, open in front of him, every detail of my precious sex on show and ripe for violation.

'My, but haven't you just the prettiest little cunt,' he sighed, 'yet she'll be prettier still stretched around my tool.'

I gave a little whimper and turned my head further away. I expected to be mounted without much preamble, his use of me without more than mental foreplay being part of the fantasy. Instead, I sensed him climb onto the bed and realised that I was going to be made to suck cock before being penetrated. Sure enough, his powerful male hand grabbed me by the hair, immediately reducing my carefully contrived style to a wretched mess. My head was dragged down and something pressed against my lips – his cock. I was deriving a lot of pleasure from resisting and feigned reluctance, compressing my lips and making little mewling noises.

He did the most wonderful thing, simply taking hold of my nose, squeezing it and then, when I was finally forced to gasp for air, popping his cock inside. I suppose I could have resisted further, but being made to open up for him was just too exciting. As soon as his big, salty cock was in my mouth I began to suck, and also to cup and stroke my breasts through my gown. He laughed, pulled my head hard onto his crotch and put his other hand between my legs.

'I knew it, you're a whore at heart, just like the rest of them,' he sneered.

I melted, trying to think of myself as being forced but not really succeeding. It was just too nice with his big cock swelling in my mouth and his fingers working on my pussy. As if to acknowledge the truth of what he had said I popped my breasts free of my gown. They felt lovely in my hands, firm and rounded with the nipples providing the peaks of sensitivity at the centre. Sucking his cock while he fiddled with my pussy was also an exquisitely submissive experience, as he was using my body as a device – readying it for his pleasure. I knew how Jasmine must have felt in a similar position and a wry thought crossed my mind. If Stan Tierney had arrived unexpectedly at that instant I would have done my best to give him service as well, or the rest of the college staff for that matter.

Telling myself I ought to be whipped for being greedy, I relaxed, letting him lead while my pleasure built. He was using his grip in my hair to pull my head up and down on his cock, which was now fully erect, hard and fleshy in my mouth. For a long time we continued the same way, both content to take our time and enjoying the sensations of our bodies. Personally I would have been happy to come that way, taking his sperm in my mouth while he brought me off under his fingers.

Rory was not to be so easily contented and after a while pulled out. I lay back, rolling my legs up as I continued to fondle my breasts. He took me by the knees and pushed them apart, bumping his cock between my legs. I felt it push between my cheeks, right over my bum-hole, and for a moment I thought he was going to try and take me anally without lubricant. I gave a squeak of protest, but his cock had already changed angle and was burrowing into the mouth of my vagina.

I sighed as I filled with cock, opening my legs wide to accommodate him as that delicious feeling of being full swept over me. He began to fuck me, moving slowly. My head was propped up against the wall, my hips sticking out over the edge of the bed. I could see myself, my naked, penetrated pussy like the centre of some enormous flower, black hair and pink-white skin surrounded by folds of linen and a froth of lace, then rimmed with crimson where the edge of my inverted gown showed. It was a superbly rude sight, compounded by the presence of Rory holding me by the legs and fucking me and of my little round tits peeping out from the top of my bodice. As before, he took his time, sliding in and out of me until I was groaning wantonly. Occasionally he would break his rhythm, either pull out and once more penetrate me or to give a flurry of sudden, hard pushes that would make me whimper and pant with pleasure.

'Are you ready for it up the bum?' he finally asked, bringing me a sharp reminder of what I had promised.

'No,' I replied, eager to try but more than a little scared by the thought of his thick, wide penis being put up my tight bottom-hole. 'Beat me first, and maybe tie my hands, then you can do it, but be gentle.'

'Just so long as it goes in,' he replied and pulled his cock from my vagina.

He put his hands under my knees and turned me over, arranging me bum up on the bed with my skirts flared out around my waist. The gown was over my head and I could see nothing, only feel the cool air on my naked bottom and thighs. I waited, listening to him whistling to himself as he made whatever preparations he felt necessary for my degradation. The first was to have my hands tied in the small of my back. He made me cross my wrists and lashed them firmly together with sticky tape and the cord from my nightgown, then pulled my skirts up between my arms to keep them out of the way. My drawers he pulled wide, using safety pins to keep them open. Even in the shame and ecstasy of having this done to me I thought it odd that he should use effectively the same technique as Caroline had to keep my buttocks available while being punished in Victorian underwear. It worked anyway, leaving my bottom feeling big and prominent, displayed in a way that I knew full well left everything showing.

His next trick was to uncover my head and tell me to look round. I did, discovering that he had arranged my dressing mirror and table lamp so that I could see my rear view. It was a cruel touch, showing me my swollen pink pussy and the tight brown ring of my anus, which looked far too small for his huge cock. He was nursing his erection in one hand while he admired my bottom. The head was slimy with my juice, a glistening knob of reddish-purple meat just perfect for putting in girls' pussies. Too big for their bum-holes though, I was sure of it.

Girls' bottom-holes are really not designed for cocks, yet they fit, just about, and I suppose it is inevitable that men are tempted by the tightness of a girl's anus. Walter Jessop had felt big up my bottom, and he had one of the smallest cocks I'd seen. Rory was much bigger, and now seemed huge as he pointed the monstrous thing at my rear and stroked it to keep it hard for my penetration. Also I had been drunk when Walter buggered me. Now I was stone-cold sober, and although I was high on sex I badly needed the beating that I have always felt should precede intercourse.

'Spank me, Rory, use the hairbrush,' I breathed, although I knew just how much the hard, wooden implement was going to hurt my bottom.

'Hard,' I added, knowing that only after being taken to my limits of pain would I be able to accommodate his cock in my back passage.

He gave a non-committal grunt and picked up the hairbrush, then, with a methodical calm he began to beat me, never once taking his hand from his cock. The first smack made me yell, and I was quickly squealing and cursing him as my bottom was turned to a ball of agonised, flaming heat. I was on the point of total loss of control when he stopped as suddenly as he had begun.

'Shut up, Isabelle,' he urged. 'Don't be such a baby! Besides, there are people around.'

'You'd better gag me,' I managed in-between frantic gulps of air.

'You're not joking,' he agreed. 'Which is your panty drawer?'

'Top left,' I told him, feeling a fresh stab of humiliation at the thought of being gagged with my own knickers again.

'No, I've a better idea,' he said and lifted the lid of my linen basket.

'Rory!' I protested as he carefully picked out the panties I had been wearing the previous night, holding them delicately between forefinger and thumb.

He took no notice but came over and rubbed them in my face. Not only had I cycled a considerable distance in them, but I had been wearing them while I watched Jasmine with Rory and Stan Tierney. They were thoroughly soiled and tasted of me as he pressed them against my lips.

'Open up, or do I have to pinch your nose again?' he asked.

I opened my mouth, resigning myself to the added dirty touch. After all, I reasoned, if I was about to be buggered, then having a pair of dirty knickers in my mouth could only add to my pleasure at being used. Rory went back to beating me, now getting only muffled squeaks in response to his firm smacks. It was a fine spanking, both painful and humiliating for the victim, as it should be. I had quickly passed the point of caring about my immodest position or of how pathetic my wriggles and bucks made me look. All that mattered was that I was being beaten and that my naked buttocks were throbbing with the most exquisite pain. At the beginning of a spanking the surrounding atmosphere is everything – clothing, exposure, rude remarks on the girl's anatomy, the knowledge of what is to happen and who is going to punish her, contempt for her submission, all of it adding to her excitement and shame. By the end such things should seem insignificant, her whole world being centred on her flaming bottom and the feelings in her pussy.

When he had finished that was how I was, whimpering and mewling into my mouthful of soiled panties and feeling thoroughly sorry for myself, also more than ready to accept him inside me. Throughout my beating he had been playing with his cock and it was still rock hard. I had expected him to immediately start preparing my bottom for entry, but he took hold of a handful of my drawers with one hand and used the other to guide his cock into my pussy. As his erection once more filled my vagina I wondered if he wasn't going to let me off, perhaps because of the state the spanking had put me in. I wasn't actually crying, because it hadn't been a punishment and the mental stimulus was wrong, but I was shivering and making little choking noises.

Then I felt something cold between my cheeks and knew that his intention was simply to sheath his cock in me while he opened my anus. He used a lot of lubricant, smearing it over the hot skin of my buttocks while the first squirt dribbled slowly down my bottom cleft. The sensation was strange, blissfully soothing yet at the same time revoltingly slimy and alarming because of what it portended.

'I have always wanted to do this,' he sighed, placing a finger on my anus and starting to rub the grease around. 'Back home, every boy in the village fancies you, but I'm sure you know that. We hardly dared to talk to you, you were so cold and superior – let's face it, stuck up. We used to think about you though. You know Ronald Peters? Well, he wanted us to catch you down by the burn and squeeze blow-jobs out of you. He reckoned that if we lifted your top and took a photo you'd be willing to do it, not that he'd have ever dared try. They got quite heated discussing it, saying how they'd come in your mouth and make you swallow it, then how they'd gangbang you.'

I let out a whimper. I had always known the village lads fancied me, but had assumed that it was with a distant yearning, as for something they knew to be above them and so unobtainable. It was a shock to learn that what they had actually wanted to do was very different and a good deal less complimentary. The idea of being caught, bullied into sucking cock and then taken turns with was terrible, yet compelling. The thought made me burn with outrage and humiliation as Rory popped the top joint of his finger into my anus and began to lubricate the ring.

'They all wanted to fuck you,' he continued, 'but I wanted to put it up your tight, hoity-toity little arse, to make you squeal with pleasure and come with a prick up your bottom. You wouldn't have been so high and mighty then would you?'

I nodded my head in miserable agreement, thinking of him making me kneel among the long grass by the burn and buggering me in front of his friends – or he might have caught me while I was swimming nude up on the moors and had me over a rock. Now he was going to do it for real, perhaps not in the same setting, but his cock would still be going up my bum.

He was still riding me, moving it slowly in my pussy as his finger delved into my rectum. He had put it all the way in and was wiggling it inside me, an exquisite sensation yet also unutterably rude. I was glad he had beaten me, because not only had the pain brought me on heat but the fact that he had punished me made me feel chastened, under his orders and so less responsible for the filthy act in which we were to indulge. A second finger slid up my bottom, pulling the hole wide. I groaned deeply as he stretched my anus open and squeezed a worm of lubricant right into the hole. It felt cold and slimy, then, as he pulled his fingers out my anus closed and I felt the jelly ooze out.

'I'm going to do it now, Isabelle,' he breathed. 'How does it feel to know that my cock's going up your arse?'

I could only whimper faintly through my panties, although my head was filled with panic, lust, shame, need, regret and above all, naughtiness. Slowly, he pulled his cock from my pussy, leaving me feeling wide open and empty. I felt the shaft laid between my buttocks and rubbed in the lubricant, then it began to move lower, the tip sliding down my greasy bottom cleft, ever closer to my anus. It touched me, a round, firm cock head against my bum-hole, the hole into which it was about to be put. I was shaking hard and whimpering deep in my throat as he began to push. As my anus began to stretch my mind was swimming with emotion, all of it centred on the sheer filthiness of what I was doing – accepting a man's penis up my back passage!

It was rude, dirty, depraved, blatantly sexual – everything a nice girl should shun, yet I wanted it desperately. I was getting it too, whether I liked it or not. Rory had taken hold of the binding on my wrists and was pulling himself into me. I tried to relax, feeling my bum-hole stretch wider and wider, gamely trying to accommodate the head of his cock. I really wasn't sure I could do it, then my sphincter gave way and he was in. I groaned deeply. It had been done, for the second time I had allowed a cock into my back passage. I was being buggered.

Slowly, methodically he inserted his full length into me, a half inch or so at a time. With the head in, he pushed until I jerked and tried to yelp, then pulled back, making my anus evert. Again and again he repeated the process, easing his erection up my bottom bit by bit until finally his balls bumped against my empty pussy and I knew he was right up. My bottom felt full to bursting, and as he began to move it inside me I was quickly out of breath, unable to get the air I needed with my mouth full of my now-sodden panties.

Realising my problem, he reached forward and pulled them out. I thanked him, both for allowing me to breathe properly and for being so careful about entering me. He said nothing, but took hold of me by the hips and once more started to bugger me. I let out a long, gratified sigh and stuck my bottom up to make sure he got in all the way.

Drunk and with a small cock in me, the sensation had been powerful to say the least. Sober and with a much bigger cock to stretch out my poor bottom-hole it was overwhelming. The last thing I wanted was for Rory to take it out, yet as he began to speed up I simply lost control – a sensation both exquisite and terrifying. Grunting, panting, and gasping in the most unladylike manner imaginable, I submitted to the use of my bottom for his pleasure. From then on I had no power over the situation whatever. He simply used me, enjoying my bottom as a receptacle for his cock while I writhed and gasped beneath him. To me, my beaten buttocks and straining anus were everything, all centred on the magnificent cock that was putting me in such a state. I felt incredibly submissive to him, worshipful even, with my whole being dedicated to his pleasure – a bare pert bottom in a flower of petticoats, offered in supplication for his pleasure.

It was at that point of fervent, reverent ecstasy that somebody knocked on the door, a firm triple rap. The door was locked, yet for an instant I felt a sensation of panic at the thought of what whoever it was would see when they opened the door. I was about to call out that I wasn't decent when Rory spoke first.

'Hang on,' he called, 'I'll be with you in a second, I'm just bum-shagging my tart.'

'Rory!' I exclaimed in horror.

'Don't worry,' he assured me, 'it's just Jasmine.'

'Jasmine!' I exclaimed.

'She wanted to watch,' he explained quite casually. 'Hang on, I'll just let her in.'

'You bastard!' I managed as he pulled his erection from my bottom.

I was much too far gone to care. Just as she had been, I was beyond the point of being capable of prissiness. The fact that he had betrayed me was unimportant, all I wanted was his cock back inside me while Jasmine watched me used.

'Hi Isabelle, you dirty little slut – nice dress,' Jasmine remarked from behind me.

I tried to find a suitable answer, but Rory was already mounting me and as he once more began to force his penis into my rectum all I could do was moan. Jasmine laughed and locked the door again.

'You like it up the bum, don't you?' she said, coming to sit on the bed.

I could only grunt as Rory's balls began to slap once more against my empty pussy.

'I've got a pressie for you,' she continued blithely and began to rummage in her bag.

I watched, wide-eyed and panting as she pulled out a grotesque object. It was a dildo of sorts, a huge black rubber thing complete with a scrotum and a set of leather straps. I'd seen it in her playroom and wondered how it would feel to fuck Caroline with it. I could guess exactly where it was going.

'Don't come yet, Rory,' she addressed him. 'I want her to lick me a little.'

Rory slowed his pace as Jasmine pulled off her tights and panties and wriggled into position between my head and the wall. Making herself comfortable, she pulled the front of her skirt up and presented me with her bare pussy. Sliding forward, she pressed herself against my face and I began to lick, finding her clitoris with my tongue as Rory's pushes once more became urgent.

'You can come now, if you like,' Jasmine sighed. 'Do it up her bum while she licks me.'

Rory's response was to take a firmer grip on my hips and increase his pace. Once more I lost control and could only vaguely rub my face into Jasmine's pussy. My anus was on fire, and the power of his thrusts was beginning to hurt, bringing the tears to my eyes. Just when I thought that I could take it no more he grunted and gave a final, hard push into me. I knew he had come up my bottom, and as he stopped and the pain receded I felt an overwhelming rush of chagrin at the sheer filthiness of the act.

'That was good,' he puffed and began to pull his cock out.

I felt it slide out, a sensation nearly as dirty as having it put in. My anus was left gaping, sore and wet. Unable to resist, I turned, seeing myself in the mirror. My bottom was a flaming red, and centred on my anus, a black hole leading into the recesses of my body, the ring pulsing slowly. Choking on my own shame, I went back to licking Jasmine.

My bum-hole closed slowly and I could feel the sperm dribbling out and down over my pussy. Then a new pressure was applied and something slid up my bottom – the handle of the hairbrush that had been used to spank me. With my eyes shut I continued to lick Jasmine. I was in a state of total surrender, aware that I had had the tables turned on me with a vengeance, but unable to resist. Suddenly, Jasmine pulled away and I opened my eyes to see what she was doing.

'Watch this, little slut,' she said teasingly. 'It's for you.'

I watched as she held up the dildo and removed the rubber plug at the back of the scrotum. Reaching once more into her bag, she produced a small bottle, which I recognised as barley wine. She opened it and carefully poured some into the dildo, filling it to the brim before replacing the rubber cap.

'Jasmine!' I moaned weakly as I realised what she was going to do.

She simply laughed and put the bottle to my lips, forcing me to drink the rest of it before taking it away. I could do nothing, only wait kneeling on the bed with my smarting bottom and penetrated anus a willing target for her perverse intention. Rory laughed as Jasmine fixed the strap-on into place. Looking back, I could see her, the cock-shaped dildo projecting out from under her skirt, giving her a bizarre, androgynous appearance like some monster from Greek legend. Beyond, I could see the mirror and my own reflection, with my bare bottom the centre of an expanse of red silk, white linen and lace, the cheeks pink from spanking, my pussy swollen and pouting, the hairbrush at the centre, protruding obscenely from my anus.

Jasmine moved behind me, obscuring my view. I faced forward and buried my head in the bed, full of shame at my behaviour and the pleasure I was getting from being used. The hairbrush was pulled out of my bottom, once more leaving me gaping and ready for entry. I gave a little sob as Jasmine's dildo bumped against my anus, just as I had been expecting. It was as thick as Rory's cock, yet it slid in without much trouble, providing me both relief and sorrow for the state of my bottom-hole. Once it was wedged into my rectum I could feel the scrotum pressing against my pussy. She kept it in, deep inside me, my anus stretched around the shaft. I couldn't help it, I dipped my back in, pressing my vulva against the rough rubber and starting to rub so that the ridges bumped over my clitoris.

'That's right, Isabelle, come on it,' Jasmine said, her tone mocking my inability to control my needs.

I began to wriggle my bottom, indifferent to the lewd display I was making of myself, happy to accept anything as long as it led to my orgasm. Neither of them had touched my clitoris, nor allowed me to stimulate it, so doing so came as an exquisite release. My pleasure built fast, rising, making me whimper and squirm my bottom more and more. Then, just as I was on the brink of explosion, Jasmine squeezed the scrotum and filled my rectum with barley wine. I was already beginning to come when the sudden sensations of weight and pressure hit me, an extraordinary feeling that made me scream with reaction. I was coming, my thighs and buttocks clamping onto Jasmine's intruding dildo, my back passage feeling fit to burst, my clitoris burning and sensitive. Yet the contact between the rubber and my flesh was less than I really needed. My ecstasy rose, near to breaking point, then subsided, rose again as my wriggles became more frantic still, only to subside once more. Vaguely I heard Jasmine's laugh, a cruel, mocking sound. Then she took mercy on me and pressed the scrotum to my pussy, finally allowing me the friction I needed. I screamed aloud as my orgasm finally burst in my head, then again and again as I came, lost to everything but the sensation of my body. My mouth was open wide, then suddenly full of my wet panties as Rory stuffed them in to shut me up.

One last climax hit me and then it was over. I was dizzy with alcohol, which had hit me with extraordinary speed from the barley wine up my bottom. My anus was on fire, my muscles burning from holding myself in position for so long, my bottom throbbing from the spanking. I was also exhausted, both physically and mentally. Jasmine pulled out, telling me unnecessarily to hold tight.

As I slumped to the floor among the litter of discarded clothing, torn wrapping paper and the various devices that had been used to punish and probe my bottom, I became aware of something that I had not previously noticed. It was a card, large, thick and printed with several lines of text in an elegant copper-plate. Focusing on it with some difficulty I managed to take in enough to realise that it was a dinner invitation from Walter, and that the dress code was effectively what I was wearing – or rather what I had been wearing before being so thoroughly taken advantage of.

Thirteen

Jasmine had put me back in my place fast, firmly and effectively. The way she had had me used in my room had been perfect. Once more I could feel my need to accept her as my Mistress growing inside me, and over the week that preceded Walter's party this sensation became increasingly strong. With no academic concerns I had no reason not to be with her, and she made sure that my time was well spent. Over the days, she not only insisted that I followed my domestic regime in scrupulous detail – including numerous punishments – but trained me in several other erotic disciplines. These were invariably humiliating and often painful, although always kept carefully within the bounds of that delicate balance between pleasure and pain.

With Caroline's assistance she taught me to strip properly, including the subtleties of erotic dancing and generally showing off to men. This included putting on shows at the Red Ox, and the better I was received the more humiliating I found the experience. Another favourite game was to make Caroline and I her puppies, fetching balls and rolling on the ground for our tummies to be tickled. Variants of this game included being her pony-girl and piggy-girl, both of which seemed to be complex and intense fantasies yet neither of which we explored more than superficially, both requiring warm weather and lonely outdoor sites. There were also uniforms, both nurses, army and – of all things – traffic wardens. These were generally used as an accessory to punishments, for instance with Caroline and I dressed as army privates from the waist up and in boots but bare between. She made us drill like that, which was humiliating to say the least with our pussies and bottoms on show beneath the hems of our shirts, but not so humiliating as the subsequent spankings.

By Friday, I had learned more about erotic display and sadomasochistic games than I had ever guessed existed and was coming to appreciate the sheer depth of Jasmine's expertise. She was twenty-three, yet she had managed to take in and refine enough knowledge of extravagant erotic practises to make her worthy of a Master's degree in the subject, were such a thing to exist.

It doesn't, of course, but I was painfully aware that the equivalent was for her to have the right to call herself Mistress. I was a mere novice by comparison, and so the justice of me serving her and learning at her feet came to seem increasingly correct. Also, a good proportion of her knowledge seemed to have come from Walter Jessop, at least the technical side of it. This explained a lot about their relationship, which clearly transcended conventional social boundaries.

By the Friday, I was deeply in awe of her and beginning to understand the unquestioning devotion that Caroline gave her. Her assertion that my absolute submission to her was the natural order of things no longer seemed so outrageous and I had begun to think of myself as hers.

Having been either her servant or sexual plaything all week, I was surprised to learn that I was not going to be expected to act as maid during Walter's dinner party. Instead, Jasmine treated Caroline and myself as equals, helping us dress and even putting Caroline's unruly curls into some semblance of a Victorian style. In full costume – myself in red, Caroline in a rich yellow and Jasmine in royal blue – the three of us looked perfect, every inch Victorian young ladies. Beneath our gowns, our underwear was correct in every detail, and simply wearing it all made me feel as if I was floating.

The dinner was conducted with a correctness and formality that only the furnishings and paraphernalia of Walter's shop made possible. The table was mahogany, the service silver, the glass genuine late nineteenth-century Austrian. Walter sat at the table's head, Jasmine at the tail and Caroline and I to either side. The meal was excellent, consisting of a number of covers each apparently authentic and certainly delicious. Walter also provided wines of a quality that I could not fault, selecting styles, if not vintages, appropriate to the last century.

For all this magnificence and for all the relaxed, friendly atmosphere, I couldn't help but feel nervous, increasingly so as the meal progressed. Knowing the company, I could not believe that there would not be a strong sexual element to the evening, and that whatever it was it would include my submission. The uncertainty and suspense were exciting, but also unnerving. Given the depths of submission to which Jasmine had already introduced me, it was hard to see what she could do, yet bitter experience showed me that she always had something new up her sleeve.

As I washed a mouthful of pheasant down with fifteen-year-old Burgundy I was thinking how hopeless had been my quest to impose my will on her. She had every advantage; age, experience, the home territory . . .

My thoughts changed tack abruptly. How, I wondered, would she have managed in Scotland? Less well, I was sure. In Oxford, she could effectively call the shots as she pleased and that was exactly what she had done. To her it had all been a game, my attempts to wriggle out of the trap simply adding amusement to the chase. Yet had she been – say – a guest at my parent's house the situation would have been very different. She would have had no friends to help her, nor equipment to help bring out my submissive feelings. We would have been matched woman to woman, where my strength and intelligence might have counted for something. What props there were – a quantity of Victorian clothing, endless expanses of moorland and improvised bits and pieces – would have been mine as well.

One thing was for certain – once I had got her alone on the moors it would have been a different story, and it would not have been me who ended up underneath . . .

'More wine, Isabelle my dear?' Walter asked, extending the decanter towards me.

'Yes, thank you,' I replied, my train of thought coming to an abrupt halt at his words.

I accepted the glass and sipped it, finding the rich, earthy-tasting wine at once soothing and enervating. After dinner, and perhaps a while to digest, I might perhaps have to give them all a strip-show, demonstrating my new skills to Walter before crawling naked to his feet and begging for the privilege of sucking his penis. Alternatively, they might put me through some unusual punishment, perhaps taking a dog whip to my bottom. Then again, I might be told to strip naked and made to do the clearing up while they sipped brandy from cut glass. Whatever came, I knew that I would accept it, meekly and submissively as befitted my status.

Something deep within me rebelled at the thought, a lingering determination to conquer despite all. True, everything was against me, even the responses of my own body, yet my submission was not yet complete. I glanced at Jasmine, who appeared totally unconcerned. In her gown and in such surroundings, it was hard to see her as I knew she appeared to the outside world. She was a stripper and corsetière, neither wealthy nor born to rank, yet in her rich blue velvet with her delicate face framed by her blonde hair and her lips set in a slight smile, she looked regal – a princess enjoying the attentions of her lesser fellows. As she noted my attention the quality of her smile changed, a tiny alteration, but one that seemed to me deeply sinister.

I tried to be fatalistic, putting aside my worries in the knowledge that they could ultimately be trusted to take me no further than I wanted at heart. The meal progressed, Sussex pond pudding with Sauternes following the pheasant and stilton and vintage port following that. I was feeling distinctly full by the time Walter served out measures of Cognac and was hoping that I would at least be given time to digest. As I sipped the brandy, my thoughts returned to their earlier line, Jasmine on the moors, set against me, huntress and prey.

Three glasses later I was feeling drunk and mellow and in the mood for something naughty if not particularly energetic. Jasmine showed no signs of doing anything and I was wondering if the three of them would appreciate oral sex from me. I would start with Jasmine, perhaps, while Caroline gave Walter a helping hand, then . . .

'Do you like Caroline's tattoo, Isabelle?' Jasmine asked suddenly.

'Yes, it's pretty,' I answered, somewhat surprised by the question, which had come from nowhere.

'Good,' she continued, 'because I'd like you to have one just like it.'

'It's not really . . .' I began, intending to decline her offer as politely as possible.

'The tattoo,' she interrupted, 'is what marks Caroline as mine, and after a lot of talking we've decided to make you the same offer, to be my slave-girl.'

'Please, Isabelle,' Caroline added.

'Aren't I already?' I asked, remembering the number of times I'd knelt to her, kissed her feet, kissed her anus.

'Not truly,' she continued, 'not in your own mind, are you?'

'Well, no,' I admitted, 'but I do like submitting to you . . .'

'We know,' Jasmine smiled, 'but to really be mine you need to be marked. Believe me, it may seem a little thing, but carrying my sign on your flesh will be a really strong feeling. You'll be mine, and you'll know it. I want your complete submission, Isabelle. I want to own you.'

I could find nothing to say. The idea of having a jasmine flower tattooed on my bottom was every bit as strong as she said, while the idea of actually declaring myself to be owned by her had me trembling. I could feel the dampness in my panties and I could also feel the tears in my eyes.

'There's nothing like it,' Caroline urged. 'Come on, Isabelle, be with me, be fulfilled.'

'I . . . perhaps . . .' I stammered, unable to turn them down.

At that point I knew I was in love with them, both of them. To join their relationship was the thing I most wanted in the world. I also knew that once that little tattoo was on my bottom I would truly be hers. It was the final seduction, the act that drew me to the centre of her web. Yet I still wanted Jasmine as mine and knew that without her submission the relationship could not be perfect.

'You hesitate,' Jasmine said sadly.

'No . . .' I said quickly. 'I love you, I love you both, I just need . . .'

'Once you are marked you'll need nothing more,' Caroline broke in.

'I know,' I replied, 'but . . .'

'Walter, is the horse accessible?' Jasmine spoke. 'I think Isabelle needs to be on heat to really admit her own feelings.'

'I don't really,' I blustered, deciding once and for all that I had to admit my feelings. 'I adore being submissive to you, Jasmine, but I need to dominate too. I want to spank you, Jasmine, regularly.'

Caroline giggled and then went suddenly quiet.

'That will change,' Jasmine answered firmly. 'There must always be a mistress, the strongest, the one with the most powerful will. Oh, I recognise that you like to dominate, Isabelle, and I may allow you to spank Caroline occasionally, but to me you will always be slave. It is nature. Is that not so, Walter?'

There was a catch in her voice though, a catch that told me that whatever she said the idea of being spanked by me had touched a deep chord.

'Indeed so,' Walter answered. 'Surely, Isabelle, after all this time you see that Jasmine is by nature dominant to you?'

'Yes, she has been, but . . .' I protested.

'You will see it when in ecstasy,' he continued, 'as I know you do. Yes, Jasmine, the horse is accessible.'

'Do you feel,' Jasmine asked me, 'that in the heat of passion you could resist begging to me?'

'Yes, if needs be,' I answered hotly.

'Then shall we see?' she teased.

'Certainly,' I answered, 'put me over your birching horse or whatever it is. Do as you please, try to get me to say ... let's see, would "Please, Mistress Jasmine, I beg to be your slave-girl," suit you?'

'Let's go for, "Please, Mistress Jasmine, your slave-girl begs to come," ' she answered, 'and if you don't say it, you don't get your orgasm. You have a stop word too, which is "red", yet if you say that first I will know that your love for me is not genuine.'

'Fair enough,' I replied, 'but this is to your rules. If you really want to prove it you'll have to do it on my terms.'

'Which are?' she queried.

'Hunt me down out in the country,' I replied. 'It's always been my favourite fantasy. A team of you can chase me, catch me and then use me as you like. If you can make me say it then, I'll be yours.'

'Completely?' she asked.

'Completely,' I answered, and knew it to be true.

For a moment there was silence, with Jasmine and I looking into each other's eyes. I felt intensely emotional, deeply in love yet frightened and fragile, also unworldly, with the flickering candlelight and the scents of perfume, wine and Walter's cigar. The scene was perfect for me, expressing all my fantasies, Victoriana, sexually uninhibited girls, the prospect of erotic physical discipline ...

'We can still play with the horse, can't we?' Caroline broke in cheerfully.

'Sure,' Jasmine answered and got to her feet, 'but you don't go over it, Isabelle, you go on it.'

I followed, nervous, excited, keen to see what she would do. Walter came behind, joining us in the room at the back of his shop, where be began to rearrange things. After a fair bit of puffing and blowing he managed to extract various bits of wood from the clutter, which he assembled with bolts to form a tall frame on a sturdy base.

'The Berkeley Horse,' he declared proudly.

'Or rather a variant on it,' Jasmine put in. 'The original was built for Mrs Berkeley, a professional domina who used to run a specialist brothel in London. The design became popular, as it allowed her clients to be whipped by one girl while another played with their cocks.'

I could see how it worked, the frame allowing the victim to be attached in an upright, spread-eagled position that gave access both to their bottom and their front.

'This one was built at some time just after the turn of the century,' Walter continued. 'I picked it up in seventy-two as part of a house clearance. The old lady was moving into a retirement home but she was already in her eighties. I can only imagine that she had run the house as a brothel when she was younger and then retired, leaving her equipment in the attic. I got plenty of other things there too, including some of the clothes and Jasmine's box. I believe you've tried the box?'

I nodded, remembering the depth of the experience. The terrible dependence it had evoked in me was the one single thing that had done most to make me feel submissive to Jasmine. I had shown my feelings at the time – I had had no choice – yet I had never admitted to the sheer power of its effect.

'The horse is less subtle,' Jasmine remarked, 'but even more fun. Come on, on you go.'

I stepped forward, trembling slightly as I lifted my wrists to the heavy leather shackles at the top of the inner part of the frame. Jasmine made quick work of securing me in place, strapping my wrists, ankles and waist firmly to the horse so that I was held immobile in the centre of the frame.

'The straps can be adjusted with these slides,' Walter explained, as he altered the tension to pull my arms out to the maximum. 'We had it set for . . .'

'Caroline,' Jasmine cut in quickly, 'so we need the straps further apart to make up for your height.'

I suppressed a smile, realising that the last victim of the infernal device had not been Caroline but her, presumably during one of her periodic punishment sessions with Walter.

'I estimate that it can comfortably take a man of six and a half foot,' Walter continued as he made the final adjustment to my straps, 'but the really clever feature is this . . .'

He pulled a lever and without warning the entire room turned upside down. I yelped at the sudden feeling of instability, then I was upside down, my skirts had fallen and all I could see was part of the floor and the gloomy red space beneath my upturned gown. Caroline was laughing and Jasmine chuckling as the device once more became stable, only with me upside down.

My weight was on my ankles and waist, yet the thick leather straps held me in moderate comfort. More alarming was being unable to see and having my split combinations the sole protection for my sex. Not surprisingly they didn't stay covering me for long. Eager fingers quickly had them apart and I sighed as my upturned bottom and pussy were laid bare. All I could do was wait as they were sewn back, leaving me vulnerable to both beating and molestation, just as the designer of the horse had intended.

Upside down, with my legs spread and my pussy bare, I felt more vulnerable than ever before. They could do as they liked, and I couldn't even see, much less resist.

'Let's make her a candlestick!' Caroline suggested enthusiastically.

'Patience, darling,' Jasmine responded, 'you know she needs a good whipping before she can really let herself go. Walter, be a dear and fetch a riding crop, a nice old-fashioned one with a broad leather end.'

'Certainly, my dear,' he answered, 'I have just the thing.'

For a long moment I was left to shiver in apprehension, then Walter came back and Jasmine spoke again.

'Thank you,' she said. 'Now, Isabelle, this is what is going to happen. First I'm going to beat you, and not just your bum, but your pussy too. Don't worry, I'll be gentle at first. When you're nice and warm Caroline will pop candles up your pussy and bumhole and light them. Once you've had a taste of the wax, I'll use a vibrator on you. At any time – from the first smack of the crop to when you feel the candle flame on your bare skin – you can stop it all by saying what we agreed. "Please, Mistress Jasmine, your slave-girl begs to come," – wasn't it? When you do, I'll stop the punishment and bring you off with the vibrator. That will be my half of your submission, yours will come on Sunday, then on Monday it'll be time for a visit to the tattoo parlour. Fair enough?'

'What if I won't say it?' I asked shakily.

'Oh, you will,' she replied, 'not because of what we're doing, but because you want to.'

'Yes, Mistress,' I sighed, determined to prove her wrong. 'Start it then.'

The thrashing was slow and agonisingly frustrating. She beat me carefully, starting with gentle slaps on my bottom, then increasing the severity but never allowing my pain to exceed my pleasure. Her expertise was extraordinary, a skill doubtless built not only of long sessions with Caroline but during her own beatings from Walter. My bottom warmed slowly, my pleasure rising with it and my breathing becoming increasingly strong. Half drunk, unable to see more than dim red light and dizzy from hanging upside down, I quickly lost all sense of reality. All that mattered were my bonds, Jasmine and the rhythmic slaps on my naked bottom.

I was in a daze by the time she started to work on my pussy. My bottom was already burning, and the last few slaps had been hard, so hard that had they been applied when my buttocks were fresh I would have been squealing with pain. As it was they had just made me moan. I had never had my pussy slapped and imagined it to be agony. Instead it was hot, sharp and erotic, a sensation that rapidly built on my sense of helpless submission and sexual need. She would slap the leather on my pussy lips, then on my mound, making my flesh sting and swell and bringing a truly desperate need to come.

Yet for all my state of abject submission and feelings of sexual torment I held back from the final submission, again and again choking back my words just as I started to say them. It got worse once Caroline had poked the candles up my bottom and pussy, the rude sensation of being penetrated in both holes adding to my woes. I could feel my muscles squirming, both around my vagina and anus, and knew how wanton a sight I made for them, Walter in particular, it being far more humiliating to show myself in ecstasy in front of him than with just the girls.

Then the first drop of hot wax touched me, landing on the sensitive, freshly whipped skin where the tuck of my bottom curves down to my anus. I yelped and writhed, spilling more drops onto my open pussy and spattering them onto my bum and thighs. Immediately they were blown out, and after a moment for me to regain control of myself I heard Jasmine's voice.

'Do you want it to end, little one?' she purred. 'If so, just say the words.'

'Never,' I managed breathlessly, drawing a cruel laugh from Jasmine and a delighted chuckle from Caroline.

Once more they lit the candles, only this time I was ready. The wax was hot, yet not hot enough to burn, and I knew that I could take it. Jasmine loved me, and for all her cruelty she would never really hurt me, while her expertise was too fine for her to make a stupid mistake. On these hopes I set my faith and gritted my teeth to endure my punishment.

They let it happen in silence, the only sounds the sputtering of the candles, the occasional smack of leather on flesh and my whimpers. Jasmine, I knew, was waiting for me to break, yet I was determined that I would not, that I could set my boundaries of resistance beyond what she was prepared to inflict on me.

Only when she started the vibrator did I begin to doubt my resolve. With the first touch of the hard plastic on my pussy I almost came, but she whipped it away, denying me my orgasm. The process was repeated, again and again, while wax ran into my pussy and down between my bum cheeks and Caroline applied the crop to my bottom, making me squirm, whimper and sob but never, never speak out. Yet all my feelings were building, approaching a crescendo of sensation that would be my orgasm, an orgasm to end all others. I had to have it, but Jasmine continued to deny me, ignoring everything except the words I simply would not say.

I could feel the heat of the flame on the inside of my thighs. The wax was trickling down my bum, filling the crease, also clogging in the hair of my pussy. A dribble lodged between my sex lips just as

Jasmine dabbed the vibrator onto my clit. I screamed and then I was coming, only for the feeling to withdraw as she hastily snatched the vibrator away. I cursed her, receiving only a light laugh for my trouble.

'Say it, Isabelle,' she said, 'say it now and you can come.'

I managed only a whimper in response as she once more applied the vibrator. Again my orgasm welled up inside me and again she snatched it away at the last instant. I felt the warmth of a new runnel of wax, but it was just that, warmth, no hotter than my own body heat. I was coated with it, all my most sensitive areas protected by the very thing that had assaulted them. With that realisation I knew I had won. The peak was past. I could resist.

Twice more Jasmine brought me to the edge, then I felt Caroline's soft breath on the inside of my thighs. The heat from the candle flame waned and I was left hanging upside down, panting, hot-bottomed, smeared with wax, yet unconquered. For all my pain it had never even occurred to me to say 'red' and bring it all to a halt. Nor would I, I had done it, shown that I could resist all her efforts, and now was the time to submit.

'Please, Mistress Jasmine your slave-girl begs to come,' I breathed softly.

She gave no reply, but an instant later I felt something against my pussy, not the hard throbbing plastic of the vibrator, but the firm, fleshy resilience of her tongue.

Fourteen

I had agreed to visit a tattoo parlour on the Monday. There, I would be tattooed with a jasmine flower on the tuck of my bottom. It would mark me as Jasmine's, her slave, her property. It had no legal meaning, yet to me it would be the admission of my subjugation by her and somehow I knew that once marked I would truly regard her as my Mistress. It was extraordinary feeling. I was on the verge of an irrevocable decision, one which, once made, there would be no going back on.

Two things occurred on the Saturday. First I was invited out to lunch by Dr Appledore, who took me to a country pub, paid for a fine meal washed down with a bottle of Chablis and then suggested a walk on the downs. Only when we were a good mile from the road did he steer me into a convenient beech hanger, lift my skirt, pull down my tights and panties and give me a firm spanking. His technique was different this time, with his hand smacking my buttocks upwards, glancing blows, each of which had the effect of making my cheeks wobble and tugging at my pussy. It stung terribly yet turned me on more rapidly than had his previous, more admonitory, hand spanking. Once I had been reduced to a state of snivelling, red-bottomed submission he put his cock in my mouth and made me give him a slow, leisurely suck. He came in my mouth and I finished myself off, sitting splay-legged among the fallen beech leaves with my tights and panties around my ankles and my top open to show my breasts.

He was in a thoroughly good mood as we set off again, remarking on the beauty of my bottom and the pleasure of spanking me, in a manner very different from his usual reticence when obliged to say anything even remotely suggestive. The area we were in was the same section of downland I had seen from the far side of the valley on the day I had seduced Caroline. As I had suspected, it was ideal for my purposes and I insisted on taking a long route back to the car, chatting cheerfully and all the while memorising the landscape.

The second thing was that Sammy Adel came to stay with Rory. They visited me that evening and were clearly a couple. Despite a slight pang of jealousy, I refrained from telling her that he and I had been having sex for most of the term. Jasmine and Caroline were less reticent, and invited both of them on the hunt. Sammy was a little shocked at first, yet agreed to join in. She then told everybody how I had spanked her and how she would enjoy her revenge, which delighted the others. Before they left, I was put across Jasmine's lap and spanked, simply to amuse and titillate Sammy. Afterwards, as I stood in the corner nursing a smarting bottom, I realised that with Rory and Sammy together my one remaining emotional reason for not being with Jasmine and Caroline was gone.

The morning was bright and clear, cool but not actually frosty. Jasmine had the event planned with her normal thoroughness, and even had my clothes ready. These were shorts and a crop top in pink fleecy material. Not only was the colour girly in the extreme, but they left my midriff bare and a good deal of my bottom spilling out from the sides. They were also so tight that my nipples and the cleft of my pussy showed clearly through the material. Once dressed I felt worse than naked, being dressed in a manner deliberately calculated to draw attention to my sex. I had also been allowed to keep my panties on underneath, not to reduce my exposed feeling at all, but because they knew how I would feel when they were eventually pulled down. As a final touch, she made me put my hair in bunches and tied them with scarlet ribbons, leaving me looking like a particularly wet schoolgirl. Caroline thought all of this hilarious, but I managed to catch her in the bathroom and get in a couple of good smacks across her plump seat before Jasmine appeared.

The next shock was that she had invited Stan Tierney. As he stood there leering at my outfit she explained quite casually that his presence was to complete my punishment for tricking her into sucking his cock. Once caught and bound in the woods, he was to be allowed to use me, just as he pleased. Seeing his meaningful leer I found myself swallowing hard and began to wonder just what I had let myself in for. Yet it was too late to back down.

Walter arrived a few minutes later, bringing Rory and Sammy with him. After a few introductions we set off, driving south to the site I had selected for my final surrender.

It was a fair way, and my adrenaline was flowing from the start, leaving me in a state of nervous agitation by the time we reached the road that runs along the foot of the downs. We pulled into a convenient lay-by and climbed out of the cars. To our left the downs rose in a great sweep, marked with bare hedges and beech hangers. The horizon was an undulating line of pale green against a sky of cold, duck-egg blue. It looked bleak, lonely and exposed, very far from the noise and clutter of the city.

Bending to check my laces, I ran an eye over my hunters. Sammy and Caroline, with their short legs and curvaceous bodies, were built for comfort rather than speed. The same was true of Walter, with excess weight and his age added to his disadvantages. Stan Tierney, a heavy smoker, would have had trouble running down a tortoise. Jasmine, although slender, lacked muscle. Rory alone had the slightest chance of actually catching me.

Their tactics seemed likely to involve Rory running ahead while the others spread out into a line. He could then catch me and simply sit on my back until the rest caught up, probably treating himself to a good feel while I lay pinned to the ground, or possibly tied up. The others could then use me at their leisure, following which I would make my second submission to my status as Jasmine's slave-girl. I would be made to kiss her anus in front of the others, and photographed doing it.

Then, on Monday, the little yellow flower she used as her brand would be placed on my flesh, my final surrender.

Just the thought made me shiver. For all the intensity of my experiences, none were so permanent, nor so absolute. Once tattooed I would have been marked as Jasmine's property. Whatever came later, however long or short the relationship proved, I would always know that I had once willingly given myself as property to another woman. True, I might explain to future lovers, even a husband, that the little yellow jasmine flower on my bottom was simply decorative, yet I would know its significance and that would be what counted.

'Are you ready, Isabelle?' Walter enquired as he approached me.

I nodded, unable to find words because of the hard lump of tension in my throat.

'We will be giving you five minutes, as agreed,' he continued. 'You may run where you will, your sole restriction being the boundaries set by tarmac roads. All clear?'

Again I nodded. He put his hand into his pocket and brought out a large stop-watch. I stood up and glanced towards the ridge above us.

'Then you had best be on your way,' he said and depressed the knob at the top of the watch.

I ran, crossing the stile onto the open downs and running up the hill with every ounce of muscle I had. Elation replaced nervousness as my blood began to warm. I was fit, much fitter than Jasmine, and I was used to hills far taller and far steeper than those before me. To the west and my right I could see the beech hanger in which Dr Appledore had spanked me the previous day. I angled for it, running flat out across the short, springy turf. Dashing into the shadows of the bare beech trees I paused, glancing back to the road. Already they were coming, spreading out into a wide arc beneath me. Roughly as I had anticipated, Rory was ahead, acting as a runner. Behind him, Walter was at the centre of the arc, with Caroline and Sammy to his sides. Stan Tierney was nearest to me, Jasmine furthest, well out on the right flank.

Turning once more to the hill I ran for the hedge that lay parallel to the skyline, a long, dense tangle of thorn beyond which lay a track. With my silly pink outfit and scarlet ribbons I knew I stood out like a sore thumb against the green-white downland and the grey-brown trees and bushes. Reaching the hedge, I ducked through and scrambled over a fence, then struck out once more, not away from them but to the left, across the front of their line.

I ran desperately, until my legs ached and my lungs burned, all the while ducked low to keep out of sight and not stopping until I had reached the shelter of another beech hanger. The centre of this was a shallow bowl, carpeted with fallen leaves and with a decaying trunk lying across the middle. I scrambled to the far side and cautiously poked my head over the rim, looking out across the spread of the downs. Sammy was some two hundred yards down the slope from me and a little to my left, Jasmine well to my right. I crossed the beech hanger and crouched down behind a tree, more or less directly in Jasmine's path. Working fast, I removed the ribbons from my hair and pulled off my running shorts and panties, then hastily replaced the shorts.

Moving out from the beech hanger I once more ducked low behind the hedge. Jasmine was visible through the bare twigs, watching to her right and then returning somebody's signal with a wave of her hand. She changed course, angling towards the beech hanger. I followed, my elation rising to a wild surge, my teeth set in a manic grin. She was no more than twenty yards away, moving slowly into the shadow of the beech hanger, quite unaware of me behind her. Beyond the trees I glimpsed Sammy, moving away. I darted behind a massive beech, skipped quickly to another and froze. Sammy had gone through the hedge, Jasmine was crossing the beech hanger, no more than ten yards from me. I balled my panties in my hand, stepped out and ran.

Jasmine heard me an instant before I reached her but it was too late. As she opened her mouth to call out I stopped it with my panties, wadding them in. For an instant her expression was one of surprise, then of outrage as I grappled with her. She managed a muffled protest, but my hand was clamped over her mouth, keeping the panty gag firmly in place and preventing her from getting help. My other arm was around her, pinning one arm.

She lurched, pulling us off balance. We fell to the ground, rolling in the chalk mud and leaves. Her hand locked on my free arm, pulling, trying to force me over. I knew her intention, to twist my arm up into the small of my back. Then I would be sat on, my shorts pulled off and my bare bottom smacked and smacked until the others caught up. I resisted, keeping one hand clamped over her mouth as I set one arm against both of hers. Her eyes showed fierce joy, a true delight in the forceful conquest of her slave, the girl who she was going to punish and who would then accept her mark of ownership.

I set my muscles against hers. Slowly her expression changed from triumph, to surprise, to alarm. Gradually I bent her arms back, letting her feel my strength, letting the realisation sink in that I was not going to allow myself to be overpowered. Our eyes were locked together, hers showing disbelief – disbelief that her willing little plaything was fighting back. Then she went over, helpless against my strength.'

Forcing her onto her back, I straddled her and set my knees onto her forearms. I was hot, panting, my muscles burning with the effort of my run and of overcoming Jasmine. Yet I had done it, and now she knew that there was a girl who could make her feel as helpless as any man could.

Taking a ribbon from the waistband of my shorts, I made quick work of tying her panty gag into place. I then rolled her over and tied her hands behind her back, rendering her utterly helpless. Finally, I could rest, and I sat back, squatting on my haunches among the leaves. I was wet with sweat and filthy with mud, my hair bedraggled and one thigh marked with a long scratch. Yet I felt absolute triumph.

Had it gone the other way that would have been it, my submission complete, overcome physically as well as mentally. I would have surrendered meekly to the subsequent punishment, to being stripped, to having to satisfy her, Caroline, probably Rory and Sammy, Walter and even Stan Tierney. Then, naked and filthy, I would have kissed Jasmine's anus, pathetic in my surrender, entirely conquered. Now it was going to be different, very different. Jasmine was mine, and the others were not there to help her. Nor would they be, unless my deliberate feint to the west failed.

She lay in the mud, breathing hard through her nose. Helpless, she had given in, preparing to accept whatever I intended for her. I supposed she fondly imagined that eventually the others would find us and I would get my just desserts, but by then she knew that she would have been thoroughly punished and humiliated. I rolled her onto her back again and stood up to look down into her sweat-streaked, mud-smeared face.

'If you don't want to take it just nod,' I told her, 'but if you don't let me I don't think I could ever really be yours.'

It was the same choice she had given me, time and time again – submit or risk losing the precious, sweet sex that so few can give. She made no sign, but simply relaxed, accepting her fate but doubtless thinking of how sweet her revenge would be.

I started by pulling her jumper and sweatshirt up and popping her breasts out of her bra, making her sigh and blush slightly. Her jeans came next, pulled down to reveal black silk panties quite inappropriate for running around on the downs.

'How sweet,' I remarked, tracing a line down the front of her knickers with one finger, 'but hardly suitable. I think they'd better come off, Jasmine, don't you?'

She squirmed a little but made no real effort, clearly aware that to do so would merely mean making an undignified display of herself and that her panties would come down just the same.

'Kick a little, try and push me off,' I suggested. 'Come on Jasmine, where's your spirit? Think of the shame of it, having your panties pulled down in the open. Having your fat little bum all bare outdoors. Anyone might see you, a farmer, a hiker, perhaps even some dirty old tramp who'd go and pull himself off over the thought of what he'd seen. Or maybe I'd let him have you. You'd like that, wouldn't you Jasmine darling?'

She kicked, goaded into response by my taunts. I grabbed her legs around her thighs, squeezing hard, using my strength to quieten her.

'Think, Jasmine,' I continued, maintaining my grip. 'I can hold you. I can make you helpless. You can't even move your legs when you're in my grip. Feel it, Jasmine, try and kick, try and move your thighs. Come on, struggle, you little slut!'

I ended my speech with a hard smack on her bare thigh. She kicked out but I held her thighs firmly, clamping her between my elbow and legs as I reached up for her panties.

'Down they come, Jasmine,' I mocked. 'Just think, a girl is pulling down your panties and you can do nothing. When you pull mine down I have to let you, but I can do it to you whenever I like, Jasmine, any time I please. Just think, I could grab you and put you over my knee. You could kick and struggle all you liked, even scratch. You'd still get your spanking, and you'd get it bare bottomed!'

She was frantic, squirming not just with her legs but her whole body, trying everything to prove me wrong. I adjusted my grip, turning her completely face down in the mud and starting to pull her panties down. She thrashed crazily as they slid off her bum, exposing the neat cheeks to the air, bare and pink and ever so spankable. With her bottom naked, I made a sudden adjustment of my position, cocking one leg under her belly. She jerked to the side, desperate not to be put into a spanking position.

There was an instant's struggle and then I had wrapped my other leg around her thighs, locking her in place with her bare bottom the highest part of her body. Taking her wrists in one hand I paused, laying the other across the swell of her cheeks.

'Spankies time, darling,' I teased, giving her bottom a gentle pat.

It was an excellent position, both helpless and humiliating. Jasmine's face was pressed into the mud, as were her naked breasts. Her bum was high and her back dipped, forcing her cheeks apart to provide a view of her pussy and the pink dimple of her bum-hole to the world at large. In the same position I would have felt utterly humiliated and extremely turned on, whether I had been told to assume it or made to. Jasmine needed to be made to, that I knew, and yet she was still struggling, desperate not to succumb to what I was doing to her.

'Just nod and it will all stop,' I said once more, determined that her submission would ultimately be of her own choice.

She made to move her head and then stopped, only to renew her struggles with increased fury. I laughed out loud, knowing exactly how she felt. Stopping our play was a failure, she had to overcome me either physically or by sheer force of personality. Neither was possible. I had her tight and her mouth was stuffed with a pair of somewhat sweaty panties. All she could do was submit to her spanking.

I started, using the firm, upward slaps that Dr Appledore had used to such good effect on my own bottom. I knew they stung the skin and jerked at the pussy, not too painful but irresistibly thrilling. Jasmine responded well, wiggling and trying to kick at first but quickly beginning to exhibit the signs of excitement. I paused to dip a finger between her legs, finding her pussy warm and wet.

'Think, Jasmine,' I said as I went back to the task of slapping her trim bottom up to a glowing red, 'I can do this to you any time I like. I can hold you down. I can take your panties off and spank you, just like a big, strong man would. You can trust me too, just like you can trust Walter to spank your little bum without insisting on fucking you afterwards. I can do all of that and more, but only if you accept my right to punish you.'

She suddenly went berserk, thrashing, kicking, wriggling, bucking. I held on grimly and continued to spank her, ignoring her struggles. Finally, she subsided to lie limp across my lap, breathing heavily through her nose, having only succeeded in plastering her face and breasts with even more mud.

Her bum was colouring up nicely, both cheeks flushed red and covered with goose-pimples. It was a beautiful view, the pretty, haughty Jasmine bare-bottomed across my lap, her face and chest filthy with mud, her hair a bedraggled mess, her bottom pink and sore and naked against the green of the downs and the blue of the sky. I paused to admire it and once more put my hand down between her legs, finding her pussy even wetter than before.

'It's pleasant to be spanked outdoors, isn't it?' I remarked, starting to play with her pussy. 'There's nothing like a bare-bottom spanking outdoors for a punishment is there? Not only do you get to show your bottom off, but there's always the chance that someone might see you. Think of it, Jasmine, your pretty little bum all bare with your pussy and bum-hole on show. Think what they'd see, Jasmine, you being spanked, with every little fold of your sex showing. Your pussy pouts out from between your thighs ever so sweetly, you know, like a little fat apricot with your sex lips and clit showing in the middle. Your bum-hole shows too, all pink and rude, like a little pair of pursed lips, just ready for a nice, fat cock.'

I finished by sliding my finger deep into her pussy, then once more started to spank her. She had given in completely, and was moaning deep in her throat as her bottom wobbled and bounced under my hand. She was pushing it up too, further spreading her cheeks. I could smell her scent, rich and musky, the aroma of excited girl.

'I'd let them do it, you know,' I continued. 'If a hiker came past, I'd ask him if he wanted to fuck you. I'm sure he would accept. After all, who could resist that swollen little pussy and this pretty red bottom. I'd tell him I'd had to spank you for being naughty but that you were now turned on and in need of his cock. After all, it's true, isn't it?'

She nodded and gave a tiny, subdued whimper, a response that suggested complete surrender.

'Actually, that's what I'll do,' I announced, abruptly stopping the spanking. 'I'll find someone to fuck you.'

She made no protest and I knew her surrender was indeed complete. With some difficulty, I managed to get her onto my shoulder, yet managed to feign ease as I set off. I had left her top up and her bottoms down, so that her muddy breasts and pink bum were bare for all to see. Not that there was anyone there, which was just as well, the accidental appearance of a hiker being one of the few things that might have spoiled my plan.

Of the others there was no sign whatever, my feint to the west having evidently successfully drawn them off in that direction. The wind had freshened and was rustling the bare branches of the beeches, adding to the wonderful sense of loneliness of the place. Jasmine was whimpering, evidently badly in need of her orgasm. She had responded beautifully, as I had anticipated, only with greater passion. Possibly she would now be ready to acknowledge me as her equal, which was what I had set out to achieve, yet I had another card to play and it seemed a shame to waste it.

My muscles were burning with the effort of carrying her, but I managed not to show it. Checking that there was nobody about, I left the beech hanger and started down the track, aiming for a dense clump of thorn where the hedge met another. I had scouted the place while with Dr Appledore, and knew it to be well shielded from view and also sheltered.

Despite my outward calm, I was seething inside, elated by my success and highly excited by having spanked Jasmine. Yet I was determined to hold my poise, just as Jasmine did when she dominated Caroline and me, never slipping until she was actually coming. I dragged her into the shelter of the thorn bushes, adding to our scratches and muddiness in the process. With her laid down in the clear area of muddy earth at the centre I quickly checked that the downs were clear.

Pulling off her shoes, trousers and panties, I made fast work of securing her in place. Rolling her onto her face in the mud, I pulled her legs apart. Her shoelaces allowed me to tie her ankles to two sturdy thorn bushes, leaving her thighs wide and her pussy spread out like a juicy tart, ripe and ready for entry. I would have liked to strip her nude, but taking her top off would have meant untying her hands, so I contented myself with making sure her jumper, sweatshirt and bra were well up and that her breasts were naked in the cool mud underneath her chest. I used her panties as an improvised blindfold, remembering my stay in her box as I tied them off behind her head. Her trousers and shoes went under her belly, raising her bum a few inches and helping to open her cheeks, make a yet ruder display of her pussy and showing off her anus properly. It also left her back dipped, her spine making an elegant curve down from her back and then up to the divide of her bum.

Satisfied that she was completely helpless, I went to scout the copse, finding a whippy hazel shoot and a large crow's feather. The downs were still empty, only the distant sound of a car betraying the existence of any human outside Jasmine and my little world. Returning to her, I sat back in a comfortable lotus between her legs. Her flushed bottom was right in front of my face, the cheeks humped up and open, her pussy swollen and moist, her bum-hole pulsing slightly.

'Right, Jasmine Devil,' I announced. 'There's nobody around to fuck you, so I'm going to make you come myself.'

I reached out and rubbed my knuckle against her clitoris, drawing an instant reaction as she tried to

232

rub herself on me. Pulling my hand back, I gave her a gentle smack with the hazel switch, leaving a faint line of yet redder skin on her already flushed bottom. She squirmed, rubbing her breasts in the muck in a frantic effort to excite herself.

'Wanton little thing, aren't you?' I remarked coolly, although I was fighting an urge to bury my face between her thighs and lick her to the ecstasy she so badly needed.

She nodded and wiggled her bottom in response, an enchanting sight that again made me want to give in. Instead, I gave her three strokes of the switch, leaving her bum decorated with three new red lines.

'Let me see,' I continued, 'what shall I do with you? Something up your bum, I think, for starters. I'm afraid I haven't any barley wine, nor a nice big dildo, not even a candle, hm . . . no, I'm sorry, but if you're to be made to submit properly you need to be buggered. Stay here.'

For the third time I went to scan the downs, but this time I saw what I was waiting for. Coming up the hill from the road, slowly, lugubriously, was the heavy-set, bearded figure of Dr Duncan Appledore. I waved and he returned my signal.

I waited as he approached, occasionally peeking in among the thorns to check on Jasmine. She was squirming, her near-naked body clearly at the same level of exquisite torment that she had brought me to so many times. I left her there, waiting until Duncan had arrived.

I greeted my tutor with a friendly kiss and led him into the copse. The sight of Jasmine – near naked, mud-spattered and obviously freshly spanked – made him draw his breath in, despite me having briefed him on his role as a supposed local farmer the previous day.

'Are you er ... certain?' he queried, pointing at her.

'Completely,' I assured him. 'Jasmine darling, I've found you a nice big farmer. If you want it just lift your bum.'

Her bottom rose immediately, although the groan she gave suggested that sort of helpless excitement that I knew so well.

'You see,' I went on, 'she's game. In fact, she's a little slut, so enjoy her without reservation.'

'Very well,' he replied, 'I shall.'

It had taken me a long while to persuade him the previous day, but now that he had agreed he gave of his best. I sucked his cock hard for him and then sat back to watch as he mounted Jasmine. Under his weight with his big cock inside her, she was soon grunting loudly through her nose, a noise that I told her reminded me of a pig. No over-eager youngster, he stayed in her for the best part of half-an-hour, riding her slowly with only the occasional burst of speed to make her grunt and moan.

When he was near to coming, I asked him to dismount and quite casually informed Jasmine that she was now going to be buggered. I used her own juices to open her anus, poking my fingers in and wiggling them until she was loose and receptive. As he mounted her I reminded her of how she had egged Walter Jessop on to bugger me and how she herself had used my bottom for her dildo.

It was wonderful watching her entered anally. I asked him to kneel behind her, allowing me to see every detail. I watched in mingled disgust and delight as his erection pressed against her anus and it opened slowly, like a fleshy pink flower, gradually accepting his cock. When the head was in she was already in a fine state, mewling and squirming her bottom. As he mounted her and began to work it slowly up her bottom I could stand it no more. Quickly pulling off my shorts I moved to her head and slid down so that her face was pressed against my pussy. I bent forward to untie the ribbon that held my panties in her mouth and pulled them free, leaving her gasping for air until I took her by the hair and pulled her face against my pussy.

She began to lick immediately, tonguing me with a frantic passion as she was sodomised. He had stayed upright, although it can scarcely have been comfortable. I could see his cock disappearing down between her bum cheeks, which were squashed together by his weight. With each push, they moved up, two plump red balls of girl flesh, spanked and now with a cock thrust between them.

'How does it feel, Jasmine?' I demanded, pulling her head back by the hair. 'How does it feel to have been spanked across my knee with your pants down? How does it feel with your bare tits rubbing in the mud? How does it feel tied and helpless while you're mounted? How does it feel with a farmer's cock up your bottom? Answer me!'

'Lovely,' she moaned, ending with a gulp as I once more pushed her face in-between my thighs.

'And will you do it again?' I continued. 'When I say? As my plaything?'

Her only response was a muffled sob. I was close to orgasm yet trying to hold back, keen to extract every ounce of pleasure from the situation. It was impossible, her tongue was working on my clitoris, bringing me closer and closer to the edge. Abandoning myself to it I quickly pulled off my crop top, leaving myself nude except for shoes and socks. Duncan grunted and Jasmine gave a sharp exclamation, perhaps of ecstasy, perhaps of despair. I knew he had come up her bottom, and with that knowledge I was coming myself. Forcing Jasmine's head hard into my crotch, I took a breast in my hand and simply let it happen. My muscles locked around her face, my back arched and my sight went blurred. I was coming, screaming out my pleasure without a thought for where I was or who might hear. I didn't care, content as long as the waves of pure bliss were flowing through me.

When I came down from my peak, Duncan had already pulled his cock from Jasmine's anus, leaving her in a state of utter desperation. Unable to get at her pussy, she was squirming herself into the ground, motions that abandoned all pretence at dignity or restraint. Crawling round to between her legs I picked up the crow feather I had found and touched it to her clitoris, provoking an instant reaction.

'Please, Isabelle!' she begged. 'Do it! Make me come!'

'Please who?' I queried, again brushing the tip of the feather directly onto her clitoris.

She squealed, a long drawn-out noise of ecstasy and frustration, but did not reply.

'Please, Mistress, I think you want to say,' I chided her. 'In fact, let's have "Please, Mistress Isabelle, your slave-girl begs to come".'

She wriggled and I once more applied the feather to her clitoris. She was a fine mess, her red buttocks thrust up and apart, her bottom-hole pulsing and oozing sperm, her pussy wide and wet, swollen with need. I took a handful of mud and rubbed it in-between her buttocks and over her cheeks, soiling her bottom.

'Come on, darling,' I teased, tickling her again.

Her pussy contracted, the first hint of orgasm. I pulled the feather sharply back and she gave a hollow, despairing moan.

'Come, come,' I taunted, 'ask nicely and I'll bring you there.'

'Oh, God, OK,' she yelled suddenly. 'Make me come, Isabelle, please make me come. Isabelle, Mistress Isabelle, anything you like! Just make me come!'

Her words had risen to a scream of frustration and need, but I simply applied the feather again, just giving her a light tickle.

'Please, Mistress Isabelle, your slave-girl begs to come!' she blurted out, her words coming brokenly as she gave the same final surrender she had demanded of me.

I chuckled as I reached out and pressed my knuckles to her pussy, only to pull them away the instant she began to rub.

'No,' I said calmly, 'I don't think you really mean it.'

She gave a desperate sob, lifting her bottom in the hope of my caress. I ignored her and went to untie her feet. She made no resistance, but allowed me to roll her over in the mud and once more spread her thighs.

'Please, Isabelle, Mistress, I said it!' she begged.

'I know,' I replied, 'but I want something more.'

I stood and turned, straddling her face so that she was looking directly up between my legs.

'No, please,' she said softly as she realised what I intended.

'Oh yes,' I answered.

I dropped into a squat, slowly, then reached back and pulled my bottom cheeks open, presenting Jasmine with my anus. She groaned and spread her thighs open but made no move. I was picturing what she would be able to see, my spread bottom with my anal lips a puckered brown ring in front of her face, like my pursed mouth but at the wrong end.

'Kiss my lips, Jasmine,' I said.

She groaned again, deep and passionate as she tried to resist. I squatted down an inch further, but no more, determined to make her do it of her own choice.

Then I felt it, Jasmine's soft, pretty mouth on my anus, kissing, gently then more firmly. The camera which Duncan had taken from his pocket clicked as Jasmine's lips pressed against my anus. She gave a long moan of despair and ecstasy and began to tongue my bottom. The sensation was bliss, yet more than physical bliss, and as I closed my eyes and threw back my head in pure, perfect pleasure my thoughts were centred on that fact that it was Jasmine whose tongue was tickling my anal ring.

I stayed enthroned proudly on her face for a long moment, then knelt forward and put a merciful knuckle to her pussy. She started to come immediately, rubbing herself on my fist with a desperate need. As her climax hit her she threw her head back and screamed, just as I had done, only with her, at the very peak, the very moment of least control, she called my name aloud, yelling 'Isabelle' out across the empty downs.

Epilogue

I took a sip of Armagnac and lay back into the comfort of the leather armchair. Naked but for my corset of jet black silk, stockings and high-heeled boots, I had one leg thrown over the arm of the chair, spreading my thighs to allow Caroline to work on my pussy. She had been licking for a while, using her tongue with an expertise born of long practice. I was coming towards orgasm, but not hurriedly, instead slowly, sipping the fragrant brandy as my pleasure rose. Caroline was nude, her fine bottom stuck out to the room, the skin of her plump cheeks flushed pink from the spanking I had given her. It had not been a punishment, but done simply for my amusement.

Beyond Caroline knelt Jasmine, also naked but with her petite bottom towards me so that I could admire it while I came. Her knees were apart, opening her buttocks and affording me a fine view of the rear of her neatly pouted pussy lips and the tight pink hole of her anus. Her cheeks were also pink, flushed from spanking and decorated with a half-dozen sets of tramlines, the evidence of the caning I had given her that morning. The lowest of these lines started at the left of her bottom, travelling down at a slight angle. A brief gap showed where the cane had crossed the cleft of her bottom and then the lines started once more, to end at the neat tuck of her right cheek. There, at the point where the red cane mark faded to pink, lay a small, fresh tattoo, a cursive 'I' in the vivid red of newly spilt blood.

NEXUS NEW BOOKS

To be published in May

INNOCENT
Aishling Morgan

Innocent tells the story of the young and faithful lady's maid Cianna and her haughty mistress Sulitea. Shipwrecked in the kingdom of Alteron, Cianna must wrestle other women for the entertainment of the masses. But as the fur flies in her world of gladiatorial combat, the distinction between her bizarre sport and her life is confusingly and thrillingly blurred. A filthy gothic fantasy tale from the author of *Pleasure Toy*.

ISBN 0 352 33699 4

UNIFORM DOLL
Penny Birch

Jade is usually a confident young lesbian, very aware of what she wants, and what she doesn't. Unfortunately her taste for being bullied can very easily get out of hand, and when she decides to compete with her filthy uncle Rupert in collecting the uniforms of sex partners, it quickly does. What starts out as a playful if provocative hobby leads to her finding herself obliged to accommodate men as well as women, and ending up in a seriously sticky mess – literally.

ISBN 0 352 33698 6

ONE WEEK IN THE PRIVATE HOUSE
Esme Ombreux

Jem is a petite, flame-haired, blue-eyed businesswoman. Lucy, tall, blonde and athletic, is a detective inspector. Julia is the slim, dark, bored wife of a financial speculator. Each arrives separately in the strange, ritualistic, disciplined domain known as the Private House. Once they meet, nothing in the House will be the same again – nothing, that is, except the strict regime of obedience and sexuality. A Nexus Classic.

ISBN 0 352 33706 0

To be published in June

RITUAL STRIPES
Tara Black

Mesmerised by the punk diva in a Seattle club, Cate Carpenter stumbles into a world of erotic cruelty. Thrilling unexpectedly to their use of instruments of chastisement, she gains admittance to an SM club linked to an ancient fertility rite. However, once recruited to work in their library of arcane fetish erotica, Cate makes enemies of everyone with her ruthless manoeuvrings and vicious canings. With the boot on the other foot, Cate must learn to temper her impulses, and come to understand that a true domina will seek out, from time to time, the pain that she inflicts on others. An arousing look at SM politics!

ISBN 0 352 33701 X

PALE PLEASURES
Wendy Swanscombe

Three sisters, Anna, Beth and Gwen Camberwell, are willingly imprisoned in the German schloss of their master, Herr Abraham Bärengelt, who is obsessed with the alabaster whiteness of their skin. They endure the most extreme torments and tribulations therein as the half-mad, half-genius Bärengelt gives free rein to his twisted imagination. Arcane, inventive erotica from the author of *Beast*.

ISBN 0 352 33702 8

AMANDA IN THE PRIVATE HOUSE
Esme Ombreux

Drawn from her sheltered life when her housekeeper Tess goes missing, Amanda goes to France in an attempt to find her. During the search Amanda meets Michael, an artist with bizarre tastes who awakens in her a taste for the shameful delights of discipline and introduces her to a secret society of hedonistic perverts who share her unusual desires. Amanda revels in her newfound sexual freedom, voluntarily submitting to extreme indignities of punishment and humiliation, but does not realise until too late the full extent of the society's depraved and perverted plans. Can Tess and Michael save her from the ultimate degradation the society has in store? A Nexus Classic.

ISBN 0 352 33705 2

If you would like more information about Nexus titles, please visit our website at www.nexus-books.co.uk, or send a stamped addressed envelope to:

Nexus, Thames Wharf Studios,
Rainville Road, London W6 9HA

NEXUS BACKLIST

This information is correct at time of printing. For up-to-date information, please visit our website at www.nexus-books.co.uk

All books are priced at £5.99 unless another price is given.

Nexus books with a contemporary setting

ACCIDENTS WILL HAPPEN	Lucy Golden ISBN 0 352 33596 3	☐
ANGEL	Lindsay Gordon ISBN 0 352 33590 4	☐
BEAST	Wendy Swanscombe ISBN 0 352 33649 8	☐
THE BLACK FLAME	Lisette Ashton ISBN 0 352 33668 4	☐
THE BLACK MASQUE	Lisette Ashton ISBN 0 352 33372 3	☐
BROUGHT TO HEEL	Arabella Knight ISBN 0 352 33508 4	☐
CAGED!	Yolanda Celbridge ISBN 0 352 33650 1	☐
CANDY IN CAPTIVITY	Arabella Knight ISBN 0 352 33495 9	☐
CAPTIVES OF THE PRIVATE HOUSE	Esme Ombreux ISBN 0 352 33619 6	☐
DANCE OF SUBMISSION	Lisette Ashton ISBN 0 352 33450 9	☐
DARK DELIGHTS	Maria del Rey ISBN 0 352 33276 X	☐
DIRTY LAUNDRY £6.99	Penny Birch ISBN 0 352 33680 3	☐
DISCIPLES OF SHAME	Stephanie Calvin ISBN 0 352 33343 X	☐

Period

CONFESSION OF AN ENGLISH SLAVE	Yolanda Celbridge ISBN 0 352 33433 9	☐
THE MASTER OF CASTLELEIGH	Jacqueline Bellevois ISBN 0 352 32644 7	☐
PURITY	Aishling Morgan ISBN 0 352 33510 6	☐

Samplers and collections

NEW EROTICA 3	Various ISBN 0 352 33142 9	☐
NEW EROTICA 5	Various ISBN 0 352 33540 8	☐
EROTICON 1	Various ISBN 0 352 33593 9	☐
EROTICON 2	Various ISBN 0 352 33594 7	☐
EROTICON 3	Various ISBN 0 352 33597 1	☐
EROTICON 4	Various ISBN 0 352 33602 1	☐
THE NEXUS LETTERS	Various ISBN 0 352 33621 8	☐

Nexus Classics

A new imprint dedicated to putting the finest works of erotic fiction back in print.

AGONY AUNT	G.C. Scott ISBN 0 352 33353 7	☐
BAD PENNY	Penny Birch ISBN 0 352 33661 7	☐
BRAT £6.99	Penny Birch ISBN 0 352 33674 9	☐
DARK DELIGHTS £6.99	Maria del Rey ISBN 0 352 33667 6	☐
DARK DESIRES	Maria del Rey ISBN 0 352 33648 X	☐
DIFFERENT STROKES	Sarah Veitch ISBN 0 352 33531 9	☐

- - - - - - ✂ -

Please send me the books I have ticked above.

Name ....

Address ....

....

....

.... Post code....................

Send to: **Cash Sales, Nexus Books, Thames Wharf Studios, Rainville Road, London W6 9HA**

US customers: for prices and details of how to order books for delivery by mail, call 1-800-343-4499.

Please enclose a cheque or postal order, made payable to **Nexus Books Ltd**, to the value of the books you have ordered plus postage and packing costs as follows:

UK and BFPO – £1.00 for the first book, 50p for each subsequent book.

Overseas (including Republic of Ireland) – £2.00 for the first book, £1.00 for each subsequent book.

If you would prefer to pay by VISA, ACCESS/MASTERCARD, AMEX, DINERS CLUB or SWITCH, please write your card number and expiry date here:

....

Please allow up to 28 days for delivery.

Signature ....

Our privacy policy.

We will not disclose information you supply us to any other parties. We will not disclose any information which identifies you personally to any person without your express consent.

From time to time we may send out information about Nexus books and special offers. Please tick here if you do *not* wish to receive Nexus information. ☐

- - - - - - ✂ -